THE WOMAN AT NUMBER 19

J. A.

B
Boldwood

First published in 2019. This edition first published in Great Britain in 2023 by Boldwood Books Ltd.

Cover Design by Head Design

Cover Photography: Alamy

A CIP catalogue record for this book is available from the British Library.

Paperback ISBN 978-1-80549-152-1

Large Print ISBN 978-1-80549-148-4

Hardback ISBN 978-1-80549-147-7

Ebook ISBN 978-1-80549-145-3

Kindle ISBN 978-1-80549-146-0

Audio CD ISBN 978-1-80549-153-8

MP3 CD ISBN 978-1-80549-150-7

Digital audio download ISBN 978-1-80549-144-6

Boldwood Books Ltd
23 Bowerdean Street
London SW6 3TN
www.boldwoodbooks.com

To Amy and Charlotte, the people who made this book possible. This one's for you, ladies!

Remembrance of things past is not necessarily the remembrance of things as they were...

— MARCEL PROUST

A clear conscience is the sure sign of a bad memory...

— MARK TWAIN

I don't know what's worse: to not know what you are and be happy, or to become what you've always wanted to be, and feel alone.

— DANIEL KEYES

PROLOGUE

She sits in the garden, her face tilted towards the sky. Staring at the cloudless swathe of blue above, her eyes are drawn towards a distant flock of swallows as they swoop and dive in perfect formation, graceful and elegant, like tiny ballerinas dancing on the thermals. She is fascinated by them and watches as they twist and turn effortlessly; sees how their small bodies are perfectly adapted to their environment. She marvels at their speed and agility. It's one of the most beautiful things she's ever seen. It makes her feel calm and at peace. Not full of rage and dread, or full of murderous intent: just relaxed and at one with herself and the gentle forces of nature.

The distant song of the blackbird floats closer: a soothing, light chirrup carried on the breeze. It's like having somebody close by, their warm breath next to her skin as they whisper poetry into her ear. She's reminded that it's the small things in life that count, that make her feel human. Being amongst the flora and fauna helps her get by, giving her a brief respite from her thoughts: the torturous ones, the dark, intense ones. The same thoughts that constantly remind her of who she is and what she did.

She blanks those thoughts out, denies any of those memories space in her head. Doesn't want to think about any of it. Those terrible days. Those awful, unforgivable deeds...

Letting out a trembling sigh, she continues gazing upwards, breathing in the gentle warmth of the sun that kisses her face. A series of smoke trails criss-cross the cobalt sky thousands of feet above. She thinks of how wonderful it would be to be one of those passengers, to be transported somewhere exotic, somewhere beautiful. Somewhere far away from here.

Closing her eyes, she pictures the exquisiteness of it all, the decadence of having people wait on her hand and foot, catering to her every demand, speaking tenderly to her, smiling and asking if everything is to her liking. Making her feel as if she were the most important person in the world. Then her eyes abruptly snap open and she lets out a small gasp.

No.

She will not allow herself to feel that way. If she lets those happy thoughts in, then she will be playing into their hands, allowing herself to feel trapped and desperate by dreaming of another world where she is free. It's all about making the best of what she has in here. That's the only way she will make it through, the only way she can carry on living her life as a prisoner. Because for all the fancy terms applied to the reasons for her being held here, that is exactly what she is. She isn't a patient; she is a detainee, a captive interred here against her will. And if she allows herself to dream about how much better her life would be if she were elsewhere, she knows for sure she will undoubtedly go mad, her mind too brittle and damaged to face the truth, to live up to the realisation that she is trapped, stuck at this place indefinitely until they decide what to do with her. Until they decide whether or not she will ever be able to leave.

So she shuts out dreams of happiness and contentment, the

thoughts she has where she can fly like a bird, soaring through the skies like the swallows that feed on the wing, and forces herself to be happy, to make do with what she has in this place. The place she has been forced to call home.

She blinks repeatedly. And what is that? What exactly does she have?

That is a good question.

What she has is a roof over her head, a bed to sleep in at night, food to eat, and her thoughts. At least they are her own. Nobody has control over them. As much as the people here in this place would like to climb inside her head and work out what she's thinking, what it is that's going on inside her mind, she can rest easy, knowing she's the only one who has the key to that particular area of her life. And as long as there is breath in her frail body, it will stay that way.

Her thoughts are all she has. They are hers and hers alone.

She leans down and carefully bends the stalk of a nearby flower towards her face, its silken, golden petals yielding to her touch, the pale, light scent billowing up and enveloping her in a delicate, perfumed haze.

Taking a deep, gratifying breath, she opens her fingers and releases the thin stem before sitting back up. The welcoming arms of spring reach out, temporarily lifting her mood. Soon it will be summer. She smiles, her face tight, unaccustomed to feelings of happiness. Summer reminds her of good times, better times. A time when she was loved and content. A time when her family was still together.

And then it's gone. Her happiness in that moment vanishes like the last gasp of breath from a dying man, and in an instant, a thick mantle of misery descends, shrouding her, suffocating her, slowly killing her as it hooks its talons deep into her soul, tearing and shredding it into tiny pieces. One small memory, one rogue thought is all it takes to burst her bubble of brief contentment – the sound of birdsong, the smell of a garden, the memory of her fragmented family and shattered life. Her life before she came here. The life she lost and will never get back.

Suddenly, she's consumed by sorrow, by raw, undiluted anguish that rushes up her abdomen, travelling up her throat and forcing its way out of her mouth. She sees them out of the corner of her eye: the people who jump up out of their seats and race across to where she sits, alerted by the noise escaping from her burning lungs. Her scream gains in pitch, a hollow, distorted, wailing sound, growing and growing until it reaches a crescendo. Their faces are full of anger and frustration when they reach her. They don't like it when she does this, when she allows her demons to escape. They want her to stop, to keep it all under control and not shatter the illusion of equilibrium they have worked hard to create, the delicate balance that separates sanity and madness in this place, and she's aware that they'll do anything to make that happen.

But then, they don't truly understand her plight or how she thinks. They don't understand that she doesn't want to stop the noise, or for the dark thoughts to subside and simply vanish into the ether. She wants them all to hear, to be exposed to her burning anger and unending terror, and be subjected to the desperate, hollow shrieks that emanate from the bottom of her gut.

Because this is how she is now and how she will always be from this point on. The spells of happiness and calm she experiences are short-lived. The memories of those painful, murky days are ingrained in her soul, entrenched forever. They'll never leave, pushing instead any fresher memories and feelings aside, stomping on them and grinding them underfoot.

So now these people need to listen to her, to be sympathetic to her cries and howls, because they're the ones who made her this way. They're the people who forced her to see what took place, to realise what actually happened. This is all their fault. They are the ones who made her see what a monster she had become.

And she hates them for it.

She hears them talking to her, their voices distant and distorted, their pleas and whispers for her to calm down simply washing over her like liquid mercury. Their pedestrian persuasive techniques are a waste of time. She won't respond. She knows it and they know it and yet still they persist. It's just another hoop to jump through, a ticked box that says they tried with her, that they did their utmost to talk her around, and it didn't work so they were forced to up their game. To do what she and they both knew they would end up doing from the start.

She continues screaming, roaring into thin air at the injustice of it all. She brings her hands up and uses her long, ragged nails to scratch at her bare skin, tearing them down her arms, tugging and digging until she is covered with blood, sickeningly warm and oleaginous, smeared over her thin, pale flesh.

Still the people plead with her. Still they try. And still she screams and tears at her own skin, ignoring their pleas for her to be silent and to take heed of their words.

Only when their begging and talking doesn't work do they eventually move towards her. She thrashes about, bucking and bending her body as they pin her down and restrain her. She screams some more, swearing and cursing. They don't stop. The small gang of people wrap their big, strong arms around her slight body, pulling at her shoulders to stop her from moving. An arrow of pain rips through her spine as her upper body is held fast. It doesn't bother her. Doesn't quieten her. She embraces the burning pain that shoots through her body. She deserves this. She deserves all of this and so much more.

In the end, they're too strong for her. She can't keep it up. No energy left. Exhaustion swamps her. She goes limp and feels herself being hoisted into the air and carried inside. Soon she'll be given sedatives and will fall into a deep, synthetically induced sleep. She will drift off into a world of darkness, into a place where the full reality of her life repeats itself over and over again. And then she will wake into a hell of her own making. A hell from which there is no escape.

1

NUMBER 19

They sit, side by side, terror coursing through their veins. Today, they don't feel so well, especially the boy. Their innards twist and roil as they watch her move about the room. She's volatile, completely unpredictable. That's what causes their fear, makes them feel on edge. Is today one of her better days or will today be the day she raises her voice to them and shrieks that they don't deserve to have somebody like her in their lives? There's no pattern to her moods, no set rules they can live by. What works one day can go against them the next.

The girl leans over and squeezes her brother's hand. His skin is cold. She places her palm against his forehead. He's trembling and his flesh is clammy. She listens to his breathing, ragged and uneven, as he pushes air out of his lungs and forces more in. Breathing is meant to be easy, effortless and reflexive, yet the rattle of his chest sounds like the death throes of a dying man. She shuffles closer to him. He is so small, so helpless. She wants to take care of him, to be the older sister he needs her to be, and she is doing her best, really trying to help him get better, but it's so difficult. Nothing is easy in this house. The smallest of indiscretions can cause a tsunami of bitterness and punitive sanctions. There's no way of knowing what lies ahead. No way of predicting her mother's next move.

She wishes things were different. She has friends who do things with their parents – trips to the seaside, days out in the countryside, cinema visits with popcorn and big bags of sweeties. She feels sure there must have been times when they did those sorts of things together as a family – had fun, laughed, ran around the garden playing hide and seek. But if they ever did, those memories are lost in the mists of time and they certainly don't do them now. It's been a long, long time since they smiled or sang or did anything other than stay in the house, watching and wondering. Watching their mother's growing irritation. Wondering what their next punishment will be; wondering what they did to deserve it.

She's considered telling somebody about their situation but can't seem to find the strength to articulate what it is she so desperately wants to say. The words simply won't come. Besides, her teachers are all too busy to listen, their time taken up with other children who are already on their radar – the scruffy kids, the naughty kids, the skinny underfed kids. The girl with holes in her shoes, the quiet boy with no friends who sits alone in the playground; they are the ones who fit the bill. Not her and her brother who live in the nice house and are always on time with the correct equipment, ready to learn. They aren't the children that people worry about. And it scares her. They are the forgotten ones. She knows that they're slipping between the cracks of the system, falling so far down that one of these fine days they may never be able to find their way back up.

And anyway, what would she say if she were to tell somebody? How would she ever be able to verbalise the subtle ways that are used to reprimand them? The hidden bruises, the name calling, the sudden acts of love when their father is around. And their mother is always well-kempt and quite glamorous when she takes them to school. Her hair shines; her make-up is flawless. People rarely suspect the highly polished ones, the pretty, fashionable ones. Bad parents look bedraggled. They turn up in the playground with unwashed hair and dirty clothes, reeking of alcohol. Their mother is far too wily to be caught out by such a schoolboy error. Standards must be maintained and children need to present well. Wagging tongues at the school gate are a dangerous thing.

So their lives continue on a downward spiral, gaining in momentum with each passing day. It's her brother she fears for. He is so small and defenceless. And there is something else that's happening to him; she knows it by his laboured breathing and grey pallor. It's just that she can't quite put her finger on what it is that's wrong. Perhaps he's ill and needs medication? Treatment that will rid him of his awful cough and bring some colour back into his cheeks. Their mother takes him to see the doctor regularly, or if he's too ill, the doctor comes to the house, but even that's not enough. Something else is wrong. Something that frightens her. Something that she feels sure is worse than her mother's shouting and unexplainable mood swings.

The girl swallows down the lump that has risen in her throat. She hasn't the energy for tears. Tears will only get her into trouble. And she doesn't like being in trouble. All she wants is for things to be back how they were before everything became too difficult, back to a time when they were happy and their mother remembered how to smile.

2

ESTHER

I'm always surprised by how cold it gets at this time of year. I shouldn't be, I know that, but after a long hot summer, autumn and winter always catch me unawares. While I am still reminiscing over how glorious the garden is, or how pretty the children look as they march past my window in their checked summer dresses and smart grey shorts, the chill creeps in along with the darkness and dampness, reminding me that nobody can stop time. We all march to the tune of the Earth as it spins wildly in space, dictating our weather patterns and forcing us indoors as the nights draw in, the cold evenings spreading their impenetrable blanket of inky blackness over us all.

Pulling my shawl over my shoulders and tugging at it tightly, I gaze outside to the early-morning sky, my mind wandering over recent events. A host of unwanted images fill my mind. I try to stop them, to keep them at bay by thinking of other things, nicer things. Things that don't involve illness and death and all the horror that accompanies such atrocities, but somehow the dreadful stuff manages to take up all the space in my head. This is how it is now – my life – day after day of empty longing. Day after day spent ruminating over what happened, how I let it happen. What sort of a mother am I?

A sudden knock at the door drags me away from my thoughts. I'm grateful for it, thankful to be heaved back into the sharp light of reality.

Amy is standing there, smiling at me, as I pull the door wide open. Amy is a natural smiler. That's what she does. My mother used to say that the world is full of two types of people – frowners and smilers – and Amy is definitely the latter.

'Morning, Esther,' she says brightly. 'Just thought I'd call in while I was passing, see if you need anything?'

I stand for a second or two, waiting for my thoughts to present themselves to me fully. I chew at the inside of my lip, giving myself some time to think. This happens from time to time. I get lost in other matters and need a couple of seconds to process everything that's constantly whirling about in my head, to assimilate my many thoughts and work out what I'm going to say or do next.

I blink and reciprocate Amy's genuine smile with one of my own. She lowers her head and gives me a sideways glance. 'Tea? Coffee? Something for your breakfast? How about those waffles you raved about last week?' she says.

'I wouldn't mind some chocolate,' I reply, knowing she'll shake her head and tell me I need more than chocolate to give me nourishment.

Instead, she smiles and nods, and tells me she might be a little while longer than expected as everywhere is really busy – lots of cars and crowds of shoppers. 'Too many people on this planet,' she shouts over her shoulder as she makes her way down the path and into town.

'I'll pay you when you get back!' I call after her.

Without turning around, she gives me a wave, her long, slender fingers massaging the air above her head. I close the door and lean back on it with a long, drawn-out sigh. Seeing Amy has boosted my spirits. Today is going to be a good day after all.

* * *

I'm in the middle of reading my book when she arrives back with a large bar of chocolate. Her hands are creased and a painful shade of pink from carrying the bags of shopping, and she's out of breath. Her mouth is set into a firm line and a sheen of perspiration sits on her top lip as she breathes in and out rapidly, her teeth clenched tight.

'Here,' I whisper as I guide her over to a seat and take one of the bags from her. 'Sit yourself down while I make us both a cup of tea.'

She nods gratefully and sets her head back against the soft fabric of the chair. 'Thanks, Esther. I'm wiped out after that walk. It was even busier than I thought. So many people about and not enough space.'

I take my time preparing our drinks. I want everything to be perfect. Amy deserves that much. She is always there for me. Amy, the young, thoughtful neighbour, the one who helps me out, listens to my tales of woe and wipes away my tears when it all becomes too much for me. This is my way of repaying her for her kindness and smiling face and gentle ways. It's a small gesture, but a gesture all the same. Amy understands me. She knows how I think. Sometimes, it's like she knows me better than I know myself.

The tea is piping hot. I arrange a plate of biscuits and set them out in a design that I saw in a magazine recently. I don't always favour women's reading material – such periodicals are usually full of mindless nonsense about celebrities I've never heard of and ridiculous medical problems that rely on natural remedies as a cure or some elusive yoga position claiming it will change your life and give you the key to immortality – but sometimes, just sometimes, I stumble across articles that interest or intrigue me. Like the one about how cooking and using food as an art form can restore balance in your thinking and help you overcome any problems you may be having in your life. And I have problems. Oh my, do I have problems. But I'm dealing with them, learning how to cope with my loss by reaching out to others and offering them as much help as I can. Occasionally, they accept gratefully, and then other times they don't. Amy always accepts, but like I said, she knows how my mind works.

I think about what I saw in the house opposite mine only yesterday and suppress an icy shiver. I have no idea if I can do anything about it, no idea where I would start to confront such a difficult issue. I don't even know if the person in question would welcome my intervention, seeing my assistance as an intrusion. I just know that what I saw was terribly wrong and I don't think I can sit back and watch it all unfold without doing anything to help.

'Everything okay in there, Esther?' Amy's soft voice brings me back to the moment, sending a slight chill over my skin.

'Won't be long,' I reply as I head back through to the living room, the china cups rattling against the metal tray with every step I take.

I place it down on the side table and hand Amy her cup. She takes it and puts it on the floor next to her feet. I offer her the plate of biscuits and see her hesitate before picking one up and biting into it.

'I shouldn't really,' she says with a slight giggle. 'I'll never get into that wedding dress at this rate.' Tiny specks fly from her mouth and land on her lap as she munches her way through the thick, crumbly biscuit, a smattering of cocoa-coloured scraps incongruous against her tight, pale trousers.

'You don't need to lose any weight,' I murmur softly, staring at her flat stomach and skinny arms. 'If you get any thinner, you'll disappear altogether.'

She shakes her head and licks the crumbs off her fingers. 'I've got another half a stone to go, Esther, and I'll never get there if you keep feeding me delicious chocolate cookies, you naughty woman.'

I laugh and shake the plate at her, insisting she have another one. 'Go on,' I say, my voice chirpy and reminiscent of my younger self, the person I used to be when I was carefree and happy, the person I was before life cut me down. 'One more won't make that much difference, surely?'

She closes her eyes, lets out a deep sigh, and reluctantly snatches up another biscuit, pushing it into her mouth and munching on it energetically. I watch her face as she savours the delicate flavour of ginger and white chocolate, see her eyes narrow as she takes a brief delicious respite from her state of eternal dieting.

'So, when is that young man of yours home then?' I enjoy talking about Amy's life, her job and plans for the future and especially the wedding. It makes me feel young again. It makes me feel as if I'm part of it even though I know I'm not. I'm allowed to indulge myself every now and again. Since losing my own family, it's one of the few pleasures I have – living my life vicariously through those around me, exploring their ups and downs, while wondering how my own children's lives would have turned out if they were here today, wondering what sort of people they would have grown into had they lived.

A familiar wave of sadness threatens to overwhelm me. I close my eyes and swallow down the lump that has risen in my throat. Not today. I won't allow myself to be consumed by sorrow today. I got out of bed feeling positive and I'll force myself to stay that way. I want the day to end the same way it began – with smiles and optimism, not grief and unhappiness. I deserve to feel contented from time to time. I may have let my family down but surely there can be moments when I am allowed a moment of respite? Days when I can switch off from the heartache and emptiness and just enjoy the moment.

'Next Tuesday,' Amy replies, her eyes sparkling with undisguised excitement and love. 'I hate that he has to work away but we need the money so what can you do? We're going shopping for his wedding suit. I was thinking pale blue to match the bridesmaids' dresses. What do you think?'

'Sounds perfect,' I murmur, my eyes filling up unexpectedly. I turn away so she can't see it. I'm the older person here, purportedly wiser and more reserved emotionally. I have to keep myself in check. I find myself wondering what sort of wedding Harriet would have had. Would she have gone for a large, elaborate celebration or simply slipped away to a small hotel somewhere remote with just a handful of close family and friends by her side?

I drain the last of my tea and turn to look at Amy. So young and trusting. I can't remember being like that. I must have been at some point, before it all happened, but it seems like such a long time ago. I feel as if I've been a thousand years old for so long now. There's no end to it.

'Anyway,' Amy says breezily, unaware of my creeping distress at her youthful excitement. 'Must be off. So much to do. I really do need to get moving.'

'How's that job of yours going?' I ask, swallowing down memories of my absent family and thoughts of things that will never be.

'My job?' she replies with an element of mild surprise. 'Oh, you know. Same old, same old.'

'I hope those patients are behaving themselves and not putting you under too much pressure.' I raise my eyebrows and watch her face for a response.

She leans forward and pats my knee affectionately. 'They're okay, Esther, but thanks for being concerned. If only everybody was as considerate as you, eh?'

I want to hug her, to keep her here with me where I know she will be safe, but I'm aware that's not possible so I give her a weak smile and stand up to follow her as she walks towards the door.

'See you again soon?' My voice is weaker than I want it to be, showing my desperation, my vulnerability, a side of me I'm not proud of. I was a strong woman once, somebody who was in control of her life. And now look at me. At what I've become.

'Of course,' Amy replies enthusiastically.

Her smile is infectious. I hope she remains forever innocent and never has to suffer the irreparable heartache of loss. I lean forward to hug her but she slips out of the door before I can reach her. All that remains is the scent of her perfume, an invisible trail of cologne that wrenches at my heart and leaves me feeling marginally bereft.

I close the door and return to the living room where I set about clearing the cups and plates away, putting everything back in order, back to how it was before she arrived.

3

I wonder if she knows I'm watching her?

After Amy left, I decided to sit by the window, hoping to catch sight of my new neighbour as she went about her business in the comfort of her own home, doing dreadful things, despicable things that had shocked me, taken the breath right out of me. She didn't disappoint.

And now I have been sitting here now for over an hour, gasping at the gall of the woman. She obviously knows no shame, treating people in such a terrible way.

That's the beauty of living where I do – I have the benefits of living in a relatively quiet area, with less traffic and fewer houses, whilst having the convenience of shops close by. My house was built in the 1970s and although many think it ugly, with its large picture windows and flat roof extension, I adore it. I also love this area. It is so wonderfully handy. Everything is accessible. I can see All Hallows Church over the road and admire the beauty of its ornate, redbrick architecture. If I crane my neck, I can just about see the end of the busy, pedestrianised high street with its many quaint shops and large, squat war memorial, and when I sit by the window to watch the world go by, I can see into my neighbour's house and witness her warped behaviour. Slightly elevated, I have the advantage of height and also the beauty of not being visible. If I perch myself like this, slightly to one side, partially hidden behind the curtains, nobody can see me. I can observe the secrets of people who pass by my home undetected. I can observe her secrets. And from what I've seen, she has quite a few.

I considered telling Amy about it when she was here but, after giving it some thought, I reckoned it was too soon. She hasn't lived here long, this new person, having only moved in a few weeks ago. I need to see what else she gets up to, to see what she's truly capable of, before I disclose my findings to somebody else. She doesn't know it, this new neighbour, but I'm onto her. After watching her only a handful of times, I've discovered she has many secrets that I'm almost certain she would rather remain private and undetected. She can rest easy on that score. For the time being, anyway. I need more evidence before I start speaking to other people about what I've witnessed. For the moment, I'm content to just sit and watch and wait.

I open my chocolate bar and bite into it, the creamy texture gliding over my tongue and slipping down my throat. I enjoy the slightly heady kick of the sugar and cocoa, then swallow and wipe my mouth with the back of my hand, my eyes never leaving the window. Things have been quiet in the last fifteen minutes or so. Before that, however, she was very active, throwing her hands around in the air like some sort of demonic force, shouting and yelling at those poor children. I picture their little faces, their terrified expressions, as she vented her spleen on tiny people who were in no position to defend themselves. They looked so frightened; their little bodies bent in terror.

Saliva suddenly fills my mouth as the image of her contorted features and angry, puckered face fills my mind. I throw the chocolate to one side, a wave of sickness filling my entire body, starting at my gullet and travelling down to my abruptly distended stomach. Some people don't realise how lucky they are, how full and fortunate their lives are, with their lovely houses and beautiful offspring. I too have a lovely house but it's empty and lonely without my family here to fill it. No small footsteps parading through the hallway, no calls of excitement as they troop in from school and drop their bags on the floor with a thump before rushing into my arms to greet me. Just a never-ending silence once the day draws to a close and everybody has closed their curtains, leaving me alone in my large home. Just me and the shadows and deeply painful, interminable silence that has stayed with me since the death of my husband and beautiful children.

I hold my breath and close my eyes, trying to fight the misery and gloom that threatens to engulf me. I promised myself that today would be a good day. I am tired of being miserable. I want to feel happy and untroubled; I really do. I crave contentment and happiness but sadness and despair always seem to win, slithering their way into my pores and clinging to my bones.

I do my breathing exercise – in through my mouth and out through my nose, in through my mouth and out through my nose – over and over and over until it starts to work and I feel an air of calm spread through me, cooling my burning veins and throbbing brain.

Opening my eyes, I take one final, deep breath and lower my head until everything begins to clear. I don't like it when my body refuses to respond to my commands. I'm a grown woman. Despite suffering a massive trauma, I like to think I'm always in control, able to handle my grief and deal with the devastating losses that rocked my life. But obviously not. Obviously, I'm weaker than I thought. That's to be expected, I suppose. After everything that's happened.

I stare over at number 19. It seems quiet in there. Nothing to report. Unlike earlier, when she was raging at her children who looked utterly horrified, the room is now empty and still.

Standing up, I look around my living room. A notepad. That's what I need. I've decided that I'm going to start jotting down times and dates to monitor this woman's movements. I would end up looking more than a tad foolish if I contacted social services and the police with no more than my word as evidence. I know from my time spent teaching that recording as much as you can is crucial in situations like this. And Amy has told me many times that when she is at work, she has to make notes about her patients and fill out heaps of paperwork. Anecdotal ramblings or gut instincts simply aren't enough. We live in a world of official forms jam-packed with small boxes that have to be ticked, categories into which people and their actions are neatly slotted. And if that's what it takes to keep those children over the road safe in their own home, then that's what I'll do. I will tick as many boxes as I can, fill in enough forms to sink a battleship, and sign every single one of them because some people don't deserve to have children just so they can abuse them when mine are buried deep in the ground.

I wipe away tears I didn't expect to fall and stalk over to the bureau in the corner of the room. There'll be plenty of paper in there. Pens and paper and everything I need to get the ball rolling on my new project.

I open the door of the bureau and stare at the mess in there. So much stationery. Years and years of accumulated stuff that I have no need for. Snatching up a sheath of paper and a half-decent pen, I head over to the small table next to the window and set everything down. I write the date at the top and then stop. I need a title. And my neighbour needs a name. I can't keep calling her *the woman over the road* or *the new neighbour* or *the woman at number 19.*

Sitting for a few seconds, I take the pen and write *Veronica* at the top, then underline it. I have no idea where that name came from but it looks right and the more I say it, the more fitting it seems. I like the way it rolls off my tongue as I enunciate it loudly in the quietness of the room. Anyway, from what I have seen, she looks like a Veronica should look, so from now on, that is how I will refer to her. She will no longer just be the woman over the road. She now has a proper name – Veronica.

I shuffle the pieces of paper until they're in line with each other and then fold the corner over to keep them in place. A small sliver of excitement rushes through me. This is a positive thing that I'm doing. It's not spying or intrusive. It's called neighbourly kindness, looking out for one another in times of need. That's what people living in close proximity do for each other. They rally around, do what is required to keep everybody safe. That's all I'm doing here – keeping those youngsters safe from what appears to be a mentally unstable mother. I've had more than my own share of heartache so I know how important it is to have help and assistance when you're at your lowest ebb. If only somebody had done the same for me when my sister was with my children and husband. Maybe then Harriet and Dexter would still be here. Maybe then I'd be happy.

Feeling empowered, I sit there, pen in hand, poised, waiting to scribe my thoughts, to put down on paper exactly what is taking place inside that house.

On the edge of my vision, a shadow disturbs my thoughts, causing me to shift in my seat. I glance over to the window, my legs suddenly weak at the thought of what I might see. I wait a couple of seconds, bracing myself, before I peek around the side of the curtains where I'm confronted with a sight that turns my stomach.

In the living room opposite, I can see Veronica standing over a man who I presume to be her husband, and she is throwing things at him. My heart taps out an uncomfortable beat as I try to catch my breath and make sense of what it is that I'm witnessing. He's sitting on the sofa, staring up at her. His face is turned away from me and I can't catch his expression or see whether or not he's injured, but his body language says more than his expression ever could. He's slumped in the seat, his position submissive, his back arched and twisted away from her.

I watch transfixed as Veronica reaches down, picks up some sort of object and hurls it at him. He ducks to one side, his hands covering his head. The large object skims past him and bounces off the back of the sofa, missing his face by inches. I can't work out what it is and whether or not it's heavy enough to do any real damage but the size of it is enough to make me go cold.

I stand up and move away from the window, stumbling on unsteady legs over to the bureau. I open it and rummage through the contents. I know that somewhere in here I have something that could help me. It's been so long since what I'm looking for was last used, I'm not even sure if I still have them. I have no recollection of throwing them out, but then after all the turmoil and upset after losing my entire family, anything is possible.

Grabbing handfuls of letters and papers and boxes that contain old documents, I push them aside and drag my fingers into the back, sweeping them back and forth, side to side, hoping to land upon something bulky, something that feels like a leather case that holds Julian's old binoculars. I grasp at anything, pulling out fistfuls of papers and throwing them behind me in desperation.

After a short while, my hand lands upon something that feels promising. With a flutter in my chest, I snatch it up and drag it out and am disappointed to find it's no more than an old calfskin wallet that has seen better days. Throwing it onto the floor in annoyance, I continue searching until the bureau is empty save for a scattering of yellowing papers and a couple of torn envelopes.

I spin around, trying to think where else the binoculars could be. It would be unthinkable that I would have got rid of them. I kept everything of Julian's after he died – everything. But of course, my mind was in such a state that I may have scooped them up in a fit of pique along with many other unwanted items, unaware his things were in there, and thrown them out. An army of people trooped through this place after it all happened: police officers, social workers, all manner of officials who worked on the case of my dead husband and children. Perhaps they removed items and failed to return them? I was in too much of a mess to do anything, to do an inventory of my belongings and ask for my property back. For all I know, Julian's precious binoculars could still be sitting in a filing cabinet somewhere in the bowels of the local police station along with many of my other household items.

Feeling torn between anger and frustration, and a sense of resignation at my predicament, I return to my seat by the window. I look down at the mess on the floor, at the papers strewn everywhere, and let out a sigh of annoyance and frustration. I'll tidy up later when I've observed Veronica some more. Some things are too important to ignore and right now watching her is more important than anything, especially tidying my living room. A handful of old documents and torn papers can wait.

I pick up my pen and begin to write down what I've just seen. This is what I have to do now. I have made it my business to keep those people safe, to report what I see and pass it onto the relevant authorities, and that is exactly what I will do. Everything else can wait.

4

NUMBER 19

The woman stares at her husband as he eats his evening meal, loving and loathing him in equal measure. There was a time when she adored him. Now she's not so sure. Does she still actually truly love him? It's so hard to tell. She doesn't think she can even remember what love feels like any more. She is tired, jaded. Perhaps she is just used to him, conversant with his ways, and thinks she couldn't live without him. The more she thinks about it, the more certain she is that that is how she feels. Familiarity, that's what they have. And don't people say that familiarity breeds contempt? Maybe that's what she feels for him but it's dressed up as love in her aching, confused brain. And yet if that's the case, then why is she so consumed by jealousy? Why is she so loath to let him go?

She saw the message on his phone. Does he know that she has seen it? Does he even care? She's not going to confront him about it – not just yet. She wants to be sure, not make some wild accusation that could be thrown back in her face at every available opportunity if she happens to be wrong.

She follows him into the living room once he's finished eating.

She doesn't even clear the dishes away. She has no energy for it. The kids are upstairs and she has decided that she wants to talk to him, to have it out with him once and for all.

He slumps down onto the sofa, his legs splayed open, his mind completely closed off. It's not like it matters. She knows exactly what he's thinking. He's thinking of his fancy woman, his bit on the side. He's certainly not thinking of her, his wife, the woman standing before him; the woman he chose to marry fifteen years ago. His mind is focused solely on *her* – his mistress.

She watches him as he leans down, picks up a newspaper and starts reading it. He's doing it on purpose, being deliberately evasive, pretending he hasn't picked up on her declining mood and ever-growing temper. What he doesn't realise is that his avoidance techniques are actually making things worse, causing her more hurt and resentment, but then she supposes he doesn't really care about her at all. If he did, he wouldn't be kicking her aside for somebody else, would he?

The seconds tick by, turning into minutes. The silence is deafening until at last, he looks up and asks her what's wrong. His tone is forced, his manner contrived. He's trying to sound kind but she can see beyond his façade, beyond his sickly-sweet manner, and something inside her suddenly snaps. She grabs at the first thing she can reach: a heavy ornament, the one he bought her for their tenth wedding anniversary. The solid block of heart-shaped granite with their names engraved into it flies past his head, missing his head by inches. It lands on the back of the sofa, lodging in a cushion and causing minimal damage to the thick fabric.

His eyes widen but he doesn't flinch. A lot of men would have reacted, done something – shouted, screamed at her to fucking cut it out, to pull herself together and stop acting like such a psycho. He doesn't do any of those things. Instead, he picks the object up and lays it back in its original place. Then he puts his arms around her and leads her out of the room, assuring her that everything is okay and asking her if she needs to go for a lie down. Her blood boils. Is that his answer to everything? That she needs to take to her bed and stay there until her anger passes? All this does is rile her all the more, augmenting her anger a hundredfold. She shrugs him off and throws his arm away from her, then watches as he shakes his head despondently and shuffles off into his study, muttering about her being difficult and refusing help.

Silently seething, she follows and stands in the doorway watching him, waiting for him to say something directly to her instead of mumbling under his breath. She can read his every thought. He's thinking of *her*, wishing he could be wrapped in her arms instead of here with his deranged wife. Has it ever occurred to him that she wouldn't be so deranged if he wasn't such a cheating, lying bastard?

Her face burns as she watches him open his laptop. He taps away at the keyboard, his long, slender fingers gliding across it with practised ease. She has to control her breathing. He's probably emailing his girlfriend while his wife is standing here watching him. That's how low he has sunk. That's how bad their marriage has become. They have plumbed new depths and it seems that there's nothing she can do about it. Not a damn thing. The harder she tries to keep it all together, the worse everything becomes. It's all spiralling out of control: her marriage, her life, her state of mind.

She turns her back on him, thinking about her next move. She won't go down without a fight. This is her marriage and her husband. And if his lady friend thinks she can step in and usurp her, then she can think again.

5

ESTHER

The sound of the ticking clock fills the room. I've been sitting here now for over an hour and seen nothing.

By the time I settled myself back down after practically ransacking the house to find the binoculars, Veronica and her husband had disappeared out of sight and their living room has remained empty ever since.

Nothing to see, nothing happening. I've briefly written down the past events and am sitting here waiting for more but it looks like that's it for the time being. I'm mildly relieved. There's only so much I can take.

I glance at the clock and let out a slight shriek. My appointment! In my bid to monitor my neighbour's escalating propensity for violence, I have clean forgotten that I am due at the doctor's. It's 1 p.m. I've got precisely quarter of an hour to get ready and over to the surgery in time to see Dr McRae.

It doesn't take me long – a quick comb of my hair, a check in the mirror and I'm almost ready to go. An ageing face, bare and pale stares back at me as I look at my reflection. I rarely wear make-up these days. There doesn't seem to be any need. Nobody to impress, no job to go to, and few friends to meet up with. Those things are all part of my history, pastimes of the person I used to be before life trampled me underfoot, leaving me looking and feeling like a washed-out old rag.

Slipping on my jacket, I head over to the surgery. It's a five-minute walk away and I doubt it will be busy just after noon on a weekday. Everybody is either at school or at work. Only retirees and stay-at-home parents will be there in the waiting room, forlorn-looking with pasty skin and a look in their eyes that tells me they are weary of life and the hand it has dealt them. I don't mind visiting the doctor at all. It makes me feel as if I'm not the only person in the world with problems. Not the only one with issues and sadness trailing in their wake. I can sit, surrounded by illness and a collective sense of weariness, and feel better about myself.

I close the door behind me and with an uncharacteristic lightness in my step, I set off, enjoying the brief feeling of freedom at being out of the house. The distant hiss of traffic beyond the nearby railway bridge and the chatter of shoppers on the high street echoes in my head. Far enough away to not bother me, but close enough to stop any feelings of isolation from setting in. I should make more of an effort, get out more. I do know that, but whenever I venture outside, I always imagine bumping into families and having a meltdown in the middle of the street as I watch them interacting with each other, being happy and loving and doing all the things that normal families do. Either that or I have to suppress the overriding need that bubbles inside me to snatch their children away and take them home to live with me and be the family I no longer have. So, more often than not, I stay indoors and watch the world from the safety of my own home, a place I'm familiar with, somewhere I know I can relax and be myself. Not what I had planned for myself when I was younger, but at this point in my life, it works. It has to. It's all I have.

The surgery is full. I squeeze in through the door and am met with a room full of people who are undoubtedly nursing a variety of minor ailments that would simply clear up naturally if given time. They come here for company and reassurance, to have somebody listen to their woes and dole out sympathy.

The lady behind the desk takes my details and tells me to take a seat. I look around at the lack of places to sit and sigh loudly. It's always the same. Too many people, too few seats. The sound of sneezing and old people snuffling into their handkerchiefs fills the waiting room. One chap, in particular, coughs so long and hard I have visions of him bringing up a tobacco-coated lung. All around me, people sniff and moan and make small talk with the person sitting next to them about their illnesses, competing for escalating levels of seriousness. They stare at me as I shuffle myself between a scruffy-looking man with dark, suspicious eyes and a young woman wearing tight jeans and a strappy top that is wholly inappropriate for the current weather and shows way too much flesh on her taut abdomen. Some people have no shame.

The man opposite tries to engage me in conversation. He tells me about his job as a counsellor and how he enjoys chatting to others, then he asks me how I'm feeling. I almost laugh out loud. I'm sitting here in a doctor's surgery waiting to see my GP. How does he think I'm feeling? I want to reply that he would do well to mind his own business but instead, inform him of my latest problem – my crumbling spine, otherwise known as cervical spondylosis. He cocks his head to one side, looks at me sympathetically, and says all the right things about how debilitating it must be, his eyes creasing at the corners as he tells me that his mum has arthritis and has to take all kinds of supplements and visit a physiotherapist to stay mobile.

I feel more than a little relieved when my name is called and I can extricate myself from his unwanted probing and near proximity. I'm sure he means well but I'm a closed book when it comes to chatting with strangers. If it's company he's after, he'd be better off talking to one of the older people who seem to love telling the world and its wife about their litany of illnesses and complaints. He gives me a nod as I stand up and head into the hallway that leads to the doctor's room.

My appointment doesn't take long. I'm given more anti-inflammatory tablets and told to keep rotating my head to keep my spine mobile, something I do anyway. Dr McRae makes some strange comments, similar to the man in the waiting room, and for a second, I think I'm going mad.

'So, how is everything, Esther? I mean, how are you?' Her tone is deliberate, her words slow and soft with a definite undertone of condescension.

I narrow my eyes and stare into her face, my expression stone-like as I enunciate every syllable. 'My husband and both of my children are dead, Dr McRae. How do you think I am?'

If I expect her to recoil or show a modicum of sympathy, then I will have to wait a long time. I am way off the mark with that thought. Her face doesn't change. She sits, rigid, her eyes unblinking as she scrutinises me and remains worryingly silent. I shift in my seat. What exactly does she want from me? Does she expect me to smile insipidly and tell her I'm fine? Or to put on a brave face and tilt my head while trying to suppress a tidal wave of misery so large I fear it might engulf me and drag me away never to be seen again? I am done with putting on a show for others to save them having to rake through their own emotions and summon up some compassion. I am done with trying to preserve the status quo and save them from embarrassment at being privy to my car crash of a life. I'm sick of it all.

'Are you doing the exercises the physiotherapist showed you? Making sure you stay mobile and don't seize up?'

'Yes,' I sigh loudly. 'I do them every morning.' She knows this is the case as she asks me every time I visit her. I hate this silly, pointless scenario almost as much as I hate Dr McRae. Seeing her feels futile but each time I leave, she insists I make another appointment. If I didn't know better, I would swear she is on commission and making a million out of my mental anguish and rapidly crumbling spine. I enjoy the walk to the surgery and being out of the house, but always end up disappointed and upset when I get here. Disappointed at her lack of concern and upset at her cutting attitude regarding my situation.

'Good,' she says quietly as she writes on her notepad, the pen making a thin, scratching sound against the dry surface of the paper. 'Exercising the body can help clear the mind, push the difficult thoughts to one side. You know what I'm saying, Esther?'

I suppress an eye roll. This is another thing that irritates me – being treated like an errant six-year-old. I'm a widow and mother of two dead children, not a bloody imbecile. Still, at least these visits get me out of the house. Better than sitting in day after day and stagnating. That's the only positive thing I can say about it.

She lets me leave the surgery without attempting to call me back in to go over some old injury or previous illness. Neither does she try to talk me into seeing a therapist. Not after last time. I brush a lock of hair back out of my face and shiver.

The sun emits a weak ray of warmth as I make my way back home. I take my time walking there. No need to rush, nothing to get back for, nobody there waiting for me.

A train rushes past on the bridge above me as I step under the archway. The almighty whoosh as it passes overhead at speed sends a bolt of fear through me. The clank of metal against metal ricochets around the damp brickwork. An image of Julian and the children forces itself into my brain, their bodies trapped inside the twisted metal, their agonising screams and faces contorted in terror as their lives slowly ebbed away while I stood close by, unable to do anything. Unable to save them.

Anguish threatens to take my legs from under me. The raw sense of loss and complete dread doesn't get any easier. It never dissipates or becomes diluted no matter how often I try to quash it, no matter how many times I tell myself that there was nothing I could have done.

No amount of therapy will alter my situation or lessen my loss. What's done is done. No turning back the clock.

And of course, there was her. In the last moments of my children's lives, she was the one sitting close to them when it should have been me. My husband and my sister, sneaking one another secretive smiles and messages while my children were sitting in the back of the car. They were the innocent ones; completely oblivious to what was really going on, thinking they were on their way to Aunt Charlotte's house when, in fact, they were being whisked away from me, taken from the one person who loved them more than life itself.

By the time I emerge from under the bridge, tears are coursing down my face, a river of suppressed memories and unending torment that, if anything, gets worse as time passes. They are all dead – my husband and my children. My family cruelly ripped away from me. I will never see any of them again. And it's all her fault.

6

I wish I could say that by the time I got back home, I had managed to pull myself together and the memories had gone but that's not how grief works. Being bereft is a yawning abyss of loneliness and endless pain that increases in strength with the passing of time. It's a huge falsehood that time is a great healer. All the passing of time does is increase the longing and the hurt. There are good days and bad days, of course. And yesterday started off as a good day but ended terribly. That's just how it goes and it's something I have little or no control over, which is why I stopped going to see a therapist. No amount of talking is ever going to bring my family back, to piece together the shattered fragments of my broken life and make me whole again.

I spent the rest of the day holed up in my bedroom, the quilt wrapped tightly around me to protect me from the vicious blows of the world in which I live. I sank deeper and deeper into despair until my pills gave me a modicum of respite and I fell into a dark, silent slumber.

And now I am lying here in my bed, desperately trying to

ignore yesterday and how it ended, and doing my utmost to 'put a brave face on it'. Those are the words people use to try and cajole me, to stop me being miserable and making such a nuisance of myself – doctors, psychologists, medical professionals from all walks of life who have no idea of how deep my suffering is or how difficult it is to walk away from the fear and darkness. If it were that easy, I would willingly do it. I'm not like this out of choice.

I drag myself up, unaware of what time it is or even what day it is. I probably overdid it with my medication but what the hell, I'm still here. Not dead yet, although sometimes that does feel like an easier option.

I look in the bedroom mirror and heave a sigh. An old woman stares back at me. There was a time I was considered quite glamorous with my hazel eyes and full mouth. My hair was thick and dark, falling in wide sweeping curls down my back and, even though I do say so myself, a fair few heads would turn whenever I walked in a room.

I rarely look in the mirror these days and whenever I do, I'm always shocked by the image I see there. My eyes have lost their shine; they are lacking in lustre and permanently stained with sadness. My skin is dull and the long tresses that used to frame my younger face have now turned a dull brown colour, streaked with grey that wires its way through each and every strand, giving me the appearance of somebody much older. I'm actually only forty-five years old but look and feel like twice that age.

Trying to force myself out of the mire of misery I have found myself in, I shower and put on clean clothes. I even drag a brush through my stiff, unmanageable hair, tugging at the knots and pulling free large clumps to untangle my matted barnet. I consider putting on a smear of lip gloss and stop myself. A step too far. Perhaps tomorrow, once this current veil of gloom has passed. But not today. I just can't face it. Lipstick feels wrong. Lipstick is for happy times. For days full of sunshine and promise. Not days like today.

Breakfast is half a slice of toast with a cup of coffee. I stare outside as I swallow, each bite sticking in my throat like lumps of cardboard. The sun is low, emitting a watery hue as it rises in the sky. The kitchen clock tells me it's 8.30 a.m. A handful of teenagers pass by on their way to school. They huddle together, gathered around their phones, giggling at something on the screen. They never fail to make me smile with their infectious laughter and genuine love of life.

I think about my years as a teacher, trying to work out whether or not I miss it. Perhaps I do. It's all a bit of a blur really. Maybe I miss the camaraderie of the staff and the hustle and bustle of the working environment but I don't miss the workload. I couldn't go back to it. Not now. Seeing all those children every single day, knowing they would be going home to their parents and knowing I would return to an empty house. It would feel so unfair.

I finish the toast and tidy the dishes away. When I return, the road is empty, the pupils now gone, disappeared around the corner and heading for the school just five minutes away. I sit for a few seconds, my mind empty.

A sudden flicker of a movement in my peripheral vision catches my eye. And then I remember – Veronica, the woman over the road. I quickly grab my notepad from behind the curtain and watch with bated breath as she steps into her living room, dragging one of her children behind her. A bubble of air catches in my throat and my heart steps up a beat. I know that I should do something, go over there and demand that she stops what she is doing, but like all cowards, she would undoubtedly lie and cover her tracks, denying all knowledge. She may even close the curtains and that would be much worse for those poor youngsters. At least this way, I can keep track of her movements, make detailed accounts of her brutality and when I have enough information to go on, then I can take it to the police or social services. I can hand it over to somebody who will step in and actually do something.

She pushes the small child down onto the sofa and stands, shouting at them. Annoyance pricks at me. I wish to God I had those binoculars, something to help me determine what is going on over there. I can see that it's a small boy she's yelling at. She says something to him and he stands up, his back rigid. I can't tell whether or not he is crying but it's obvious by his stance that he's distressed and frightened; the way his small body is bent to one side, the way his arms are wrapped around his tiny frame. An unuttered scream of protest roars in my ears. I want to run over there and snatch him away from her, to tell him that everything is going to be all right and that he will be safe here with me. But of course, I can't. For now, I have to sit and watch and wait. It's killing me, not being able to do anything, but once my log of misdemeanours is finished and I have enough evidence against her, then I can do something. Not yet, though. For now, I'll have to be content with watching and writing. For the time being, I am simply a voyeur with an ulterior motive. Somebody who wants to help and make all of this better again. I just need to be patient and see my plan through to the very end.

I find myself smiling – something I don't do very often. This is a good thing that I'm doing, watching Veronica and noting how she treats her children. I can monitor the woman at number 19 and be the saviour of those poor kids.

I feel buoyed up. I have a purpose. No more moping about, no more endless days of pining or drowning in loneliness. I can throw myself into this venture. And one day, some good will come of it.

People will thank me instead of viewing me with pity. I now have something to give.

It will feel good to get out of bed knowing somebody somewhere needs me. Being alone can feel overwhelming, like being lost on a high cliff. There are days when I am fine and the sun shines and everything is manageable and then there are days when I stumble along, wondering where I'm going to, thinking it would be for the best if I just leapt over the edge into the impenetrable darkness.

I continue to watch her movements. She's still shouting at him and he's still standing there, frightened and frail-looking. I can see now that the poor kid is still in his pyjamas. He must have overslept and now he's going to be late for school. Perhaps that's why Veronica is angry. Maybe he has upset her routine and she is furious. It's no excuse, however. He's just a child. She is the one who should have set the alarm clock and got him up. She's the adult in the house. None of this is his fault. He's a child. Just a child.

Moving farther back behind the curtains, I continue watching, hoping she calms down and gives the poor kid a chance. She doesn't. If anything, she becomes more agitated and animated, leaning towards him and pointing in his face. Then she does something that makes me feel quite sick. She rushes towards him and yanks down his pyjama bottoms. I let out a slight shriek and bring up my hand to cover my mouth. I watch horrified, as he stands there half naked. His small body shakes as he steps out of the pyjama bottoms and sits back down on the sofa, his small arms covering his skinny, naked limbs.

With trembling hands, I make a note of it all – Veronica's body language, his terrified stance and the final cruelty of leaving him standing there, the lower half of his body cold and exposed in the middle of the living room.

I continue watching as she stalks out of the room and then comes back in seconds later holding something aloft. She begins to rub him down, her movements sharp and jerky as she towels his bottom and the top of his legs. A breath judders out of me as I realise that he's being punished for wetting the bed. A memory spears through me. Dexter sometimes used to wet the bed but rather than shout at him and blame him, I'm almost certain I simply changed the sheets and gave him dry nightclothes, all the while explaining to him that it wasn't his fault. Which it wasn't. Why on earth is Veronica punishing him for something that is completely out of his control? My memory sometimes gets a bit hazy but I'm sure I never carried on with my children like this woman does. She has no compassion, any maternal instincts she should possess, seemingly absent.

She throws him a pile of clothes and he quickly steps into them, undoubtedly grateful for the warmth of the dry fabric against his cold, wet skin. I want to rush over there, gather that poor child up in my arms, hug him and bring him back home with me, but I know that's not possible so I will just keep on doing what I'm doing: watching over him and his sister from a distance until the time is right and I can step in and put a stop to it all.

Once he is dressed, they both leave the room and that's the last I see of the children for the rest of the day. I feel so helpless, just sitting here waiting for them to re-appear. I only hope they're both at school. It must be a reprieve for them, being away from their mother for those few hours every day. I bet they treasure their time in the classroom, being spoken to nicely, being treated fairly, playing with the other kids, knowing that no gruelling punishments are going to be meted out when they get back inside. I'll bet that school is their sanctuary.

* * *

The hands of the clock seems to move so slowly as I watch and wait for it to be 4 p.m. I'm ready by the window to record more of that awful woman's shenanigans when the children get in from school. She doesn't know it, but I am onto her. It may take some time to collate everything but as I have nothing else going on in my life and I've made it my mission to nail her, her downfall may well come about sooner than I could ever hope or she could ever realise.

It doesn't take long for her antics to kick in. I'm sitting, poised, pen in hand, as she sails into the living room, closely followed by the two children. The older child, a girl, looks to be about nine or ten years old. The boy looks much younger. I would say he is about five or six. Difficult to tell from this distance but they are both definitely too young to defend themselves.

They look at one another before turning to face their mother. Suddenly, the boy begins to retch. He bends over and holds onto his stomach, his head dipped as he leans forward and throws up on the floor. My heart leaps up my throat as I wait for Veronica to do something terrible to him, to raise her hand to him or push him away or scream at him while pointing in his tiny, terrified face.

Every second is an age as I watch and wait for her reaction. Time slows down. I can hear the sound of my own blood as it pulses around my body. Then something happens that takes me unawares. Rather than shout at him and be her usual angry self, Veronica scoops up the boy into her arms and holds him tight against her shoulder, rocking him back and forth and mouthing something to him in his ear, while the girl stands frozen to the spot.

I have no idea what is going on. A million thoughts rush through my head as I sit there watching this current drama unfold. Did I get it wrong on those other occasions? Is she really a caring mother after all and I've misconstrued her actions? Have I got it all horribly wrong? My stomach tightens. Something tells me not, but then why is she suddenly being the caring mother she should always be instead of the despicable woman I've been watching for the past few days? Confusion nags at me. Something isn't right with this situation. I just can't work out what it is.

I lean back, away from the window, and take a moment to let it all sink in. Perhaps I've done this woman an injustice and caught her at her worst, on one of the bad days that all parents have. I genuinely hope so. I genuinely hope I've caught her at her worst and things are about to improve. I make the decision to continue watching her, if only to settle things in my own mind. I'll keep vigil for the next week, just to be sure. I see it as my duty as a close neighbour to make sure those children are safe. I will give her seven days to prove her worth as a decent parent.

I close my eyes for a couple of seconds, trying to suppress the sensation that is rising in my gut. I shouldn't be feeling this emotion. It's wrong, I know it is, but I can't help how I feel. Disappointment tugs at me. What if her behaviour was just a blip and it turns out that she is a kind woman at heart and parent of the year? Where will that leave me? I suddenly had a purpose, a reason for living. I had focus for the first time in months, if not years. God forgive me for thinking it, but part of me prays this woman, this Veronica person, goes back to being a monster and doesn't take my reason for getting out of bed in the morning away from me. I want to help these youngsters, to save them. Because if I can save them, it will feel like rescuing my own children. And although I didn't know it until now, that is exactly what I need to do in order to heal my damaged soul. I want to be the saviour of these poor little mites because, difficult though it is to admit to it, I badly failed my own children and now they both lie in their graves, cold and alone with nobody close by to keep them safe. I let them spend time with my sister, their aunt. I let them think they were going be safe when in fact, they were taken from me, involved in a car crash, and now they're both dead. I hope they're looking down on me right now and can find it in their hearts to forgive me, because I know for certain that I can never, ever forgive myself.

7

NUMBER 19

The girl feels her body go cold and her skin prickle. She watches her mother cradle her younger brother. The woman holds him close to her chest and rocks him back and forth like she used to when he was a baby and she still loved him. Because although the girl is confused about many things, like why her mother is so angry all the time and why her brother is ill so often, she is certain of one thing – that her mother no longer loves anybody who lives in this house. She would even go so far as to say that she hates them all, even their dad. She can tell by the way her mother looks at him when they're all sitting at the table eating, and by the way she goes out of her way to pick arguments over any little thing.

The stench of vomit invades the girl's nostrils. On instinct, the youngster goes into the kitchen and comes back carrying a bucket of hot water and a scrubbing brush. This is the second time in a week her brother has heaved his guts up all over their floor. The doctor has been out to see him twice already for his fainting fits. He passed out at school and their mother was called to come and collect him.

He was surrounded by a group of concerned-looking teachers

when she arrived at the school wearing her best clothes and charming smile. The daughter had been waiting outside the office, her stomach in knots. She watched as her mother spoke at length with the headteacher and other members of staff, assuring them he was being seen by a medical professional and that yes, she would take good care of him when they got home and yes, she would definitely take him to the doctor again and get him sorted. She nodded in all the right places, doing her best to look caring and unassuming. Nobody knew or could have ever guessed the real mother, the unpredictable, cruel mother, concealed beneath the warm smiles and layers of carefully applied make-up.

In the car on the way back, the girl had sat on the back seat with her brother laid over her legs, his small head cradled in her lap. He was running a fever and she was terrified he was going to die. Her mother had told her not to be so stupid when she mentioned this later at home. A lump had stuck in the girl's throat at the callous way her fears had been dismissed so quickly and without question. The boy was ill. She felt sure that one day soon, he would go to bed and never wake up.

She kneels down at her mother's feet and begins to scrub. Her mother doesn't say anything, not that she expects her to. Sometimes, the girl goes about things, doing chores around the house, trying to fix their stinking house and broken family by applying detergent and hot water to the obvious piles of dirt that her mother doesn't seem to see, and nothing is said. The girl doesn't want thanks or displays of gratitude. She just wants to feel safe and loved. She hopes that one day soon, things will improve. She hopes that if she alleviates the workload of her mother, helps her out around the house and makes her day easier, then all their lives will go back to how they once were before her constantly overwrought mum became permanently angry.

The girl bites at her lip and tries to block out the vile stink of her brother's stomach contents that are splashed on the floor before her. It's a funny thing really. When she thinks about it, the only time her mother seems to snap out of her moods is when her brother becomes ill. Perhaps she does love him after all. Maybe when he's poorly, it makes her mother realise that she needs her family and has to help them and that they need her right back.

She finishes cleaning up and rises from her haunches, watching as her mother walks to the chair in the corner and sits down with the boy. The smell of vomit still clings to the fabric of the rug but it's the best the girl can do. Her hands are sore and her back is aching. She stares over at her brother huddled up like a broken old ragdoll on her mother's knee. She's glad he's getting some form of comfort from her. He deserves it. He's such a sweet little boy. Such a gentle, unassuming soul.

The only positive thing about this is that her parents don't argue as much when her brother becomes ill. Her father is too busy caring for his son and her mother is usually tied up with speaking to the doctor and arranging the medication. She smiles at the doctor more than she smiles at any of her family. They often stand together chatting, her mother flicking her hair back into place and nodding as the doctor speaks to her, assuring her that everything will be fine and that it's probably no more than a bug he picked up at school.

The girl hopes that's the case but something deep down in her gut tells her otherwise. Something is amiss, something she can't quite put her finger on. One day soon she feels sure a terrible thing is going to happen. The thought of it twists at her innards and makes her feel sick. She wishes she could control things, make her brother better, because if he recovered then her mother might start being nice to their dad again and then everybody would be happy.

She empties the dirty water down the sink and puts the bucket back in the utility room, making sure every drop of water is wiped away. When she passes the living room, she sees that it's empty. Her brother will be tucked up in bed, her mother probably on the phone to the surgery, requesting another visit from whoever is on call. The girl feels relieved. At least he's being cared for. That's the important thing.

Making her way into her bedroom, she tries to shake off the feeling of misery that sits squarely on her shoulders, pressing down on her, making her feel clumsy and anxious as if her feet are made of lead.

Her bed feels cold as she throws herself down on it, the sheets still crumpled where she crawled out of them that morning. The doctor will sort it when he comes out again, make it all better and cure her brother. He has to. It's his job, and if he can't do anything and make it all better, then she refuses to consider what could happen to them all.

8

ESTHER

Amy looks happy as she stands in the doorway, a halo of light surrounding her. I move to one side to let her in but she shakes her head and stays put. 'Just about to start my shift and I wanted to make sure you're okay.'

I nod and allow myself a small wry smile. 'I'm feeling pretty good today, actually,' I reply.

And I am. I slept well and awoke early with a spring in my step. Last night, I took one last look into Veronica's house and there she was, at it again, hollering and shrieking at her husband. He was sitting reading and I saw her standing over him, pointing her finger at him and screaming in his face. It was easier to see their expressions as the darkness was setting in outside and the light in their house illuminated everything. It was obvious he was trying to ignore her but she simply wouldn't let up with her tirade. I knew then that I hadn't got it wrong and that she really is a bad person, permanently angry and in fighting mode almost all of the time. Relief had flooded through me. Not because she was angry but because I was right. This is a serious accusation I'm making. Lives will change beyond recognition once I submit my findings. I have to get it right. And at least this time her fury wasn't directed at the children. I presumed they were safely tucked up in bed, away from the furore that was taking place below them in the living room. I drew my curtains and settled in for the night, ready to keep watch again the next day, feeling victorious. I felt vindicated. I had been right all along.

'That's good,' Amy says softly. 'I'm glad you're having a good day.'

I smile at her. She is such a good person. A young woman with a heart as big as the moon. I can't remember the first time Amy walked past my house or started visiting. My memories of those early days after Harriet and Dexter died are blurry and vague. I'm not even sure how she found out about my predicament. I suppose neighbours must have told her about me and what happened and she somehow made it her business to help me out and keep me sane. Although who she spoke to is a mystery to me. There aren't many houses in my road. Next door is the Peterson's. They're both in their nineties and rarely leave the house. A team of carers troop in and out on a daily basis, their cars swinging into the long driveway that leads to the big old house that Harry Peterson built himself, back in the 1960s when land was cheap and opportunities for self builds were aplenty.

On the other side of my house is Nancy Eldridge. A large insurance pay-out after her husband's death means she spends most of her retirement years abroad, travelling around Europe or cruising to somewhere exotic in the South Pacific. The house next to hers is rented by a young woman who works in London during the week. I can't even recall what she looks like. And then of course, opposite me is Veronica and her husband and children. They only moved in recently, perhaps a few weeks ago, and I know plenty about them and their miserable existences, but of course, that's my secret. For the time being, anyway.

Amy lives farther down the road, I think. Beyond the railway bridge in a cottage with her disabled mother. She passes here to get to the bus stop so she can get to work. She's a nurse at the large hospital in town and I have no doubts at all that she is an asset to her team. She has certainly been an asset to me.

'Well,' she says, her hair shining under the rays of the weak sunlight. 'Best be off. Lots of patients to see to today. I'm on a twelve-hour shift so I'll have to get a wiggle on.'

When Amy first started visiting me, I was a wreck, barely able to remember who I was, what day it was or where I was. She made a call to the surgery to get a doctor out to see me and that was when our strange asymmetrical friendship really began. I'm aware of the age difference between us. Amy is in her early twenties and I'm forty-five years old but when two people form a bond, age shouldn't matter. We chat almost daily and she helps me out by getting items of groceries for me when I can't face leaving the house. She also makes me laugh, something I thought I would never ever be able to do again after my husband and children died. Many women struggle to cope with just losing their husband. I lost Julian and my two children in one fell swoop. There one minute, gone the next.

She has done so much for me and I'm not even sure she realises it. Like the time I got it in my head that tidying up the garden would be therapeutic and help me restore some semblance of normality in my life. I set about mowing the front lawn and weeding the flowerbeds. Amy came along, saw that I had omitted to get changed out of my nightclothes, and helped me back inside before anybody passed by and saw me cutting the grass in my silk dressing gown. It's only when I recall incidents like that, that I realise I'm actually in far better shape now than I was after it all happened. I may spend time moping about like an old woman but at least I remember to dress myself every morning.

'I'll call by again soon. If you want me to, that is?' She looks at me quizzically. I want to laugh out loud and ask her if she is being serious. If I want her to? Without Amy, I'm pretty sure I wouldn't be the woman I am today. I may not be a fully rounded person or the most contented of individuals, but without her I know I would be a shrivelled-up wreck.

'I never want you to stop coming to see me,' I say a little too sharply. Part of me is always afraid that she will move on with her life and forget about me. She's young and has everything to look forward to. Soon, she will get married and possibly move away from here. She's talked before now about living nearer to where her boyfriend works. I swallow and shrug off those thoughts. She's still here and I have to focus on that, be thankful for her visits. I don't want to think about what will happen to our friendship in the future. I need to stay positive and be thankful for what I have here, at this moment in time, and not pre-empt things that may never materialise.

'You are a funny one, Esther,' she says, her nose wrinkling up as she smiles at me. I don't think of myself as even remotely humorous or amusing but I'll take her compliment if indeed that was what it is meant to be.

I watch her leave, then settle myself down by the window with my pen and paper. I quickly make a note of the time and wait for the next occurrence to take place at number 19. Veronica's living room is empty but that doesn't worry or faze me. Time is something I have lots of. I will sit here all day if I have to. Since leaving teaching, I haven't worked and don't plan to return anytime in the near future. I have enough money to see me through. I'm not wealthy, not by any stretch of the imagination, but my mortgage is paid and I can afford to live comfortably without having to get a job. Especially a job that involves working with children. I know I wouldn't be able to do it. Seeing their little faces and hearing their small voices would be too much for me. I like to watch the children as they pass by my window every day but being amongst them would probably tip me over the edge. Leaving my teaching career was a decision I took after Harriet and Dexter died, and one I know I'll stick to. I have no desire to return to an environment that will serve only to remind me of what I have lost.

I return my gaze to number 19, to the large picture window that allows me to see straight into their home. As expected, it's empty.

I sit for another half hour or so, keeping watch, and am just about to get up and make a cup of tea when there's a loud knock at the door. A splinter of anxiety slips under my skin. It can't be Amy. She's already been and as she said, she is on a twelve-hour shift today. I'm not expecting anybody, or at least I don't think I am. I do occasionally get visitors but I'm not prepared for this one. I like to know how my day will pan out. I'm not a fan of unexpected surprises. I like order in my life. After my tragedy, I need to know who or what is lurking around every corner.

The knock comes again, echoing throughout the silence of the house. Putting my pen down, I march through to the front door and open it, annoyance at my being disturbed oozing out of every pore. If it's somebody selling something then I'm afraid they will get short shrift from me. I don't agree with people going around knocking on doors without being invited. An old-fashioned way of thinking perhaps, but it's one of those simple rules I have in my life to preserve my privacy and keep my fragile sanity intact.

I turn the handle, pull open the door and feel my legs go weak. Hanging onto the frame for support, I stare into the face of somebody I dread seeing and am not prepared for.

'Charlotte?' My voice sounds distorted. My head pounds and I feel as if I've been submerged under water.

My lying sister is standing there, smiling at me as if we're still close, as if we're old friends. We are most definitely not that, nor will we ever be again. I want to scream at her to leave, to get off my doorstep, but find myself suddenly mute, shock rippling through me as a torrent of dark memories begin to bubble up in my mind.

'Esther, I thought I would pay you a quick visit. Do you mind if we have a little chat?'

I don't seem to have a say in the matter. Her mind is clearly made up. Charlotte barges past me and strides into my living room as if nothing ever happened between us. As if she didn't have an affair with my husband and then be a passenger in the car that killed my entire family.

9

'I'm moving away from the area.' Charlotte's words ring around the room. 'I just thought you should know.'

I have no idea why she came here to tell me this. I couldn't care less where she lives. She could emigrate to the other side of the world and I wouldn't care or miss her. We watch each other carefully, observing every movement, every facial tick, every single breath that exits our bodies. We scrutinise one another for signs of stress or defects. I do my best to show none. Charlotte is the last person on earth I would reveal my weaknesses to.

'Right, well, good luck,' I manage to say at last.

She nods at me and tilts her head sideways as if I'm a helpless child. Her walking stick is resting at the foot of her chair. I feel like picking it up and whacking her around the head with it. She has no right coming here unannounced like this, no right at all. More fool me for letting her in.

'Don't you want to know where I'm going to? I could give you my forwarding address,' she says, her voice sickly sweet with arrogance and an air of superiority.

I shake my head and watch her expression darken. I can't work out whether it's sadness or anger that creases her face as she tightens her lips and gives me a sharp nod in return.

'How are your legs these days?' I say.

I'm almost certain she detects the sarcasm and faux concern in my tone but she answers anyway, doing her best to keep smiling as she leans forward and strokes her damaged knee. 'Not too bad. As long as I stay mobile and don't sit around for too long, I can manage. The pain at night is quite bad but then I suppose...'

I want to jump in and finish the sentence for her by saying *But then I suppose what did you expect when you were in a car accident, on your way to God knows where, after conducting a long-standing affair with the husband of your only sibling.*

I don't say anything of the sort. Of course I don't. I'm too immersed in my own anger and misery to exert the energy needed to say it. My hands shake as I turn away from her and stare out of the window. I refuse to let her see me cry. She has no right to pity me or view me as some sort of victim. Were it not for her thoughtless, manipulative ways, Julian would be here with me today. There would be two messy bedrooms above me full of clothes and toys and the general detritus that is present in the rooms of most children.

This – my present misery and loneliness and fucking awful existence – is all her fault. I hate her for it. She got to keep her legs and her life whereas I lost everything. My entire life was crushed beyond recognition.

'I'll leave my forwarding address anyway. And when I'm back in the area, I'll come and visit you. I'm moving to Stirling in Scotland. It's about a three-and-a-half-hour journey from my new place to here, so I'm not so far away.'

I feel like screaming at her that I'm not stupid. I've lived in the North East all my life. I know exactly how long it takes to get to Scotland. When we were kids, we used to go there on holiday with

Mum and Dad. Maybe Charlotte has forgotten that? Or are those memories so unimportant to her that she has disregarded them, pushed them aside to make way for the more precious things in her life, like her boyfriend, Derek?

'Is *he* going with you?' I say. I know that he is. They're inseparable. The last time she visited me, he was with her. I can't even remember how long ago that was. Six months ago? It may as well be six years for all her visits matter to me. Charlotte only comes to me because she knows I would never ever make the effort to go and see her.

'Derek? Yes, of course he is. We've got a big old house in the middle of the countryside. We're planning to turn it into a guest house once we get in and get settled. I've always wanted to run a B&B and the new house is in the perfect location. Lots of tourists and ramblers that pass through the area.'

I purposely glance down at her leg and then back up at her face just to make sure she sees me. I allow my eyes to linger long enough to let her know what I'm thinking.

Her face burns red as she sweeps her hand over her knee and rests it on her thigh. 'Derek'll be doing most of the manual labour stuff. He used to be in the army and can make beds better than I ever could. I can work in a small office at the back of the house and take bookings and do all the paperwork.'

I would like to ask how much she paid for this new house. Did her insurance claim come in handy? If I'm not mistaken, she was given somewhere in the region of £50,000 for the damage to her leg. She and Julian had been travelling well within the speed limit when they got caught up in the middle of a police chase – two patrol cars were chasing after a stolen vehicle that was manoeuvring wildly through side streets at high speed when one of them hit Julian's car. The perpetrator got away scot-free. Charlotte lost the use of her legs for a couple of months and I lost everything that ever mattered to me. I hope she spends her blood money wisely and I hope it makes her and her new boyfriend very happy.

'I was thinking about your house.' She watches me closely, waiting for my reply.

I take a deep breath. Blood thunders through my ears as Charlotte speaks, her voice, her face, everything about her now alien to me. I can't quite believe what I'm hearing. I know exactly what she's going to say and jump in before she can go any further. '*My* house! That's exactly it, Charlotte. It's *my* house and nothing whatsoever to do with you.'

She nods and lowers her eyes. I know what she was going to suggest – that I sell it and buy something smaller, something more manageable, now I'm on my own. This is a big old house and ripe for renovating. The windows need replacing, the garden is far too big for one person to look after, and the plumbing system hasn't been replaced since God knows when. The boiler rattles and bangs and has a mind of its own. There is a lot of work that needs doing in my home but I am definitely not selling it. It is my sanctuary, the only stable force in my life. The radiators and old windows may well be in need of repair but this is my house and anything that happens to it is my decision and mine alone.

'I love living here in Warum. I'm not about to move for you or anybody.'

'But, Esther…' She narrows her eyes and spins around to look at the room we're sitting in. 'Esther, I really don't think that—'

I hold my hand up to stop her from saying anything else. I've had enough of my sister and her intrusive ways. She's taken enough away from me. I'm not about to let her take my house as well. 'Charlotte, I know you mean well, or maybe you don't. Who knows? What I am sure of is that I'm not prepared to talk about this any more. It is my house and nothing whatsoever to do with you. Now if you don't mind, I'd like to be alone.' My words are sharp, my meaning crystal clear as I catch her eye and hold her gaze.

She lets out a protracted sigh and drops her eyes to the floor, a scarlet web of embarrassment slowly creeping up her neck and over her cheeks. After a few seconds, she picks up her brass-tipped walking stick and holds it tight in her palm before hoisting her ungainly frame up out of the chair. Her legs appear weak and unable to support the weight of her body and for one awful moment, I think she might fall. I find myself wondering whether or not I would help her if she did, or whether I would let her lie there on the floor, struggling for purchase as she squirmed about to haul her injured body upright. But she doesn't fall. She stands perfectly still, her gait slightly out of kilter, as she watches me with her dark-brown eyes. I suspect she is waiting for me to back down, to say that it's a perfectly acceptable idea and that she can help me with the paperwork and perhaps even take a cut of the money.

I want to shake my head at her, to tell her that she is out of her tiny mind coming here, ordering me about. I'm not the younger sister any more, somebody she can control and manipulate. I'm more than capable of sorting my own affairs out.

I begin to edge towards the door, hoping she takes the hint and follows me. Fortunately, she does just that and we walk together in silence, our bodies so close I can feel the heat emanating from the bare skin on her arms. At one point we bump into each other and on reflex, I rapidly move away. This will hurt her, I know that, but I really couldn't care less. She caused this rift, not me. And I can't help how I feel.

It's hard to believe it, looking at us now, but Charlotte and I were once close. As teenagers, we would trail around the shops on a Saturday afternoon, a pitiful amount of pocket money burning a hole in our pockets. Charlotte, being the older sister, would always try to guide me when I attempted to spend all of my cash on sweeties and cheap lip gloss. She was always more sophisticated than I could ever hope to be, instinctively knowing what colour clothes and make up would bring out the best in her skin tone, and what sort of blusher would enhance her sweeping cheekbones. I always looked up to her, admired her knowledge of fashion and music, and unlike the older sisters of some of my friends, she was kind to me, guiding me through life and helping me to navigate my way through the snarled and often dark path of puberty and adolescence. When I woke up one morning to find a bloodstain on the bedsheets that had leaked out from between my legs, it was Charlotte I went to, not Mum. She gave me one of her sanitary towels and rubbed my shoulder softly when I told her I had stomach cramps, laughing that I had best get used to it as I had another forty or so years to go until they stopped.

There was a four-year age gap between us. When I was a gawky twelve year old, Charlotte was a glamorous sixteen year old, stylish and fashionable, and knowledgeable in the ways of the world. I felt proud to have her as a sibling.

I didn't mind being in her shadow, being the younger, slightly less glamorous and definitely more ungainly, sister. People often told me I would grow into my face, which I did. I was never going to be in Charlotte's league but I always made the best of what I had; I looked after my skin, curled my hair, kept a trim figure. People often complimented me on my appearance, telling me I had the look of a budding film star.

By the time I was eighteen and forging a life for myself, Charlotte had left home and was living with a man ten years older than her. My parents weren't exactly delighted at the age gap but he was a kind and reliable chap, and was a doctor at the local paediatric unit in town. Coming as we did, from a fairly average, working-class home, they saw his position as a real step up for their daughter. Charlotte was a legal secretary at a large solicitor's practice and loved her job. Their life was pretty rosy until one day, Charlotte came home from work to find her boyfriend dead on the kitchen floor. He had suffered a brain haemorrhage and according to the coroner's report, had probably passed away before he hit the ground.

'I'll visit again soon, Esther. I promise I won't leave you here on your own.' She turns to face me as we stand side by side near the front door. I wonder if she is considering hugging me. I hope not. The days of us being the tactile siblings we once were are far behind us. We're very different people now – the split in our pasts too deep, too cataclysmic to ever be repaired.

'Don't bother. I'm managing just fine here.' My voice is clipped, cold and distant. I refuse to make any attempt to conceal my displeasure at seeing her.

She lets out a sigh of resignation and dips her head away from me. I don't miss the flicker of sadness in her eyes or the look of disappointment as she leaves. I can see both emotions clearly in her face. I simply don't care.

Outside, a ridge of heavy clouds hangs above us, grey and ominous-looking, as a strong and sudden gust of wind pushes them ever closer. They fill the sky, causing me to shiver with a terrible sense of foreboding. Perhaps it's Charlotte's unexpected visit that's causing it or perhaps it's just how I am lately, my moods oscillating wildly from one second to another without any warnings or triggers. I try to snap out of it but it's as if an invisible hand is pushing at my back, forcing me downwards towards the cold earth beneath my feet.

A small group of people pass by the end of the garden. They stop and watch us, one of them giving me a small wave. I don't return the gesture. I have no idea who they are. Possibly neighbours from farther down the road beyond the bridge. I guess they all know about me – the sad woman who lost everything. It doesn't bother me so much, all the clacking tongues that talk plenty but say nothing. They think they know all there is to know about me. They couldn't be more wrong.

Charlotte starts to walk away down the path, her hand brushing close to mine as she moves. I can sense that she is tempted to hug me, to apologise and ask if we can start again. She also knows what my response would be, so instead she continues walking, stopping at the end of the path to chat to the group of people standing there. Their bodies and expressions are animated as they make small talk. I have no idea what they're discussing – the weather, the state of the economy. It could be anything at all. I don't much care either way. They have an air of arrogance about them and I feel sure they are discussing me despite not knowing who I am. One of them briefly glances my way before turning back to join in the ongoing conversation. I am half tempted to march over there, tell them all to shut up and move away from my house but instead I slam the door hard, making sure it can be heard from where they are standing, then I lean back on it, heave a trembling sigh, and let the tears fall.

10

It doesn't take me long to pull myself back together. I'm both surprised and pleased at how quickly I manage to talk myself back round. Not in such bad shape after all. This buoys me up, makes me realise that I'm getting stronger all the time. There was a time when an unexpected visit from Charlotte would have had me curled up in bed for days on end.

I allow myself a wry smile and think about her as she makes the journey home. Did she really expect me to succumb to her wishes and give up my home? I almost laugh out loud at the audacity of the woman. First, she takes my husband and children and now she's after my house. I don't think she expected me to stand my ground. Perhaps she wanted me to go and live with her in Scotland where she can keep an eye on me, revert back to being the older, controlling sister. Or maybe her conscience is finally pricking her and she feels duty bound to take care of me. She can think again. I'm not going anywhere and I'm perfectly capable of taking care of myself.

After the accident, Charlotte spent six weeks in hospital having reconstructive surgery on her twisted and broken legs. I was at home during that time, trying to piece together the shattered fragments of my life. I managed without her then. In fact, she was the last person I wanted to see once I realised what had been going on behind my back. Our lives became divergent at that point, never to come together again, so I'll damn well manage without her for the rest of my life.

She has been over to see me on a few occasions, all of them uninvited. Considering our differences, I have no idea why she even comes at all. My life may not be perfect, far from it actually, but it ticks along in its own strange, methodical little way. I live a fairly quiet existence and have good days, bad days, and sometimes bloody awful days but all of them, absolutely every single one of them, I scrape through without the assistance of Charlotte.

Feeling quite smug at having packed her off with the notion firmly embedded in her head that I no longer want anything to do with her, I set about tidying up the living room. The place is in a bit of a mess. I can't recall the last time I gave it a good, thorough clean. There never seems to be much point with me living alone, but Charlotte's visit has set me off on some sort of purge. I feel the need to get rid of every trace of my sister, along with the rest of the dirt in this room.

It doesn't take me too long to clear it and I decide after finishing the living room, to move onto the bedroom. Opening a cupboard that I rarely use, I'm greeted by the sight of a green leather holdall I don't recognise. My chest tightens a fraction as I lean down and drag it out onto the floor where I can see it properly. A small pulse starts up in my neck as I peer down at the alien object seated at my feet. I had hoped that by getting a closer look at it, I would recognise it, see it in a better light and suddenly remember why it's there. None of that happens. My mind goes into overdrive, trying to work out where it has come from. It doesn't belong to me. I'm sure of it. A horrible thought then occurs to me – what if it's full of children's clothes? A bag full of Harriet and Dexter's belongings that somebody put there with the intention of removing later on? In all the furore after their deaths, any number of people could have traipsed through the house and moved their things. I do have a vague recollection of asking one of the many people who descended here in the aftermath, to remove all their belongings. I couldn't bear to look at any of their favourite outfits knowing they would never wear them again. It was just too painful a reminder for me to deal with. With the benefit of hindsight, I now wish I had kept some of their stuff, even if it was just one item each, something I could hold onto in bed in the wee, small hours when the night-time seems to drag and the darkness is never-ending.

My breath catches in my throat as I kneel down and open the holdall. I peel the top back and let out a gasp. Inside is a large pile of my own clothes. Nothing belonging to my children at all. It's a bag full of my clothes that I wear every day. I pull out a vest top and my old grey trousers and hold them up in front of me as if an explanation for this bizarre find is going to drop right out of the sky and into my lap.

I swallow nervously and place the items onto the floor next to my feet. Rubbing at my eyes with the back of my hand, I stop and stare at the next layer of fabric. My nightclothes lie neatly folded on top of the pile, the same nightclothes I wore last week and hung on the back of my bedroom door with the full intention of washing them. I don't know whether to laugh or cry. My vision blurs and a lump becomes lodged in my throat as I begin to pull things out and put them down on the floor next to me. My blue sweater, my second pair of slippers, even two of my lace bras – they are all packed away in this bag that I have never seen before. Or have I?

My initial instinct is to say not, but if that's the case, then how did my clothes get in here and more importantly, why did I put them there?

Fear grips me. What if I'm suffering blackouts or going into some sort of trance and doing things without any recollection afterwards? A sob erupts out of my throat. I close my mouth and stifle it, dragging everything back in the holdall before closing it with a sudden slap.

Standing up, I kick the bag back into the cupboard and shut the door. The noise echoes through the house; wood hitting wood, the sound of a door being slammed by somebody who is confused and frightened. It's the sound of my innermost fears being dragged out into the open.

I stagger back into the living room, dazed and scared. A thought slips into my mind. Did Charlotte do this? Is this her way of making me think I need her help? But then, how did she get hold of my things? I was with her all the time she was here. She never left my sight. It wouldn't have been possible for her to try and trick me like this. As much as I'd like to blame her for carrying out such a cruel act, it simply doesn't fit.

A thousand possibilities flit through my brain, none of them feasible. I eventually run out of options and have no idea what to think. I'm almost certain I've never gone into any sort of trance or dreamlike state and packed my own clothes into a bag that I've never seen before. Why would I? None of this makes sense.

I wander around the room, wishing I had some alcohol in the house. A drop of whisky would be just the tonic right now. I can almost taste the acrid, woody flavour as it slides over my tongue and hits the back of my throat with a kick. But I have no whisky, no wine, no port or sherry stashed anywhere. Nothing to take the edge of what I find to be a wholly disturbing experience.

Instead, I make a cup of tea and sit by the window to calm my nerves. There is obviously some logical explanation for it all. I just don't know what it is yet. Sipping at the steaming liquid, I decide to not ponder over it. When the time is right, the answer will come to me. I must have put the clothes there at some point. There is no other reason and I refuse to worry myself sick over something I have no immediate answer to, so I take my time drinking my tea and let myself be carried away by the lulling effect of the ticking clock in the background.

The sun is setting and the sky is just starting to darken when I wake up. Disorientated, I pull myself upright. The empty cup is still in my hand and I am slumped down into the chair, my neck aching where I slept with it cocked to one side.

I try to rouse myself. It's rare that I sleep during the day and my mind is in a fog as I attempt to pull myself round. Blinking repeatedly, I put the teacup down and run my fingers through my hair, yawning and bleary eyed, trying to adjust my vision to the last vestiges of the dying light outside.

Viewed with the advantage of a rested brain, the holdall episode seems far less worrying than it did before I fell asleep. Even Charlotte's unexpected visit doesn't jar my emotions or send me into a tailspin. I feel completely relaxed and at ease with myself.

A flicker of movement at the edge of my vision causes me to stiffen. And then I remember about Veronica. From where I'm sitting, I can see straight into her living room, which is well lit and wide open. A frisson of excitement runs through me. How could I have forgotten about her? Charlotte's visit has totally thrown me, causing me to lose focus on what is important and what I need to do.

I settle myself back in the chair, aglow with contentment and a refreshed mindset, and watch.

11

NUMBER 19

Things are slipping away from her. She can just feel it. He's going to leave. He's not intimated it but she knows him well enough to work out what he's thinking. She'll try to stop him. He knows that she will. What he doesn't know is how far she will go, how far she has already gone. Things are in place. She has a plan, a way of making him stay, getting him to love her again like he used to when they were younger. When she was pretty and slim and had tight skin and a positive outlook on life.

Her daughter seems to be able to read her mind. She's a clever one that girl, and she will have to be careful around her, not let her get too close. She's only doing what she is doing so she and her daughter and the rest of the family can all go back to how things were, so they can return to their once happy existence. It feels like a lifetime ago since the sound of laughter tinkled through their house. When was that? Before the kids were born or just after? Everything is so difficult to pin down – the once well-defined lines in her mind now blurry and lacking in any sort of tangibility.

Whenever she thinks of her son, she gets a warm glow. Such a sweet boy. Desperately wretched at times, and the bedwetting is downright irritating, but he is a good boy. Always obedient and biddable. That part of his nature serves her well.

Right on cue, her daughter enters the room and starts to speak, disturbing her thoughts. The girl is crying and asking if her mother and father are about to get divorced. The words slice through the woman, sending a shard of ice through her, cutting deep into her bones. What happened to children being seen and not heard? Such arrogance from somebody so young. Without thinking, the woman steps forward and brings her hand up to her daughter's face, the slap taking her breath away and leaving the girl looking as if the life has just been sucked out of her. The woman moves back, shocked. She hadn't meant to hit her daughter that hard. It's just that everything seems to be slipping from her grasp like water trickling through her fingers, her once-perfect life slowly but surely ebbing away from her.

Maybe she needs to up her game, speed up her plan to keep her life on track. When she takes control of that particular aspect of things, she feels so positive, as if she can conquer the world. It makes her look caring and compassionate and brings her the attention she so desperately craves.

Her daughter backs out of the room, her palm clasped over her cheek. The woman feels her temper flare. No need for histrionics from the girl, no need at all. It's a good job her father is out of the house or she would undoubtedly go running to him for sympathy and he would give it to her without question, never asking what she may have done to deserve it, not thinking to ask his wife what had taken place. He rarely if ever, takes her side.

This is how it's been since the kids have come along, as if all the attention he once lavished on her has suddenly been handed over to their children, leaving her out in the cold. If she's being honest, that's when it all started to go horribly wrong. Once they became parents, any time they had for each other was stripped away until they became virtual strangers. So she guesses it's only right and fair that the kids pay a hefty price for it. They are ones who are to blame. They are the ones who caused the current fissure in her marriage. At least it feels that way. There must have been times when they were all happy and functioned as a family, but misery has eaten away at all the good stuff, wiped out the better times, and now all she feels is resentment and rage.

She slumps into the chair, feeling defeated at her lack of progress. He'll probably be late home tonight. He will be out with his mistress, whispering sweet nothings into her ear the way he used to with her when they were young and in love. Fury and jealousy pulses through her. She is dizzy with it.

Fuelled by her anger, she stands up and stalks into the kitchen, her mind in overdrive as she tries to work out what her next move is going to be. She needs to do more, be the loving, attentive wife and caring mother he wants her to be. That's how she'll get him back. It's the only way. It sounds easy when she says it, but being a loving and attentive wife and mother takes time and energy and that's something she is all out of. Why is it that being hateful and hurting others comes easier to her than displaying warmth and kindness?

Taking a few deep breaths, she leans into the cupboard and retrieves the hidden packet she keeps stashed behind the large bags of flour. Scrutinising it carefully, she looks for somewhere to keep it, somewhere easily accessible. This small item is the key to everything, to keeping her family intact and salvaging what is left of her marriage.

She allows herself a small smile. If she can keep her cool and get everything just right, this plan of hers may just be the best idea she has ever had.

12

ESTHER

Sadness runs through me as I observe her in action. I'm not sure if she is worse than I remember or if my nap has cleared my mind to such a degree that any act of violence feels repugnant and alien to me.

Sheer fear and dread pulses under my skin when I see her daughter walk into the room. I can tell by the way Veronica screamed at her husband earlier that something awful is about to take place, something horribly dire and grim that will turn my stomach.

She doesn't take long to prove me right. In one swift movement, she steps forward and slaps her young daughter across the face. I recoil, pushing myself away from the window, my spine pressed into the back of the armchair. I lift a trembling hand to my forehead, horrified by what I've just witnessed.

I have no idea what to do. I simply cannot just sit here and watch it all unfold without doing something to help. And yet I know I might make things worse by making my presence known, by letting this awful woman know that I'm onto her. All it will do is drive her behaviour underground, make her more secretive about her abuse. Yet it feels so very wrong to just sit here and do nothing. I think of the Edmund Burke quotation – *the only thing necessary for the triumph of evil is for good men to do nothing.*

Standing up, I pull on an old sweater and grab my boots from the hallway, pushing my feet into them as I grab at the door handle and head outside.

A cold breeze greets me when I step out into the chill of the evening. It's still quite early but once the sun sets in Warum, the temperature drops rapidly, coating the landscape with a wet mist that floats in from the nearby river, trailing over the grass and curling itself over every inch of ground.

Ahead of me, a group of people in their twenties stand chatting in the street. Probably on their way to the pub. I don't miss any of that stuff – the drinking, the crowds, the pushing and fighting to get to the bar and then the loud, belligerent behaviour from those who get drunk and can't take their alcohol, turning aggressive with everyone around them.

As I walk towards Veronica's house, one of women moves towards me, blocking my path. I try to step aside but end up accidentally bumping into her. She is a small woman with blonde hair, slightly older than Amy, and she's wearing black trousers and a sweater. Hardly clothes to go clubbing in. Maybe I've got it wrong and they're just standing there making small talk before moving onto somewhere else. I quickly apologise and carry on walking, my heels clicking loudly on the pavement.

'Everything okay?'

The voice causes me to turn around. I initially have no idea who it is that is speaking and feel sure it's not directed at me. Why would it be? I don't know these people and they certainly don't know me. At least, I don't think they do. Maybe they live locally and have heard all about my situation. My face burns at the thought of it – being talked about, pitied, having people avert their gaze whenever I walk by because they are all too embarrassed to speak to me, unsure what they should say to somebody whose family died in tragic circumstances. Unsure what to say to the mad lady who lives alone in the big old house on the corner.

I ignore the voice. The last thing I want is to get dragged into a conversation with people I don't recognise. I have never been one for chatting idly with strangers and have no plans to start doing so at this juncture in my life. Charlotte was able to make friends with the people in the queue behind her whilst doing her weekly shopping but I have always been much more reserved, preferring my own company to that of fake people and forced friendships.

'Esther? Are you okay?'

The voice rings in my head, bouncing off my skull as I hear my name spoken. My blood freezes as I stop and take stock of what is happening. Who are these people? I hear a murmur spread around the group and suddenly feel compelled to march over to them and demand to find out how they know me. But I don't. For a couple of seconds, I have no idea what to do, how to react. I want so much to find out who these people are and why they're standing outside my house calling my name but I can't seem to find the strength to move. Time stretches out before me as I wait. I hear their whispers, hear my name being bandied about as they discuss me, talking about how thin I look and how pasty my skin is. I visualise myself screaming at them to stop, shouting at them to leave me alone and get away from my home, but of course I don't do anything of the sort. The coward in me takes hold and instead, I spring out of my stupor, then turn and shuffle back inside the house, locking the door behind me, my limbs weak with fear and shock.

I can hardly breathe as I perch myself on the edge of the chair. The floor sways beneath my feet and the walls seem to lean in at a peculiar angle. I grip the wooden arm of the chair with my cold fingers, determined to make sense of what just happened out there. Everything feels so delicate, so unreal, like a bubble about to burst, shattering my fragile existence. I thought I had everything sorted. I felt so close to being strong again and now things are happening that I can't explain: things that bewilder and frighten me.

My hands tremble as I reach over and shift the curtains ever so slightly, just to get a better view of number 19. The goings on over there, I'm not imagining them. They're very real. While some things that have happened lately are mysterious and unexplainable, the woman at number 19 is someone I know to be true. Her presence in that house is the one thing I can rely on. Her and my visits from Amy. Two people who are polar opposites – one, good and caring and wonderful, and the other, evil personified. And yet the one who fascinates me is the epitome of darkness and depravity. When everything else gets me down, the thought of spying on my neighbour puts a spring in my step. It's strange and repulsive and wrong on every level, but I feel some sort of connection with her, as if I've been put in this position to step in and help her and her family.

I concentrate on what is happening over the road and push the events that have just happened outside to the back of my mind. I can't spend each and every day worrying about things that are out of my control, and besides, thinking about it too much will only distress and worry me. If those people know of me, then there's nothing I can do about it. The idea of people knowing my personal business and being talked about locally doesn't feel good or sit well with me, but there's absolutely nothing whatsoever I can do about it. Sometimes, we just have to let things go and focus on the things we can change. And I can change what is taking place at number 19. I can do something positive and help those poor children. Everything else is just detritus in my life.

13

Veronica's house is quiet for the rest of the evening, with nothing occurring, no unusual movements or the kind of bizarre activity I've come to expect from her. The children filter in and out of the living room, stopping to watch TV occasionally, but nothing suspicious or even remotely interesting occurs.

Dragging myself away from the window, I decide to spend the remainder of the night watching TV, something I rarely do. I am barely five minutes into watching some lame film about a bride who gets ditched at the altar when I hear knocking at the door. After the escapade earlier, I'm on red alert and up and out of the chair before whoever it is that's out there gets a chance to knock a second time.

I stand with my back against the wall, my breath coming out in hot, rapid grunts. I can hear voices on the other side of the door and feel my flesh prickle with fear. Amy wouldn't call this late. And there's more than one person there. I can hear snippets of a conversation. What if it's those people who were speaking about me earlier? What if they have plans to do something terrible to me, something unspeakable?

I close my eyes and inhale deeply. They didn't look particularly devious or even capable of doing anything violent or nasty, but then you never can tell these days, can you? People can appear to be one thing and be something else entirely once you start probing and dig beneath the surface; they can come across as decent law-abiding citizens while all the time, the Devil lurks deep in their souls, driving them on, making them do dreadful deeds. Alcohol, drugs – they make people do things that even they themselves didn't know they were capable of. Substance abuse almost always brings out the worst in everyone – rarely the best, always the worst.

By the time I pluck up the courage to open the door, whoever is out there has knocked again, the sound reverberating around the room causing my heart to pound against my chest like a caged animal clawing to be free.

I turn the handle, the metal slipping against my sweaty palm, and pull the door ajar. I screw up my eyes and stare at the people standing there. Two people I don't recognise are either side of Amy. Behind them, the moon hangs heavily in an inky sky. Stars are dotted around the spread of black, small twinkling lights embedded in a thick blanket of darkness.

I step closer to get a better look at the two strangers standing there and feel Amy's hand rest on my arm.

'Esther, is everything okay?'

My scalp prickles at the obvious tension in her voice. I have to make a concerted effort to stop my jaw from quivering as I reply to her. 'Of course it is. Why wouldn't everything be okay?'

I have half a mind to shut the door on her but can't quite bring myself to do it. She deserves better. I'm rankled by her manner, however, by the fact she has turned up on my doorstep at this hour accompanied by people I don't recognise. None of this feels right.

'I just wanted to check, that's all. I saw you earlier and you looked distressed. Is there anything I can get you?' She smiles at me, cocking her head to one side as she speaks to me in a slow and somewhat condescending drawl.

'I'm fine, Amy.' I glance at the people either side of her in turn, making sure my probing gaze doesn't go unnoticed. 'Aren't you going to introduce me to your friends?' I try to sound authoritative, to let them know that this is my house and I'm coping perfectly well on my own, and that they have no right turning up here unannounced.

She lets out a short laugh and shakes her head. 'Oh, Esther, you are funny. I'm pretty sure I've introduced them to you before. This is Anne and this is Rose. They've both just started work at the hospital and I'm helping to train them up.'

I nod my head and try to look knowledgeable, even though I'm certain I've never met either of them before. Amy has a busy life and is obviously confused as to who she has spoken to when she's been with these two people. I want to ask how she knows about the incident earlier but am too worried about what her reply will be. I don't like being talked about or viewed with sympathy like a small child, somebody who is impaired and not in full possession of their mental faculties. I may not be the person I once was, but after my trauma, I think I'm doing okay. I'm certain many others would have buckled under the strain, so in comparison, I actually think I'm doing rather well.

The two young women watch me, smiling dispassionately as they wait for my reply. My mind is in a whirl, thinking about who they are and how Amy saw me. Perhaps she was farther down the road, just beyond the bridge? There's a slight kink in the pavement, making the houses down there more difficult to see. But then if I didn't see her, how did she see me? I was distracted, maybe that was it. Desperate to convince myself that's the case, I return their smile and say a quick hello before making to close the door.

'So, everything is okay then, Esther?' Amy says, stepping forward before I have chance to shut it fully.

My pulse quickens and I almost choke on my own spittle as I stare at the usually reserved creature before me who has almost jammed her foot in my door. I begin to feel marginally threatened by Amy's bizarre behaviour, as if everything I thought I knew about her was way off the mark. This whole scenario feels like some sort of wild, scary dream where everyday conventions are turned on their head and anything is possible. Even the unthinkable.

'Everything is fine, thank you, Amy. Off to work, are you?' I try to keep my voice light, to keep the growing irritation I feel at this unwarranted intrusion, out of my timbre.

The two young girls smile at one another before being visibly glared at by Amy, who suddenly looks very serious. Her expression morphs into a look of somebody more senior, somebody who holds a position of authority, which I suppose she does when compared to the pair of immature and inexperienced women standing either side of her here on my doorstep. Just youngsters, not yet in possession of social graces, their emotional refinements still not fully formed, they don't quite comprehend what is required of them in the presence of near strangers.

'We've got a busy night ahead of us, for sure,' Amy says, her voice returning to its usual milder tone. I relax as I hear her speak, my chest constricting with sympathy as I think of her working through the night at that big old hospital. Amy once told me she thought the place was haunted. On more than one occasion, she has heard somebody calling out her name when she was alone in one of the rooms. I shiver and pull my cardigan tighter around my arms at the thought of it.

'Well, stick together, ladies. I don't want to hear any terrible stories from Amy about some of those patients you have to deal with. Watch out for one another and you won't go wrong.'

Amy nods at me, her eyes bright with kindness and understanding. I feel myself soften and wonder why I felt so troubled and annoyed with her just a few moments ago. She would never ever do anything to hurt or upset me. I know that for certain. Amy and I care for each other. She is my rock and I'm her project. I do know that. I'm not so stupid as to fool myself that she thinks of me as a close friend even though I consider her one of mine.

I watch them leave, Anne and Rose turning occasionally to look at me. I know that they probably think of me as a deluded, sad old woman but I don't really care. They'll learn as they get older that judging people simply blinds you to their strengths. It obliterates the good stuff and before you know it, you spend each and every moment searching for faults in people that deserve so much more than rash, sweeping judgements when all they want is to be understood and loved.

* * *

I decide against watching more mindless drivel on the TV and switch it off. A sudden silence fills the room, making me feel jittery and ill at ease. Silly, really. I have no reason to feel that way. I'm perfectly content here on my own.

I make a point of walking past the window and not stopping to look. Tomorrow, I'll look in on Veronica again but for now, I much prefer the idea of being alone, not seeing anybody else and focusing only on my own thoughts and ideas.

My mind is still tangled up with thoughts of Amy and her friends as I walk into the bedroom and stop in the doorway. Something is different. It takes a couple of seconds to register what it is that is wrong with the room, and then I see it. The bedsheets. They've been changed. And the curtains. They were open when I left the room earlier, and now they're closed. I step into the room and peer over down the side of the bed. And that's when I realise that there's something else. Something that makes my skin crawl. A feeling of disquietude seeps into my bones, settling there like molten metal. I stare down at the ground, at what's lying there. They're on the floor. I swallow hard. The photographs of my family, including Harriet and Dexter, my precious, precious children, are lying in shreds on the bedroom floor, torn into a hundred tiny pieces.

I slump down on the edge of the bed in a heap, place my head in my hands and let out a horrified, bewildered shriek.

14

NUMBER 19

Her husband stands close to her, his chest rising and falling as he watches their child helplessly. She steps forward and lifts the hand of their small son, her thumb placed against the soft skin on the inside of his wrist as she feels for a pulse. She detects her husband's presence behind her and can practically smell his fear. She's the one with the coping strategies, the one who will get them through this torrid time. He's relying on her to sort this thing out, to make everything better. Which she will. And at the end of it, he'll thank her for it, be eternally grateful for saving their youngest child from a serious illness, for saving him from certain death. And then he'll love her again unconditionally. She deserves that much.

She turns and smiles at him, eyeing him earnestly, trying to reassure him that everything will be fine. He gives her a weak smile in return, his mouth creasing at the corners as he suppresses a sob and blinks back unshed tears.

They've been here for just five minutes after finding the boy ill in bed, refusing to get up for school, his skin grey, his eyes glassy as he looked up at them from under the covers, a desperate plea for help evident in his expression.

She assures her husband that it's nothing serious but does her best to look concerned. She makes the call to the doctor, the second one this week, and tells the receptionist that yes, the boy is too ill and too frail to attend the surgery and that yes, the doctor absolutely does need to make a home visit. Yes, she is also aware that it's the second one this week but her child is ill. He needs to come. They all need him here, to care for their boy.

Husband and wife sit side by side next to the son's bedside. She listens to her husband let out a moan of despair and strokes his hand. He is grateful for it and shuffles closer to her. She cranes her neck away from him and allows herself a small grin of achievement. This will bring them closer. It will bring him back to her, back to his wife's side, exactly where he belongs.

By the time the doctor arrives, she has tidied the house, packed the daughter off to school and re-applied her lipstick, a smear of scarlet spread over her lips as she smiles and steps back from the door to let him in.

The boy's breathing is shallow as the doctor leans down to examine him. He pulls up the child's pyjama top and places the stethoscope against his chest, listening intently, his eyes screwed up in concentration. The boy's mother steps forward and watches the doctor. She begins talking to him in an animated fashion but he raises his hand for her to stop. Her face flushes hot at the indignity of being hushed. This is her child. She'll speak if she wants to. She's the one in control here. Not the doctor and definitely not her husband. At this moment in time, they all rely on her for information and support. She's the backbone of this family. She is the one pulling all the strings. Nobody tells her to shut up. Nobody.

He's been vomiting. I've slept by his side all night. Do you need a list of his ailments, doctor? I've got them all written down. I'm very organised when it comes to dealing with my children and my family.

The doctor thanks her but assures the woman that it's not

necessary. She tries to control her breathing as she watches the way all his attention is focused on the boy – her boy. This is her home and her child. Her face burns with fury as the doctor turns his back on her and takes the boy's temperature.

Then he twists his body around and stares up at her, his expression unreadable. *I'm going to get him admitted to hospital and run some tests.*

Her stomach lurches. She's unsure how she feels about this statement. Her husband stands up and shakes the doctor's hand, thanking him profusely. He says their son's illness has gone on for far too long now and he's glad somebody is finally taking notice.

She listens as a sob catches in her husband's throat. He doesn't know. He has no fucking idea. She steps closer and takes his hand. He grasps it gratefully, rubbing at the base of her thumb with his fingers, an act he used to do many years ago when they were young and in love. It was a gesture she always found to be extremely soothing and slightly erotic. The passing of time hasn't altered her reaction. She briefly closes her eyes and thinks about what they will do later, once their son is safely ensconced in his hospital bed and they're back home. She pictures her husband's naked torso, his tanned skin, the line of hair that runs over his navel, down towards an area that never fails to turn her on. It's been a while. Too long, his attention recently focused elsewhere. But now he's back. She has him exactly where she wants him, back in the fold of his family. Back in her arms.

15

ESTHER

I try to rationalise what could have happened to the photograph and how it ended up shredded into dozens of tiny pieces on the floor, but can come up with no decent explanation to help me work out what has taken place or who did it.

Carefully putting the bits of torn paper on the table, I set about putting them back together. Delicate pieces fit neatly next to one another like a miniature jigsaw, the faces of my children staring up at me as I slowly slot their features back into place. Dexter's dark hair, Harriet's wide blue eyes, their beautiful pale skin – they all serve to heighten my grief and by the time I'm almost finished, it's as if I've lost them all over again, the sense of loss as raw as it was on the day it happened. That fateful day when my life as I knew it came to a juddering halt.

My heart drums in my chest and I struggle to fight back the tears. My veins feel fit to burst as blood runs through them, hot and viscous. I feel full of anger and resentment and untethered misery as I stare down at the loosely connected fragments. I have no idea how any of this happened and can't even begin to work out what the hell is going on. Nobody has been in here and I know that

I would never do such a thing. These photos are so precious to me that I keep them in my bedside cabinet, away from the prying eyes of any visitors I may get. I make a point of keeping them safe, so why has somebody been in here and done this?

A pain shoots across my head while I reassemble the photos and go over possible scenarios again and again. The fact remains that there is no logical explanation for any of this – the change of bedsheets, the tearing of the photographs – none of it is possible and yet here I am, piecing the shredded faces of my children back together. So what the hell is going on?

Hot tears run down my face as I finish assembling the photographs. I wipe at my eyes with the back of my hand, refusing to let this latest event get the better of me. I stride across the room and go through every drawer and cupboard, looking for glue to stick them back together, knowing all the while that I don't have any. After their deaths, this house was practically stripped bare and I haven't had the energy to go about replacing things. There seems little point anyway now there's only me living here. Except I now desperately need some glue. I won't settle until the faces of my beautiful family are intact once more. Without them, I am nothing. First thing tomorrow, I will go into town and get some. It'll be my top priority. Forget breakfast or tidying this old house. My family come first. They always have. They may not be here with me in person but they're never out of my mind.

I slump into a chair and think about the whole bizarre situation, trying to be as clear-headed as I can despite feeling overwhelmed with grief and bemusement at my find.

My breathing feels laboured, my thinking muddled as I sit there in the chair, trying to clear the fog that has settled in my head. This happened when I was at the door talking to Amy. My pulse speeds up as a thought gradually plants itself in my mind. Somebody must have snuck in the back way and done this terrible, awful deed when I was busy chatting at the front. That's the only thing that could have happened. But who and why? It's a ridiculous state of affairs. I'm a widow, living alone, with hardly any family or friends. I'm no threat to anybody and practically a recluse, so why in God's name would anybody want to sneak into my house and ruin my personal possessions? I figure that I must have got muddled up with which bedsheets were on the bed. The idea of somebody breaking in my house and changing my bed linen is just too ridiculous for words, but those photographs...

A faint buzzing fills my head. Did my sister come back and do this to get back at me? It seems a little strange even for her, but then her past behaviour has shown me that she is capable of anything – any misdemeanour, no matter how small or hurtful, isn't beyond her. And yet something tells me it isn't her. I don't know why I think this, but a feeling deep down in my gut tells me she wouldn't do this. It's too petty, too silly an act even for her. When Charlotte wants to hurt me, she is upfront and full on. Like trying to take my husband and children away from me. No half measures where my sister is concerned. She wanted it all, the whole shooting match.

A small thought burrows into my mind. Has my neighbour seen me spying on her? Is this her way of telling me to back off and to mind my own business? I feel a flutter of something in my belly. Not annoyance, not even fear that she may have come in here and wandered around my home and found items that are very dear to me. It's none of those things. So what is it that I feel? I focus on my breathing, suddenly realising with a mixture of emotions that what I'm actually experiencing is something akin to excitement. The fact that Veronica may have been in here to get back at me for finding out about her behaviour stokes a fire in my soul, unleashing passions I haven't felt in a long, long time.

I shake my head and tell myself not to be so silly. The very idea that a perfect stranger would do such a thing is outrageous. If she has seen me looking at her through her window, then surely she would have just knocked on my door and confronted me, told me to mind my own sodding business and to stop peering into her living room? I'm letting my imagination run wild and thinking thoughts that are simply too stupid for words. And yet if it isn't her, then who is it that broke into my home and tore up my pictures? A frisson of pleasure at the thought of Veronica rummaging through my personal belongings continues to run through me, firing up my senses even though I know it's a mad idea. Everything is too tenuous, the possibilities too far-reaching for it to be her. And yet...

I sit for a while, trying to link everything together, aware that my thought processes are verging on madness, when I suddenly spot her. Veronica! Her movements in the corner of my eye catch my attention and before I can remove myself from the position I'm in, I find myself transfixed, caught up in her wicked spell. I watch as she strides into her living room and takes command of it, her long hair shimmering under the glare of the living room lamp, her body bending and swaying as if in time to music. Behind her, the husband walks in and sits down on the sofa, watching her. Her movements continue, effortless and elegant, her arms lifting and floating around in front of her, her eyes closed as a look of concentration takes hold on her face.

I can barely breathe. I am mesmerised by this woman. Who is she? And why is she suddenly being so graceful as opposed to the monstrous being that I'm so used to seeing?

I don't have time to work it out as she suddenly turns and smiles at her husband, then in one swift movement she unzips her dress and lets it fall to the floor, effortlessly stepping out of the pile of pale-blue fabric that lies crumpled at her feet like a snake shedding its skin.

A wave of dizziness takes hold of me, my head swimming as I

watch this woman, this perfect stranger, remove her clothing in front of me. I gasp and duck for cover behind the curtains, my skin hot with shock and surprise. I stay there for a couple of seconds but am unable to not look. Something deep inside me compels me to keep watching her. I have to. I have to see.

Very slowly, I move back into view and suck in my breath when I see Veronica still gently swaying around the room, lifting her long hair and piling it on top of her head before letting it fall again. It cascades down over her slender shoulders, framing her feline features. I want to look away but can't. There is something about her that flicks a switch in my head, something about her shape and her eyes and the way she simply moves that has me rooted to the spot.

I am locked into place, wondering what she'll do next. Her husband sits watching her, his head tipped slightly to one side, his hands placed either side of him on the sofa. I can't see whether his expression is one of lust or repugnance. I imagine it's the former or he would have got up and left by now. What is it with this woman and her seesawing emotions? One minute, she is a screaming banshee, hollering at her husband and children, and the next, she is a vixen of desire, touting her wares for all the neighbours to see.

My breath continues to come out in short, jagged bursts as I sit watching this woman who is both desirable and hideous at the same time. Beautiful on the outside but ugly and warped when you dare to peer into her soul.

The breath I am struggling to regulate almost stops when I see what she does next. Without a flicker of shame or embarrassment and with no inhibitions whatsoever, she unhooks her white, lace bra and throws it aside. It lands on the floor next to her husband's feet. He makes no move to retrieve it, sitting instead with his eyes firmly focused on his wife and her shapely frame. Her hips are narrow, her waist small – the perfect figure that many women dream of having. She stops dancing and leans down then slowly hooks her fingers either side of her tiny, white knickers and pulls them down over her hips and legs, stepping out of them, graceful as a gazelle.

I stare at her naked back and pert buttocks and legs that seem to go on forever, feeling slightly envious of this woman and her life. Despite what I've witnessed so far, despite her rages and unpredictable moods, I am consumed by jealousy. At least she has a husband and children, whereas I have nothing. Just a cavernous abyss of emptiness where my family should be. She mistreats them and is cruel, that I do know, but she can change, can't she? People have the ability to put right their many wrongs, to correct their mistakes. All the errors I made with my family died with them that day. I have no way of making it up to them, no way of telling them how sorry I am for not being there for them when they needed me the most.

Tears threaten to fall. I stop them, steadfast in my refusal to let grief own me completely. Not today. For once, I would like a reprieve from it. I don't necessarily crave complete and utter happiness but neither do I want to be permanently miserable. It's lonely and exhausting living like this. I would like some balance in my life; some joy to counteract the constant feeling of sadness that even on my good days, never actually really leave my side.

My eyes are still drawn to the naked woman over the road, to Veronica, the woman who has everything yet acts as if she has nothing at all. She is still standing facing her husband, letting him feast his eyes on her slim, nude body. Then without any warning, she spins around, faces the window and begins to dance again, her arms up above her head, her fingers twirling in the air as if conducting an invisible orchestra.

On reflex, I pull back away from the glass, my heart pounding with what? Desire? No, not desire, but something about her nakedness, her dancing, has unearthed a sensation or a memory that is buried deep within my brain and I can't work out what it is.

Nausea nips at the bottom of my belly. Why is that? I have no reason to feel this way, no reason at all, and yet a nagging sense of doom has suddenly taken a hold of me and refuses to let go. With a thumping head, I close my eyes, trying to clear the myriad thoughts that are racing around my brain, my synapses firing and misfiring, confusing and frightening me as dark images set in and scratch at my skull.

I lean back and feel a familiar heaviness descend. Sleep comes to me as exhaustion presses down, forcing me to give in to it. I close my eyes and welcome the darkness, longing for an escape from everything...

Charlotte and I are sitting in my living room. I can see her face, the grey pallor of her skin and the way her mouth is moving, but I can't hear what she is saying. Behind me, people are moving about, shapes slipping in and out of my peripheral vision. I try to reach out and touch them but they disappear before I can place my hands on any of them. I don't know who they are. I want to scream at them to go away but the words won't come. They stick in my throat, coming out instead as a protracted moan, like a death rattle, letters and meaningless phrases trying to escape out of my mouth.

Behind Charlotte stands Harriet and Dexter. Their eyes are black like marbles, unseeing, expressionless. My heart leaps in my chest. I want to grab them, to cradle them and hold them near to me but they don't seem to know I'm there. Charlotte taps her knees and they both sit, perched lightly on her lap. Dexter nuzzles his face into her neck, murmuring into her ear. I am sick with envy. I want to leap up and tear both of my children away from her, to tell them to run and hide from this woman who is about to rip them away from me.

I turn my head, looking for Julian, but he's nowhere to be seen. I hear Charlotte laughing, her cackle echoing through the house, bouncing off every wall, off every bare surface, until I can no longer stand it. I lift my hands up and cover my ears, rocking in my chair as I try to stop the tears.

Eventually, I find my voice. It pours out of me, a stream of obscenities directed at Charlotte as I tell her to leave, to get out of my house and to leave my fucking family alone.

She laughs some more, pointing at me, her finger almost touching the tip of my nose as she shouts in my face, her features contorted, her eyes narrowed in anger. Her voice is a screech as it pierces the air. 'You can't have them, Esther! They're all mine now. I'm having them. You don't deserve to have kids. You never have.'

I begin to sob, a low, whimpering sound at first until it escalates into a gut-wrenching howl. I can't stop. My throat aches and my abdomen is a hard ball of anger and self-pity. I'm horrified at the unfairness of it all. Why isn't anybody helping me? I scream at her to leave them be, that they're my children and belong to me.

A hand unexpectedly rests on my shoulder, the warm touch of somebody I immediately recognise. I stop, a deep, guttural moan caught in my chest, and turn to see Julian looking down at me. I search his eyes for signs of understanding and compassion but find none. Instead, I see hatred and anger lurking there. I want to beg him to stay with me but know that he's about to leave and take everybody I care about with him, and that pleading with him will be pointless. My voice, my requests and cries, will simply disappear into the ether. He is leaving me to go off with her. I just know it. And there's not a damn thing I can do to stop them.

He drifts past me, my flesh now cold where his hand has been, and sidles up to my sister. I watch horrified as Harriet and Dexter snuggle up between him and Charlotte as if they're a family unit. My skin shrivels up. I shriek at them to move away, to come back to their mummy. They ignore me. My own children, and they act as if I haven't spoken.

The sudden slap across my face causes me to stop. I stare up into the face of my older sister, the person I thought would help me, the person who used to protect me when we were kids. She glares down at me, her words cutting through me, digging deep into my veins, allowing my blood to ooze and leak out until there's nothing left of me.

'They're not dead, Esther. They're my children now and you'll never get them back.'

16

NUMBER 19

She leans over her husband, sees the look of desire on his face and feels a tendril of satisfaction snake its way over her naked skin. She has him back exactly where she wants him. If you want to snare a man, don't fall for the old adage about filling his stomach in order to secure the key to his heart; the way to get a man and to keep him is to lure him with sex, each and every time. Make him feel as if he needs you, can't live without you, and then give him unlimited amounts of sex, and he'll be yours for as long as you want him. And this woman wants him for life. She wants him where his mistress can't get to him: in her home, her heart and her bed. She is his wife and this is where he belongs, here with her, for richer or for poorer, for better or for worse.

She spreads her legs slightly and licks her lips, watching as he lets out a small gasp of longing, then she moves forward and climbs onto his lap, straddling him and staring deep into his eyes. She starts to unbutton his shirt, her breath coming out in short bursts. He doesn't stop her, not at first, but then something in him changes – a sudden about-turn in his instincts – and she feels his body turn rigid, sees the light in his eyes begin to dim and a coldness take hold. She stops, wondering what the problem is and what it is she has to do to keep him interested in her. What the fuck will it take to keep him by her side and in her bed?

He turns his head away from her, whispering that it doesn't feel right, not with their boy laid up in a hospital bed. He had wanted to stay the night with him, to make sure their child wasn't frightened, but she had insisted they come home. Why had she done that, he asks? Other mothers would have wanted to sleep in the chair next to their child's bed. She had chosen to come home. What sort of parent would do that? What sort of parent is she? His voice is sharp, dispassionate; his face set like stone. And then before she can stop him, he is on his feet, pushing her aside and telling her they should get a babysitter for their daughter, go back to the hospital and make sure their son is being cared for and not laid in a strange place, frightened and alone, wondering where his parents are and why they have abandoned him.

She fights back tears and tries to cover her nakedness with her hands. What is it he wants from her? She's done what she thought was necessary to please him, to keep him from that fucking woman and now it has backfired spectacularly and she is left looking like a complete idiot. When is he going to realise that she's his wife and all he'll ever need? This is their home, their marriage, and here he is, ready to bolt out of the door to see their son who is in the hands of a perfectly capable team of medical professionals.

Grabbing at her clothes, she pulls on her dress, not bothering to put on her underwear, and stalks out of the room, a tsunami of humiliation washing over her, almost pulling her under until she feels like she can no longer breathe properly.

She clambers up the stairs and throws herself down on the bed, confusion, shame and exasperation boiling up inside her, festering and building, until she is so consumed by it, she lets out a roar of anger that echoes around the bedroom, stirring her daughter from sleep in the room next door.

She hears the patter of small feet along the landing and listens to the door being opened, to the soft shuffle of the girl's slippers as she pads along the carpet and stops next to the bed asking her mother what's wrong. Is it her brother? Has he taken ill at the hospital? Do they need to go there straightaway?

The woman sits up, her face scarlet, her temper frayed. She watches the girl intently. What does she know about anything? She's just a child, inexperienced in the ways of the world. One day, she'll find herself having to do all manner of humiliating things just to keep her man at her side. Then she'll know. Only then will her daughter fully understand why her mother does the things she does.

The questions continue, her childish voice irritating the woman beyond reason. All she wants is to be left alone, to ruminate over what just took place downstairs in their living room, but the girl won't stop talking. Why won't she shut up?

The woman brings her hand up. The sound of the slap and her daughter's shriek is drowned out by the slam of the door below as her husband leaves the house and gets into the car. He's going to the hospital. She just knows it. He is so predictable, so weak and spineless. Their son is fine where he is. He doesn't need them. They're husband and wife. They need each other. The children are one of the reasons their marriage is crumbling. Everything was fine before they came along. Why can't he see that? She had kids and lost her youth and her vitality. She's spent the last few years consumed by exhaustion – the fatigue of looking after children and doing household chores stripping her of every ounce of femininity and energy until she can hardly think straight. She loves them, of course she does. They're part of her, but they've changed her. They've changed their marriage. The time they spend together as a couple has all but stopped and now every spare minute they have, they're either working or cooking and cleaning, or doing things for their children. It never seems to end, the life of drudgery she has found herself in.

She looks at her daughter, at the spread of crimson on her face, at the imprint of her hand where she struck her, and suddenly realises what she has done. Letting out a howl of anger and pity, she draws the girl into her arms and they sit locked together, their tears mingling, their fear and confusion overwhelming them both. Is this what having a family is meant to be like, she wonders? All this pain and dread and tension. And for what? All so she can keep her husband by her side and stop him from tearing their little family unit apart.

Sniffing and staring up at the ceiling, her daughter's head laid against her chest, she thinks perhaps it would be better to let him go. Let him leave her for his fancy woman and then she can begin to forge a new life for herself, just her and the kids. The thought of it makes her feel sick to the pit of her stomach. She doesn't think she could do it. She's nothing without him. He is her rock, her everything.

She straightens up and wipes at her eyes. She'll confront him about his affair once he gets back. He doesn't know that she knows but she's seen the messages on his phone from an unnamed contact, worked out what those coded texts mean. She's not an idiot. She knows that he wants his wife gone. She's a nuisance, somebody standing in the way of his future happiness with his girlfriend. And from what she can gather, when he goes, he is planning on taking the children with him. Well, he can think again. This is her life, her marriage, and she will cling onto the final remnants of it for as long as she can. She will prove to him that she is still the same woman he married, the woman he wants her to be. She can do it. She has it within her to be anything he desires. She has hidden depths that most other women don't have. She'll tap into them and do whatever it takes to keep her man. She will do absolutely anything. Anything at all.

17

ESTHER

I wake up coated with sweat, my head pounding like a bass drum. My breathing is erratic and my vision is misted as if I've been crying in my sleep. I have no idea what time it is or how long I've slept for. All sense of time has left me. I'm completely disorientated and slightly numb where I've shifted into an uncomfortable position and slept like that.

Shuffling myself up into a more comfortable spot, I rub at my eyes with the heel of my hand. Weariness gnaws at me as I attempt to rouse myself. It takes me a couple of seconds to orient myself and think straight. My thoughts are blurry, like a thick mist has descended in my head, blotting out all logic.

I blink repeatedly to clear my eyes and think about the dream I've just had, how vivid it was and how even my own mind has the ability to taunt me, making me think my children are still alive. A small sob rattles up my throat. I swallow hard, pushing it back down. Crying won't solve anything. And anyway, it was just a dream, just a cruel, callous dream conjured up by my dysfunctional brain to plague me and make me even more miserable. As if I haven't been through enough.

I look around the room. Everything is exactly as it was before I nodded off. No more uninvited guests, no damage to my belongings. Relief floods through me. I listen to the ticking of the clock on the mantlepiece and use it like a metronome to regulate my breathing. It works. My heaving and gasping gradually slows down and my pulse slowly begins to return to normal. The fog in my head begins to clear and I can finally think straight.

I methodically go through my movements before I fell asleep, what I was doing and what I was thinking, and then it hits me – Veronica; she was dancing about naked in her living room. It knocked me off kilter seeing her, causing me to feel jittery and out of sorts. It set something off in my head, made me feel an emotion that I still can't quite pin down or put into words, as if a sudden, fleeting memory jumped into my mind and left again, leaving a gaping wound behind. The sight of her bare skin, the slow waltz that she did around her living room, it unlocked something in me, something I didn't care for. Something that frightened and unsettled me to the point of exhaustion.

I shiver and try to block it from my mind. She almost had me for a moment. I was totally spellbound by her act, making me forget what a monster she really is, what an utterly depraved human being she is, treating her husband and children with nothing but contempt. I can't let that happen again. I need to stay focused, to concentrate on her behaviour so I can put a stop to her deplorable acts of cruelty. She is obviously extremely manipulative and like all good manipulators, she does it with aplomb. Her poor family must be at her mercy. And if that's the case, they need my help more than ever. Those poor kids must hardly know if they're coming or going with her undulating emotional state and rapidly changing behaviour.

My stomach lets out a howl of protest at being deprived of food. I can't remember the last time I ate anything substantial, let alone cooked myself a proper, hot meal. I don't know where the time goes lately. It slips past so quickly, it actually frightens me. If only I could stop it, turn everything back to how it was.

I make myself some cheese on toast and a cup of tea, then sit by the window watching. I have mixed emotions about this now. I'm starting to witness things that are so much more than regular abuse. This Veronica is a real piece of work, devious and cunning, and from what I've seen, rotten to the core. I have to be careful here. People like her are far smarter than the likes of me. I lead a simple life with no hidden agenda, whereas she looks as conniving as hell. I may be well educated but she is light years ahead of me when it comes to trickery and deception.

Biting into my supper, I chew slowly, savouring the salty flavour of the cheese, wondering how I could let myself go this long without realising how hungry I am. I need to take better care of myself, eat properly, sleep more, and then maybe I'll start to get a grip on my emotions and stop feeling so desperately sad all the time.

Everything is quiet over the road. The house is pretty much in darkness apart from a dim light coming from one of the bedroom windows. The curtains are closed and there are no flickering shadows, nothing to suggest that anything is happening. All is quiet at number 19 for a change.

I finish eating and clear away the dishes, making sure the kitchen is clean and everything is put away properly. Tomorrow, I'll go into town and get some glue. I really need those photographs putting back together. Everything else in this house could lie in ruins but those photographs are my world and I must get them repaired. The thought of somebody skulking in here and doing such a thing fills me with disgust.

I walk through the house, switching off the lights, ready to go to bed, thinking about somebody creeping around this place. I suppress a shiver. Shadows stretch up the walls at irregular angles, large, grey forms looming over the furniture and the floor, causing me to spin around and glance behind me. I blink and check myself. This is silly. There's nobody here. The only things that's amiss here is my nerves. I need to be calm and remember that I'm perfectly safe in this place.

I stride towards the front door to make sure it's locked and feel my knees buckle. An envelope is propped up on the table in the hallway. It's resting against the letter rack, a small, white envelope with my name written on the front. Hand delivered, no postage, no address. Just my name.

Stepping closer, I peer down at it, my eyes blurry with fear and puzzlement. I didn't put it there. I know that I didn't. At no point today or even yesterday or anytime this week has a hand-delivered letter been put through my letterbox. I would know if it had. I would bloody well remember, wouldn't I?

Torn between feeling anger and blind fury, I reach out to pick it up, then stop. My flesh prickles and my fingers tremble as my arm hovers in mid-air. I quickly tuck my fingers in my pocket and rest my other hand on the doorframe to steady myself. This is insane. This whole thing is preposterous. What the hell is going on in my house?

I stand still, refusing to let fear get the better of me. There has to be a rational explanation for this. There is always a reason for strange occurrences. Always. As bizarre and scary as they may seem at the time, there is inevitably a solid cause for things. There is no such thing as ghosts. There is logic and reason and cold, hard facts. That is what I believe in. At some point, I must have scooped this letter up and placed it there. I *must* have. Nothing else fits.

I go over it again and again, desperate to convince myself that I'm not going mad or being stalked. If anything, I'm the stalker, spying on my neighbour, taking notes, watching her, scrutinising her conduct. So how the hell did this letter get here?

A pinprick of a thought edges its way into my mind, a memory from many years ago slowly pushing itself forward, creeping through the outer reaches of my mind. It dances on the fringes of my consciousness, teasing me with its elusiveness, refusing to be pinned down: a butterfly of a memory flitting about in my head, in and out of my brain. Something from my childhood. That's what it is. Something indefinable but possibly painful or terrible? I can't be sure. Whatever it is, it feels tinged with sadness, something that, once cracked open, will be hard to put back.

I don't touch the envelope. It can wait until the morning. If I open it and it contains something that I don't want to see, it will just stop me from sleeping, putting me on edge for the rest of the night. So instead, I turn off the light and head back into the living room, my heart beginning to pound as the distant, vague memory still sits at the base of my brain, refusing to reveal itself.

I stand in the centre of the room and take a deep breath before looking around and switching off the lamp. Then I head into the bathroom where I take a hot shower, letting the water pummel my back and aching bones. I towel myself dry and slip into bed, the cool sheets a comfort against my skin. It doesn't take long for me to relax and for sleep to take me. I am floating, happy, slipping into darkness, deep into the abyss.

And then I'm awake.

I sit up in bed, my head buzzing with the realisation that I've remembered. I know what it was that was lurking deep in the back of my brain. I know. And I wish I didn't. I wish I had slept the sleep of the dead and woken up refreshed and still unable to recall any of it, but I haven't. I am here, sitting up in bed, clutching the covers and utterly horrified by the memory that is slowly unfolding in my mind. And I can't stop it. It's there. It happened. The thought of what I did makes me feel sick. And yet, it wasn't me, was it? Not really. It was a terrible event that included me. I wasn't wholly responsible for what happened. I was a child. Just a frightened child who knew no better.

Blood roars in my ears as I close my eyes, willing the memory to leave me. It's late. I'm exhausted. I'll be up all night if this image doesn't disappear from my mind. Once again, I wish I had some drink in the house. Just a small glass of something to help me sleep, to dull the effects of this stupid, fucking repressed memory that has decided to bounce back into my brain when I should be sleeping.

I scramble around, my fingers groping in the darkness, and flick on the bedside lamp. Light floods the room, forcing me to squint. My body feels heavy as I push my feet into my slippers and stand up. If I can't have whisky, I suppose a cup of tea will have to suffice.

Pulling my dressing gown tight around my body, I head into the kitchen and put the kettle on, then on impulse I walk into the hallway and stare at the letter. It's exactly where I left it. No mysterious movements, no more nasty surprises waiting for me. Just the small, white envelope propped up, waiting to be opened.

I snatch it up, shove it in the pocket of my dressing gown and stroll back into the kitchen where I finish making the tea. I carry the cup back into the bedroom, the letter feeling like a lead weight as I sit on the edge of the mattress and pull it out of my pocket. My head swims slightly as I look at the handwriting. I recognise it immediately. I don't know how I didn't see it before, how her recognisable cursive script didn't jump out at me.

My heart thumps an arrhythmic beat in my chest as I slip my finger into the corner of the fold and open it.

18

I feel as if my head is about to burst.

Clutching the letter tightly, I'm hardly able to bring myself to read the words written there. Swinging my legs up onto the mattress, I cover myself up, the chill of the evening nipping at my exposed skin and making me shiver. I put the letter down on the bed next to me and think about the memory that slipped back into my mind when I least expected it. A lump rises in my throat. I was just a child when it happened. I couldn't be held responsible. And it was an accident, wasn't it? Nothing to do with me. I ended up in the wrong place at the wrong time.

Resting my head back against the wooden headboard, I try to think about it clearly. It was a warm summer's evening. I was about seven or eight years old and my parents had had some friends around for supper. Charlotte and I had been packed off to bed after being allowed to play downstairs and mingle with their guests for a short while.

My father tucked us in after we'd had a supper of sausage rolls, cheese and crisps, washed down with a glass of shandy each, something we were occasionally allowed as a special treat. Charlotte chatted to Dad about how exciting it was to be at the party and how lovely the ladies looked in their summer dresses and sling-back sandals, whereas I was swamped with tiredness and curled up on my side, my stomach full of salt and vinegar crisps and greasy pastry.

I must have fallen asleep almost immediately as I have no recollection of anything after getting into bed. The next thing I knew, I was standing barefoot in the garden, still in my night-clothes, blood smeared over my hands. I have a vivid memory of looking down, seeing the oily spread of scarlet on my skin and screaming over and over until my throat was raw.

A sea of faces suddenly loomed over me. Adult voices came thick and fast as I continued to howl and cry. A pair of strong hands scooped me up and I turned to see my father's concerned expression change into one of horror as he spotted the blood on my skin and the dead cat lying in the bushes next to where I had been standing. A couple of the female voices grew in pitch, their disgust and shock patently obvious as they staggered back across the lawn, slipping and sliding in their high heels and thin cotton frocks. I distinctly remember their expressions, the look of absolute revulsion in their eyes as they looked from me to the cat and then back to me once more. I suddenly felt horribly guilty even though I had no idea how the body of the dead animal had got there or even how I had ended up outside in the garden. One minute, I was in bed, and the next, I was standing outside covered in blood.

I'm not sure what my exact words were but I remember crying and shouting that it wasn't me. I hadn't killed the cat. I couldn't have. I had no memory of anything at all. My face had burned and I saw in those brief couple of seconds that they had all jumped to their own ill-informed conclusions and found me guilty without any evidence whatsoever. My father had shouted that it was obviously the dog next door, that it must have done it and I had wandered outside and found the cat already lying there, mauled to death. My mother had stood there, frozen and horrified, too afraid and ashamed to glance at any of her friends, her hand clasped over her mouth, disgust and ignominy at the situation in her garden turning her cheeks a dirty shade of mauve.

I was carried back upstairs where my father washed me and tucked me back up in bed, assuring me that everything was fine and that I wasn't to worry. I had been sleepwalking, he said, that's all it was. They should have locked the back door, he whispered to me as I cried softly into my pillow, the tears soaking into the cotton next to my face. None of it was my fault.

My mother remained downstairs, hurriedly ushering people back inside and offering them more canapes and wine. She didn't come up to see me.

The next morning, the cat was gone and the patio had been cleaned. To this day, I have no idea who the animal belonged to or how it died.

My father always insisted next door's dog had done it. Always was a vicious bastard, he used to say whenever the subject cropped up. My mother never answered him and busied herself at the sink, refusing to get involved in the conversation, her back turned away from me, her eyes cast downwards.

I sleepwalked quite a few times after that incident but it all stopped once I got to my teens. The times that it did happen were a blank to me. I used to wake up in a different place with no recollection of how I got there. According to Charlotte, I was once found in the kitchen sitting on the floor, surrounded by tins of food and an array of cutlery including the sharp kitchen knives that I had retrieved from the wooden block that we kept on the kitchen counter.

Could that explain the photographs? And the holdall full of

clothes, not to mention the letter? Have I started sleepwalking again, doing strange, unexplainable, random acts with no recollection of them once I wake up? It's a distinct possibility and not something I should dismiss. It's certainly a more feasible explanation than some unknown neighbour breaking into my house, moving my things about and ruining my photographs. I'm not sure what I was thinking of with that daft idea. I also know that sleepwalking can be triggered by stress and high levels of anxiety.

I bite at a loose piece of skin on the inside my mouth. Perhaps I should have taken Dr McRae's advice and continued seeing a therapist. The thought of somebody raking through my thoughts and persuading me to talk about things that I don't want to talk about fills me with dread, but so does the idea of being out of control and wandering around the house in an unconscious state, wreaking havoc and misplacing things. The last time I saw a therapist, it was such a traumatic experience I ended up having a meltdown in his office. All I remember is standing up and getting ready to leave and then waking up in his chair with him leaning over me, dabbing at the blood that was running down my face. Apparently, I had panicked, tried to leave the room, and tripped and banged my head on the door jamb.

I look down to find that my hands are trembling. The letter is fluttering between my fingers and creased at the edges where I've grasped it too tightly. I straighten it out and try to stop the shaking but it's so difficult. I feel agitated and cold, and my head aches. I should really get some sleep, but I also need to read this, to find out what Charlotte thinks is so important she had to get it down on paper for me to read.

I skim read it, my eyes drifting over each and every word. I stop and look up. I feel too confused and upset to fully digest it. Then again, if I try to sleep knowing it's there, opened, it will nag at me all night. I won't settle properly until I know what it is that my devious, lying sister has written.

Even breathing feels difficult as I try to get comfortable and prepare myself for more lies and hurt dressed up as sisterly care and guidance. I brush a stray hair out of my eyes and begin to read it properly.

Dear Esther,

I've written this letter because you seemed unwilling to speak to me in person. Why is that what we want to say is always easiest when the person we want to say it to isn't present? Anyway, I hope you read this letter and take it in the manner it's intended. If you feel offended by anything, then I apologise. I don't mean to hurt you. I just want to help you. I've only ever wanted to help you. I hope you know that.

I look away and wipe at the tears that are already streaming down my face. Lies and more lies. Just as I expected. Deceit dressed up as concern.

I tried to talk to you about your house the other day and I know this is a difficult subject for you but I do think it's something that needs sorting out. I noticed when I was last there that the garden is really overgrown and looking unkempt. Also, the windows are ready to be replaced and some are actually leaking. I know you are really attached to the old place but it's so big and hard to maintain that I think it's time you thought about selling it. Can I just say that I know it's your house and your decision but at the end of the day, I just want to help you and be there for you. You would get to keep the money from the sale of the place, obviously. I only say this in case you think I'm trying to take anything from you. I know you blame me for lots of things, especially the accident, but all I have ever wanted to do is help you. You're still my sister and I love you. I only want what's best for you.

I also have some photos of the children that I thought you might like to see. I wanted to give them to you last time I was there but you were too upset so I thought it was best to wait.

I'll come and see you again once we're settled in our new house. Everything is upside down at the minute but we're hoping to be done in a couple of weeks.

I do care about you, Esther, and I know you blame me for everything that has happened, but you have to believe me when I say that I will always be here for you.

Love,
Charlotte

I can hardly breathe. I feel hot and cold at the same time. Who the hell does she think she is? Her arrogance, it would seem, knows no bounds. I'm shaking so badly, I can hardly muster up the strength to tear up the letter but Christ almighty, I give it my best shot. My fingers rip at the paper over and over until it is scattered over the quilt cover in dozens of tiny pieces. Small fragments of it sail into the air, fluttering like the wings of a miniature bird before landing on the floor beside the bed.

It was a bad decision reading it. I should have just thrown it in the bin. If she wanted to upset me, then she's won. Yet again, my sister has the upper hand. I'm too churned up to do anything now, especially sleep. I'll end up tossing and turning all night, my stomach in knots and my mind going over it, hour after hour.

I can't forgive her for what she did to me. I just can't. And as for bringing me photographs of my children? How dare she? How fucking dare she? Shame on her. I am horrified at her appalling lack of compassion and sensitivity. I knew she was a thoughtless bitch but this latest episode beggars belief.

My heart is still thumping in my chest as I step out of bed and pace around the room. I need to calm down, to still my racing pulse. I can't spend the night in a complete rage like this. I take deep breaths and sit back down on the edge of the mattress, trying to think it through logically. Charlotte is obviously feeling guilty, otherwise why would she write this letter? What I need to do is rise above it, be the better person and not think about it ever again. Then I can continue living my life without her. I don't want anything from her. Nothing at all. She's taken enough. I refuse to let her have anything else. She ripped my heart out and now she expects what – forgiveness? For me to sit up and start taking advice from her?

No. I would sooner die than do any of those things. I don't care what her motive is or why she has suddenly decided that it's time for me to sell up; she can go to hell. She was the one who made the decision to cheat and lie and deceive me in the worst possible way and now she can live with the consequences. As far as I'm concerned, I no longer have a sister. Charlotte is a stranger to me, a nobody. She could die right now and I wouldn't care. I hope she rots in hell.

19

Despite everything, I sleep reasonably well. It takes a little while for me to drop off but once I do, I have a restful, dreamless night and wake up feeling pretty positive, determined to forget about the whole sordid scenario.

I refuse to let my sister's name pass my lips. She means nothing to me. I have a life here. It may not be the most scintillating of existences but it's mine and I won't allow her to take it from me. She stole my previous life many months ago. She is not about to take the one I now have in its place.

I quickly drink a cup of coffee and get ready to head into the high street for a small tube of glue. I'll spend the morning putting the torn parts of my children back together. I silently apologise to them for defiling their memories and assure them I'll never ever let it happen again.

I'm just slipping on my jacket when I hear a familiar knock at the door. Amy and Anne are standing there as I open it, Amy's smile a welcome interlude from what has been an exhausting couple of days.

'I need some glue,' I say as she eyes my jacket and shoes. 'I'm just off out to the shops.'

'Right then,' she says without missing a beat, 'let's go.'

I'm not shocked or taken aback at all by her response. If anything, I've come to expect it from her. It's as if she can pre-empt my every move. This only serves to reaffirm my belief that Amy and I are soul partners. The two of us meeting was meant to be. Call it what you like – a twist of fate, kismet, give it any number of names you want to – but it's as if our strange and unlikely friendship was always going to happen. Every second spent with her is a bonus.

I make a point of smiling at Anne. She is just a young girl trying to find her feet. I remember only too well how that feels. It's a big, scary world out there and we all need every bit of help we can get. She is a friend of Amy's and despite her childish giggles and display of immaturity the other day, I consider any friend of Amy's to be a friend of mine as well.

It's hard to disguise my delight as we make our way into town and browse in shop windows that I haven't visited in such a long time, it may as well be decades ago. I feel as if I'm walking on air, having two young people by my side. Just being near them has given me a much-needed injection of vitality and optimism. They exude cheerfulness and chat constantly about everything and anything – boyfriends, work, social media. Their talk of contemporary issues and easy happiness is infectious, making me feel marginally delirious.

I scan the crowds, searching for anybody I recognise, but am met with a wall of blank faces. It's been so long since I meandered through here that the people I once knew will very probably have moved on to pastures new.

'You might get your glue in here, Esther,' Anne says as we head towards a local DIY shop that's been on the go for as long as I can remember.

We step inside, the smell of dust and varnish greeting us as we scan the shelves for a small tube of adhesive. It doesn't take long to get one that's suitable for what I need. We head to the counter, picking our way through the detritus that litters the floor – brushes and dustpans, buckets and chamois leathers and all manner of cleaning utensils – and pay for the glue.

'I'll carry it, Esther,' Amy says as she scoops it up and slots it into her bag before I can say anything. 'Why don't we go for a coffee? Seems like a shame to head back straightaway when it's such a nice day.'

'Ooh, sounds like a good idea,' Anne chips in. 'What do you think, Esther? You ready for a latte and a slice of chocolate cake?'

I nod, trying not to look too overenthusiastic at the suggestion, even though I'm ecstatic. I can't remember the last time I sat in a café and chatted like an ordinary person. I've been living half a life for so long now, I've actually become frighteningly accustomed to it. I could continue with my way of thinking and so easily go down the route of becoming an even greater recluse by wallowing in self-pity and lashing out and blaming others, but today has shown me that I'm done with all that. This moment, this very day, could be the catalyst for turning my life around and climbing out the hole of depression that I've inhabited for as long as I can remember.

We head into a small coffee shop and order three lattes and three caramel slices, then find a table in the corner with a view of the small courtyard out the back. Time seems to vanish as we drink and eat and chat, making small talk about fashions and favourite desserts, and anything and everything that is both significant and insignificant.

'What about you, Esther?' Anne says as she drains the last of her latte, leaving her with a milky moustache on her top lip. 'If you could invite anybody at all to a dinner party, living or dead, who would it be?'

I see Amy's eyes flicker as she glances over to Anne and then back to me. She's waiting for me to go silent or cry or shout that I would invite my dead husband and children and that it was a stupid question, thoughtless and crass, and that she had no right to even ask me in the first place. But I don't do any of those things. Instead, I bite into my caramel slice, crumbs spilling onto the plate in a sudden buttery explosion, and answer her through a mouthful of sugary, heavenly chocolate.

'Well, I know I'm supposed to say that I'd invite somebody who has done something monumentally marvellous. You know, somebody who has helped change the world for the better, like Martin Luther King or Albert Einstein or Marie Curie, but I'm actually going to be controversial and a little bit rebellious here and say Carrie Fisher.'

From the corner of my eye, I see Amy let out a small gasp of relief, and smile. Poor Amy. And poor Anne, not fully understanding which conversations are allowed and which ones are considered out of bounds in my presence, and blundering in like that. I did it, though. No tears, no crushing misery. Just me and two young women sitting having a regular conversation like old friends.

'Oh, Carrie Fisher is awesome!' Anne squeals. 'I would so want to be in her gang, wouldn't you, Ames?'

Amy laughs and tells us about her fiancé who is obsessed with *Star Wars*. 'I swear to God,' she sighs as she rolls her eyes and shakes her head, 'that his idea of a perfect night in is to sit with a big bucket of popcorn and binge watch as many *Star Wars* films as he can before falling asleep on the sofa. He is such a nerd, it's actually really worrying. I'm a bit concerned he'll turn up to the wedding dressed as bloody Luke Skywalker.'

I have to stop myself from leaning over and hugging the pair of them. Everything here is perfect. If I could capture a period in my life and replay it over and over, it would be here and now. I wish I could bottle it and keep this moment for all time. I really feel as if I've turned a corner.

We spend the next ten minutes chatting and laughing until Amy looks at her watch and lets out a sigh. 'Right ladies,' she says as she stands up and brushes the crumbs off her lap. 'I'll go and pay the bill. This is my treat.'

Tears mist my vision. This girl is perfection personified. I won't allow thoughts of Harriet, and how she might have turned out at the same age as Amy, to crowd my thoughts. I can't continue wading through my life weighed down by misery. At some point, I have to emerge from it and look forward instead of continually peering back at what could have been.

Anne and I wait for a few seconds in companionable silence as Amy drags her purse out and settles up just a few feet away from where we're sitting. I watch as she makes her way back, weaving through the tightly packed tables like a slalom competitor. I'm loath to leave this place. I feel as if the spell will be broken the minute we step outside, the moment of happiness we've just shared torn into shreds and thrown into the four winds.

I'm not wrong.

We get up and walk to the door. Amy ushers us along in her inimitable style, pulling at her bag and hoisting her jeans up. I stop when I get to the doorway.

A sudden chill rushes over my skin as I stare at the shops nearby, at the pavement we're standing on, at the line of shoppers who bustle past us hurriedly, their faces lined and closed off. It's happened. The moment of happiness I've just experienced has ended, disappeared in a matter of seconds like a soap bubble bursting. The fragility of it all is so frighteningly ethereal it makes me feel quite sick.

I take a deep breath, a wave of wooziness and sudden nausea threatening to take my legs from under me. I have no idea where I am. I want to take hold of Amy's arm and ask her our exact location but the words evade me. She would think me stupid, a helpless, doddery, middle-aged woman who can't remember what day it is or where she is, and I don't want that. I'm not an old woman. I'm simply grieving and finding life difficult. And besides, I feel as if I've done particularly well on this visit. I don't want to ruin it and turn it into a catastrophe by showing my fear and becoming hysterical. But this is frightening. Horribly dreamlike and utterly terrifying.

We begin to walk along the path as if everything is normal. It isn't. This isn't normal. We were on Warum High Street when we went into the café, and now we're not. Now we are somewhere completely different and I am frightened and bewildered, unable to work out where I am and unable to orient myself to my unfamiliar surroundings. It's like some sort of childish nightmare and right now, I'm the helpless youngster who has lost their parents and can't find their way home.

I spin around, trying to find the old DIY shop where we bought the glue, but I can't see it anywhere. That would help me work out where we are. It has to be here somewhere. And yet it isn't. I cannot see it anywhere.

'Everything okay, Esther?' Anne says, her voice containing more than a touch of apprehension as she spots my stricken expression and the unmistakable look of fear in my eyes. Dread is starting to claw at me. I'm fighting to conceal it and failing miserably.

Amy stops walking and places her hand on my shoulder. 'I think perhaps it's time we get back. Is that all right with you?'

I nod, too dazed to speak. I want to ask where we are and why we're no longer in Warum but can't bring myself to form the words, to say it out loud. The echo of my own voice ringing in the air like a small, bewildered child would be too much to bear. I was happy a few seconds ago. I knew where I was. And now I'm in a strange town, frightened and unable to think straight. What the hell is going on?

We continue walking, my legs trembling and quivering with the effort of staying upright. I feel as if I'm walking on uneven ground, the paving slabs swirling and rotating under me. A sign on a lamppost up ahead causes me to stop. I can feel a tremor in my voice as I read it out loud.

'Leyburn?' I say breathlessly. 'We're in Leyburn, in North Yorkshire?'

Amy takes my arm and covers my hand with hers. She is warm and her voice is gentle but what she says does nothing to reassure me. 'I thought it would make a nice change. Bit of a nightmare to get parked. I think we probably got the last spot. How lucky is that, eh?'

I don't reply. I can't. My voice has left me and I simply can't speak. I want her to tell me that this must be part of a huge joke, a horrible, sick prank, but I know that's not possible. What's happening here is real. We're not in Warum. How are we not in Warum? We walked into town, to Warum, the place where I live, not to here. How did we get to this place? How the fuck did we get here?

We continue on for a few minutes, my legs threatening to buckle under me, every breath I take a huge effort, until we stop at a dark-blue vehicle parked up in the centre of the town. It's some sort of people carrier and before I have a chance to protest or ask what we're doing, I find myself being helped inside like a frail, old lady. Anne sits next to me and straps me in while Amy climbs in the front and starts the engine. Is this Amy's car? Where did it come from?

My face burns as we set off. Anne chatters to me but I can't hear anything she's saying. A roaring sound fills my ears and I can't seem to think straight. Behind her, the ridge of the North Yorkshire hills bobs up and down and the sky gradually changes from a calming pale blue to charcoal grey.

We wind our way through the country lanes, the car rocking from side to side as Amy manoeuvres her way through the waning autumnal foliage that leans into the narrow roads, its shadows like giant intruders clawing at the car.

Rain begins to patter at the window, vertical slashes of water hitting the glass in a slow rhythm, until the heavens eventually open, releasing a torrent of water. It bounces off the sunroof and smears the windows with water, blocking out the view. Cold pulses off the glass next to my skin, causing me to shiver.

Anne has stopped her incessant chatter, which is a relief to me. I'm not sure how I would have responded if she had quizzed me for answers. I'm not good with impromptu replies. I end up flummoxed and unable to get my words out. She would know immediately that my mind was elsewhere and not focused on what she was saying. I'm doing my best to appear calm and happy but she must know that something is wrong, that I'm rigid with panic and confusion. I can hardly breathe, let alone speak.

I clench my fists and stare straight ahead. Everything is spoilt. A fabulous day is suddenly in tatters. I have no idea where I've been or how I got there. Everything is ruined.

The sound of the rain and the buzzing in my ears lulls me into a near-meditative state. I close my eyes, glad of the rest. It provides some respite from having to watch the blur of landscape that we pass as we snake through the countryside with its thinning leaves and gnarled-looking trees. It stops me thinking about the fact that I think I'm losing my grip on reality and possibly losing my mind.

* * *

A sudden jerking movement drags me back from sleep. I feel myself being helped out of the car by warm, gentle hands and guided inside the house. My eyes are watery and my neck is aching. All I want to do is curl up on the sofa and go to sleep. What just took place is too abstract and chilling for me to think about. If I close my eyes and shut my mind off to today's events, it makes it easier to deal with. I can pretend none of it happened, carry on in blissful ignorance as if it was all a figment of my imagination.

I'm too groggy to engage in any meaningful conversation with either Amy or Anne as they take off my jacket and deposit me in the chair next to the window. I want to ask Amy about the letter, and whether or not she found it and propped it up in the hallway, but I'm too tired to go into any detail, and also wary of hearing her answer, so I let them both leave and then sit slumped in the chair, desperately trying to forget the events of the past few days.

I rub at my eyes and gaze over at number 19. Nobody there and nothing happening. I'm rather relieved. I've had enough for one day. I can catch up on Veronica's antics in the morning when I'm feeling more receptive. For now, I just want to sit and do nothing. My brain needs a rest; my body needs a rest. I lean forward and place my head in my hands. Despair and dread well up inside me. I feel as if I'm actually, truly going mad...

20

NUMBER 19

Her boy is home. Her family is back together under one roof. The doctors were astounded at his rapid recovery and discharged him the following evening. Her husband took the day off work and they went together to pick him up, bundling their boy into the car, her husband smothering him with cuddles and kisses and fawning over him like he was some sort of precious work of art.

She should feel happy. She knows that. And yet none of this feels right. Something is still missing from this equation. There is a void within her that is aching to be filled. The rumblings of discontent are stirring deep within her belly. If she is being totally honest, she is silently seething. After all, she was the one who spoke at length with the medical staff at the hospital, not her husband. She was the one who thanked them for their help and listened to their theories about their child having some mysterious illness, probably viral, and she was the one who took on board their advice that they shouldn't worry but that if they had any more problems, to call the GP immediately. It was her they had wanted to speak to. She's the boy's mother, the matriarch. This family can't function without her. So why does she continually feel like an outsider?

The boy had clambered out of the car and all but skipped back into the house as if his illness had occurred a million years ago. The husband marvelled at how resilient children are, how strong their son is and how wonderful it was to have him back home, fit and healthy.

Isn't modern medicine a marvellous thing? he had said and she had nodded in agreement.

She had tried to take her husband's hand as they stood on the driveway together but he was too enamoured by their son, too enraptured by his miracle recovery, to show any interest in his wife. He snatched his fingers away as she grasped for his hand, stating they should all have a late supper together.

Scrambled eggs and toast! he had cried as they trooped into the kitchen and sat at the table while he whisked the thick, yellow mixture, made toast and even put a salad together.

And now here they are, playing at being one, big, happy family. Their daughter sits alongside her dad, celebrating her brother's new-found good health as they eat and talk animatedly, telling the boy how wonderful it is to have him back home and how much they've all missed him.

Haven't we, Mum? the girl cries happily as she links her arm through her brother's and leans her head on his small, bony shoulder.

The woman nods and swallows down her unease. She watches her young son. His eyes have lost their dullness and he's stopped being sick. He looks, to all intents and purposes, completely better. She should be elated. Any decent mother would be. But then, she knows deep down that she is far from decent or kind. She blinks and pushes the thought aside. No time for that now. No time for remorse or self-reproach. She has a family to look after. A husband to keep. A mistress to avoid.

They finish eating and the children slink off upstairs to play.

Her husband gets up and disappears into another room. She watches him go and gets up to follow him. He'll be onto *her* no doubt, his floozy, texting or emailing her, gushing about how his son is home now and that he's free to meet up.

He's sitting in the living room watching the news when she walks in. She's in two minds as to whether or not she should go and sit next to him. After last night, everything, every single movement and spoken word, feels forced and contrived. It shouldn't be like this. Marriage should be as easy as breathing. So why does she feel as if she is drowning?

She perches on the edge of the chair, holding her knees with her hands clasped around them. Her knuckles are white. She feels nervous. Out of sorts. She no longer has any idea what it is he expects from her. After last night's debacle, it's obvious he isn't interested in her body. Her face heats up at the memory.

They sit in silence for a few seconds until eventually, the tension becomes too much. She asks him if they can talk and waits for his reply. He smiles at her and nods, telling her that of course they can talk.

We're husband and wife, he says casually. *We can talk about anything. Anything at all.*

She takes a deep breath, her courage abandoning her when she needs it the most, and decides to just come out with it. There's no easy way to say what she wants him to hear, no way to sugar-coat the words she is about to come out with, so she just comes straight out and says it.

I know you're having an affair.

There is a moment's silence and then he throws his head back and laughs, stopping only to glare at her over the top of his glasses. Her pulse speeds up. A tic take hold in the side of her jaw as her anger builds, twisting and burning in her gut. This isn't the reaction she anticipated. She was prepared for lots of emotions –

denial, anger, incredulity – but not this. She definitely isn't prepared for this.

He shakes his head and stops the loud guffaws, which is just as well as it was irritating her half to death.

I'm not having an affair, he says quietly, his eyes narrowed as he watches her.

She can't be sure but it sounds like there's a hint of menace in his tone. A touch of malevolence.

Now it's her turn to shake her head. She doesn't believe him. Who has he been secretly texting and speaking to on the phone when he thinks she isn't listening? Why is he so cold towards her all the time?

Liar! she shouts. Her voice bounces around the room. She stands up and backs away from him.

Once again, he shakes his head and tells her not to be so ridiculous.

Who is it you're texting all the time? Why do you keep sneaking away from me? You're a filthy, fucking liar!

She turns away from him, her hands itching to land upon something. Something heavy to let him know how vexed she is, how fucking furious she is at his lackadaisical attitude and disgusting lies. She strides across the room, pacing and pacing up and down, around and around until she spots his trophy. It's sitting on the bookcase, half hidden behind rows of old hardbacks and general household clutter. He won it a few years ago for some golf tournament he entered and now it sits, concealed and forgotten behind piles of old bills and children's swimming certificates. Exhilaration runs through her. Glancing at him, she can see that his attention is already elsewhere – the sports paper, the TV – anything but on her. Is it any wonder she's so bloody angry and upset and frustrated all the time? He's as cold as ice. It's like being married to a corpse.

Her hands itch to pick it up and hurl it at him. Anything to get his attention, anything to make him realise that his wife is in the fucking room and wants to talk to him about their disintegrating marriage. The marriage she is desperate to save. The marriage that is slowly crumbling, turning into dust.

She walks to the bookcase, ready to grab it. Her palms are damp at the thought of it. She can practically feel its cold, smooth curves, the ridges of the square base. The reassuring heft of it.

Behind her, the door swings open and their children come tumbling through. They fall onto their father, smothering him with kisses and giggling as he tickles them and nuzzles his face into their soft skin. Her stomach plummets as she watches them, envy eating at her. She's an interloper in her own home. A stranger standing on the outside looking in.

A solid lump sticks in her throat. She has to find a way back into her own family. It's lonely being left out in the cold. She doesn't like it out here. She is lost, cast out into the wilderness. Why can't people look up to her? Take what she has to say seriously? She has a role within this family, a purpose. Everybody wants to be wanted, don't they? And she very much wants to be wanted.

Leaving her family alone, she goes into the kitchen. She'll do what she has to do to make everything perfect in this house. Soon they'll all realise how much they need her.

She comes back in the living room a short while later, carrying a tray of drinks with a glass of red wine for herself and her husband, a strawberry milkshake for her daughter and a banana one for her son. *Your favourite!* she says handing it over to him. He takes it with a smile and they all drink to his health.

When he complains that it tastes odd, she assures him it's just because he's been ill and that drinking it will help him get better. *Like medicine!* she cries, her eyes misting over as he gulps it down.

He smiles at her and finishes it quickly. The girl hands her empty glass over and the woman quickly bustles off to the kitchen and refills both, handing them back to her children telling them that there's more where they came from.

She can feel her husband's eyes following her as she moves around the room. He gives her a weak smile and she tentatively returns the gesture. They both sip at their wine and watch as their children guzzle back their milkshakes. She daren't expect too much but she does hope that this is the beginning. Things will improve. She can just feel it.

* * *

The following morning, the girl rushes into her parents' bedroom where they lie, blissfully ignorant of what is taking place in the room next to theirs.

Come quickly! she urges, her voice quivering with fear. *It's happening again. He's ill. Really ill. I can't wake him up.*

21

ESTHER

After yesterday, I find myself second-guessing everything. Every stupid, little thing. I slept well enough and woke up groggy, questioning whether or not any of it actually even happened. I concentrate so hard on the smallest of details that I end up feeling exhausted despite the fact the day has barely begun. Even walking feels measured and unnatural, as if I have to put an inordinate amount of effort into simply putting one foot in front of another and making sure I stay upright. I begin to wonder whether or not I no longer know my own mind and can trust my own logic or coordination.

Wandering around the living room aimlessly, I go over it all in my head again and again until I can no longer bring myself to think about it. It's like a form of self-torture, combing through the finest of details until my head aches with the effort. I need to find something else to do, something that will act as a distraction and take my mind off it. Then I see the picture sitting on the table, the small shreds of paper that make up the faces of my children, and I remember about the glue. Amy still has it in her bag. I feel a spark of irritation strike in my gut almost immediately. I have no idea why she felt the need to take it from me. I'm perfectly capable of carrying my own items of shopping and now I'm going to have go and get it from her, which will prove tremendously difficult as I don't have any idea of what number her house is. All I know is that she lives in a cottage somewhere beyond the railway bridge. The briefest of details, that's all I have. I close my eyes and try to visualise the houses at that end of the road, but all I can see is my own home. It's been an age since I walked up the other end of and I can't go knocking on doors to find her. A cottage can mean anything. It's often a twee euphemism for an old, terraced house. Or of course it could actually be a proper cottage with a thatched roof and climbing roses trailing around the front door. So which is it? When I go looking for Amy's house, what exactly am I searching for?

My eyes feel heavy as I try to work out what I should do. Anybody else would simply step out the door without any deliberation and go on the hunt for that damn house. But then I'm not just anybody, am I? Annoyance at my own ineptitude gnaws at me. If I do it now, without thinking too deeply about it, I may just end up being successful. Overthinking things has always been my downfall.

Without missing a beat, I snatch my coat up off the peg, put my shoes on and head outside. The breeze is bracing. It's still early and the ground and air haven't yet warmed up from a cloudless, chilly night after a huge downpour. I take a deep breath and stroll along the road like any normal person. Like somebody who hasn't lost their entire family and now lives like a recluse.

Doing my best to regulate my breathing, I begin to head towards the bridge but am stopped dead in my tracks by a shout from behind me.

'Hey! Hello there!'

I spin around to see a man staring in my direction. He's waving his hand at me as if we know each other, even though he is a perfect stranger to me. My heart speeds up. He's smiling broadly and begins to walk towards me, taking great strides before breaking into a slight run. I have no idea what to do. I can't turn back towards my front door as he is now closer to it than I am and I would look more than a tad foolish if I were to run away in the opposite direction. I'm a grown woman for heaven's sake, not a frightened child. So I stay put and try to place his voice and face whilst doing my best to still my battering heart.

'How are you feeling today? Better, I guess, since you're out and about.' His voice is calm and unrushed. I swallow down my fear. Who is he? Why is he following me?

Before I have a chance to reply, he is almost next to me, his clear eyes scrutinising me, his dark hair flopping in front of his eyes as he leans down to look at me.

'I knew it was you,' he says in a soft tone that feels artificial and condescending. 'I saw you from back there and thought, yup, that's definitely her.'

My head buzzes as I try to work out who he is and how he knows me. Or thinks he knows me. I'd like to say that I have no idea who he is, but now I can see him close up, there is something about his face that feels vaguely familiar. Perhaps I have met him before, although I can't for the life of me work out where or when. There is something about him that twists my stomach into a tight, uncomfortable knot.

'Sorry,' I murmur, my face flushing as he continues to stare at me with his bright blue eyes, 'but I don't believe we've met?'

His smile is enough to allow me to forgive him for shouting at me in the street and causing me alarm. 'Okay, sorry,' he laughs. 'I should have approached this a little better. I'm the counsellor from the other day. We spoke briefly?'

'Ah,' I reply, a flush creeping up my face. 'Yes. Now I remember. The day at the doctors' surgery.'

He nods and holds out his hand for me to shake. 'That's right. I was rather rude back then and didn't introduce myself properly. I'm Daniel, or Dan. Whichever you prefer. I generally answer to anything that isn't rude,' he says, his eyes twinkling with mischief.

'Hello, Daniel,' I say despite my nervousness and reluctance to become embroiled in a conversation with him. I don't know this guy. Not really. Apart from a five-minute chat with him in the waiting room, we're virtually strangers. So why do I feel compelled to answer him and engage in general chit-chat? Perhaps it's his easy manner and soft voice but then I guess he's trained to approach people and get them to open up to him.

He stands quietly, waiting for me to introduce myself. I consider ignoring him and walking away but on reflection, he seems friendly and harmless, so I offer my hand in return. 'I'm Esther,' I say, my voice a mere whisper.

We shake, his grasp firm and vigorous, his skin soft and cool against my clammy palm. I snatch my hand away and surreptitiously wipe it against the side of my trousers. I feel like a wayward child caught out doing something I shouldn't be doing. So silly.

'I need to go and see a friend,' I murmur, and turn to face the railway bridge, hoping he takes the hint and leaves me alone.

I start to walk away and can feel his eyes boring into my back. I know without turning to look that he's still there, standing behind me, watching me. Scrutinising my every move. I should feel unnerved by his unmoving presence, yet I don't. He isn't a threatening or intimidating figure. I do wish, however, that he would leave me alone to get on with finding Amy. I want to be able to concentrate on locating her house and having him observing my every movement will make me nervous and giddy. And surely he has better things to do than watching a middle-aged woman wander up and down the road, randomly knocking on doors?

The sound of my own footsteps echoes in the still air as I walk away and head under the bridge. I don't turn to see if Dan is still there. I have to concentrate on what I'm doing. If I think about it too deeply, I'll falter and rush off home, my nerves getting the better of me and I don't want that to happen. What I want is to put all my efforts into finding Amy and her cottage so I can collect my adhesive and get on with putting my pictures back together. Why are the simplest of tasks so arduous and difficult?

There's no rush of a train overhead as I walk through the short tunnel and emerge out of the other side; nothing occurs that drags me back to the past and leaves me feeling confused and miserable. The sun causes me to squint as I step out of the shadows into daylight. I cover my eyes with my cupped hand and stop to look around. My breath seems to leave my lungs in a sudden blast. My chest feels empty and cold, devoid of oxygen. I struggle to breathe and place my hand over my breastbone.

Glancing back down the road behind me, I'm relieved to see that Dan has disappeared out of sight. I take a rattling breath then turn around and stare at the brick wall that faces me. The brick wall where a row of houses should be. This is insane. Absolutely ridiculous. This is where Amy lives with her disabled mother. This is where a row of houses should be.

Everything swims in front of me and the pavement appears to tilt under my feet as I try to take in the scene in front of me. A brick wall. No houses, no cottage. Just a sea of red stone.

I look again, my eyes blurry as I scrutinise the curve of the wall that appears to close in on me. There are no houses here. None whatsoever. Next to the wall is a small lawn and beyond that, some sort of enclosed courtyard. I blink and run my fingers through my hair, tugging and pulling at thick clumps the way I used to when I was a small child and feeling anxious. I have no idea what to do. I can't go any further. I don't know where I am or where I can go to find Amy. I suddenly feel the urge to go home but am afraid Daniel will be waiting there for me, standing by the front door with a knowing grin on his face and that twinkle in his eye that tells me he knows all about my stupidity and declining mental health.

I leave go of my hair and nibble at a piece of ragged nail, wincing as it comes away, taking a tiny strip of skin with it. A thin line of blood immediately rises to the surface of my skin, forming into a small crimson bubble. Am I going mad? Did I imagine those houses? Or have I spent so long holed up in my own home that the town I live in has altered beyond recognition, with buildings being demolished and large walls built in their place?

I don't give myself any more time to think. I turn around and head back down the path. I don't care if Daniel is still there, outside my door waiting to speak to me; I know that I cannot continue looking at that wall for a second longer. It should be a row of houses. Last time I ventured up that way, they were definitely there. Having to stand and stare at what isn't there will be enough to convince me I'm going mad.

A lump is wedged in my throat and I fight back tears as I head back the way I came. Everything is wrong. Wrong and messed up and I fear that I'm losing the plot, forgetting who I am and no longer sure of what normal is. Everything feels like it's slipping away from me, dripping through my fingers, and I don't know how to get it back.

The pavement is thankfully empty as I stumble home. My eyes are misted over and a sob tries to escape from my chest. I shake my head despairingly and swallow it down. I grapple with the handle, wrench the door open and all but fall inside, my feet twisting under me as I slam the door shut and drop down onto the sofa. I rub at my eyes. I won't cry. I refuse to let it happen. Not again. I'm all out of tears. They don't help. All they do is leave me feeling exhausted and washed out. Sitting weeping hour after hour, day after day, strips me of any lucidity or logic that I might possess and right now, I need those attributes to navigate my way out this nightmare and escape from recent incidents that have slithered into my brain and are currently doing their utmost to convince me that I'm losing my mind.

I sit there with my head tipped back, staring at the ceiling for what feels like hours even though I know it's probably only a matter of minutes, trying to work out what to do next. Through the fog of thoughts that randomly tap at every inch of my brain, I hear something that jolts me back into the present. Sitting up, I listen again, my ears attuned to every single thing, every whisper of wind outside, every rattling breath that exits my lungs; I can hear it all here in the near silence of the living room.

It comes again, a light tapping at the front door. Standing up, I straighten my dishevelled clothes and make an attempt at looking half decent. I don't doubt for one minute that I look a complete fright, with my hair sticking up at divergent angles and my face pale and stricken-looking after suffering another shock, but I do my best to look normal as I stride towards the door, forcing myself to exude an air of confidence that I definitely don't feel.

Grabbing at the cool metal of the handle and pulling the door ajar, I'm not sure whether to be pleased or upset to see Amy standing there with Anne and Rose beside her. I no longer trust anybody or anything. I even doubt that what I'm seeing right in front of me is actually real. I'm half tempted to reach out and touch them, to feel that they are solid matter and not a figment of my imagination.

Amy rummages in her pocket and brings out the small tube of glue that I bought yesterday. 'Thought we'd pop over and give you a hand,' she says casually, as if nothing has happened. As if I didn't find myself wandering around a strange town yesterday. As if I haven't just been up the road to find myself bricked into a place I don't recognise.

I clear my throat and am tempted to snatch the glue out of her hand and slam the door on the three of them. Instead, I do what I always do – nod politely and lean forward to retrieve it.

Amy closes her fingers around the small tube before I can take it from her, then steps inside the hallway. 'We'll stay and give you a hand, Esther, won't we?' she says to the other two females who are watching me with more intent that I care for. 'We're free for an hour or so. I've been telling these two about those lovely biscuits you keep feeding me.'

And before I can stop them, all three are in my room, asking me to put the kettle on.

'So,' Amy says nonchalantly, her manner just a little too manufactured for my liking, 'let's see if we can fix those photographs.'

22

The next hour passes more quickly than I expect it to.

Amy and Anne were already leaning over the table, dabbing the torn bits of photographs with spots of glue by the time I followed them in. My fingers itched to get involved but Amy insisted I busy myself making tea.

'And besides,' she said when I tried to intervene, 'there isn't really enough room around the table. Leave it to us, Esther. We'll have it sorted in no time at all.'

I was all fingers and thumbs as I made the tea and did my usual job of arranging the biscuits in a pretty pattern on the china plate but as I arrived back in the living room, the chatter and smiles of the three young women had a calming effect on me. The buzzing in my head began to dissipate and the uncomfortable swirling sensation in my stomach gradually stopped.

So now I'm sitting here making idle chat with Rose who, it appears, can eat her own bodyweight in cookies and biscuits and yet somehow remain as thin as a rake.

'Oh, Esther! Amy wasn't wrong about these biscuits. They

really are lush. I could eat a full pack of them,' Rose says as she licks at her fingers and finishes her tea with a loud slurp.

I'm sorely tempted to lean back and catch a glimpse of the goings-on over at number 19 but don't want to appear rude or draw attention to my interest in their domestic arguments so, instead, pretend to be interested in what Rose has to say about her boyfriend and her impending visit to Leeds Festival and how she wishes she could afford to buy her own house. Her voice is a long stream of syllables and sounds in the background as my mind drifts back to the lack of houses beyond the railway bridge, the brick wall, and Daniel, the counsellor, and his sudden appearance right outside my house.

'So, what do you think about it, Esther?' Rose is staring at me, her expression eager as she waits for me to say something. I let out a small gulp and rub my hands together, locking and unlocking my fingers to give myself some time to think. I have no idea what she was talking about, the thread of her conversation completely lost on me.

'We're almost done!' Amy shouts and suddenly I'm on my feet with Rose close behind me, her question already forgotten as she chatters about the camera on her phone and how wonderful it is. Brilliant for taking selfies, apparently.

My heart leaps up in my chest and tears burn at my eyes as I look down at the repaired photographs of Harriet and Dexter. I want to hug Amy and Anne and thank them over and over but my throat feels tight and I fear I might cry for an age if I open my mouth and try to say anything.

I reach out and run my fingertips over the images, carefully avoiding the lines of glue that hold them together. 'Thank you,' I manage to mumble at last. 'Thank you so much. These are perfect.'

'Not a problem,' Amy replies breezily. 'Not a problem at all.

Anyway, we'd best get on. Lots to do.' She looks at Anne and Rose, who nod enthusiastically.

'Amy, can I ask you something?' The words are out before I can stop them, before I've had a chance to fully think through what it is I want to ask her without sounding like some sort of imbecile.

'Course you can!' Her voice is like a chirruping bird, always happy, always light and breezy. Never tinged with sadness or misery. Life has yet to crush the Amys of the world, to grind them underfoot and turn them to dust.

I try to formulate the words, to say what it is that I want to say, but nothing comes out. I want to ask her where she lives and why her cottage isn't where she told me it was. I want to ask who it was that tore my photographs up and scattered them on the floor. I also want to ask her who the people were outside my front door and how we ended up in Leyburn on our shopping trip when we started off in Warum. And how did she know I wanted glue for the photographs? So many important questions vying for space in my head but all of them too silly and embarrassing to say out loud.

Shaking my head, I attempt a wide smile. 'Never mind,' I say with a slight tremble to my voice. 'Maybe another time. I'm just overthinking things as usual.'

'Aw, Esther. Don't let stuff ever get you down. You know we can always chat, don't you?' She quickly glances to Anne and Rose, then back to me. Both young women are immersed in conversation, their voices too rapid and quiet for me to hear what they're talking about. I'm almost certain she knows I don't want to speak in front of them. I'm an open book to her. I hope she calls back later when she's on her own. Things haven't been quite the same since these two have started accompanying her on visits here. I look forward to a time when it's back to being just me and Amy.

'Right,' she says to her acquaintances, 'shall we make a move?'

I muse over where they're going and think about that hospital and what sort of things they have to do when they're there. It's not the kind of place I would ever want to visit. I visualise it as a cold, soulless place, stripped of anything remotely resembling warmth or compassion. Apart from Amy's presence, obviously. But I'll bet some of those doctors are brusque and difficult to work with. I can't imagine they show a great deal of sympathy and kindness towards their patients. I just hope they're pleasant to Amy and treat her well. She deserves that and so much more besides.

The three women saunter into the hallway and step outside, a blast of cold air forcing its way in as the door gets opened.

'Call again soon,' I say to Amy as I hold the door ajar. It's not that I don't want the other two to come calling; it's just that I'd like to see Amy alone. I need to speak to her in private, to tell her all the things that have happened lately. My mind is in turmoil. So many events, I won't know where to start. And that's without going into detail about Veronica over at number 19. That is something I definitely need to speak to her about. I can't let that sort of abuse continue for much longer. Everything that's happened to me lately has knocked me off balance and made me lose focus on what's important. Once I get Amy alone, she'll know what to do about Veronica. She has knowledge of those kinds of things. When I was a teacher, I was well versed on the machinations of the social services team and their rules and regulations and safeguarding issues, but since leaving the profession, I've lost the knack and feel more than a bit helpless. I really do need Amy's guidance and assistance on this one.

'Right,' Amy says with an authoritative air to her voice, 'let's get moving, shall we?'

I watch as all three stride down the path. I lean out of the door to see where they head off to but a sudden movement over the road catches my attention – a person running through the living room, a silhouette dashing about manically. By the time I look back, Amy, Rose and Anne have all gone, disappeared out of sight.

* * *

I'm really desperate to have a look at the newly repaired photographs but I also need to see what's going on inside Veronica's house, so rather than sit and study the pictures of my children, I march past the table where they still lie and get settled in my seat by the window.

My heart leaps in my chest as I watch the drama that is currently unfolding in the living room of number 19. Veronica and her husband are holding the boy in their laps, stroking his face and tapping at his hand. The girl is bending down in the corner of the room and appears to be scrubbing at something on the floor.

My eyes are drawn back to the boy laid across their knees. His body looks floppy and unresponsive. I can't see if he's awake or not but judging by his body language, or rather the lack of it, he appears to be in some sort of unconscious state.

A flash of luminous green fills the room as a medic marches in and leans down over the child's body. His bulky frame obliterates my view but I don't need to see what's going on. I can easily imagine the terror that will be present in that room. Perhaps the boy has a long-standing condition that on occasion requires medical attention. I pray it's nothing serious and that he'll be up and about in no time. A quiver of fear stirs deep within me, something I can't quite put my finger on. I don't think he has any sort of condition. I don't know why I think that. I have no reason to feel this way, but somewhere deep inside me is a niggling sensation of a memory that I don't care for. It's like an insidious creature as it worms its way through me, growing and expanding until it eventually gets so big, it takes over completely and there is nothing left of the original me. I try to shake the feeling away but it sits there like a great big weight, growing and ballooning inside me.

Over at number 19, the medic continues to attend to the boy, every so often leaning down in his bag to retrieve his instruments before turning his attention back to the patient.

My stomach tightens. Why, when I don't know these people, do I feel so drawn to them? What is it about their lives that fascinates me? I feel compelled to watch them. Even if there was no abuse going on, I feel sure I would still want to watch the minutiae of their lives as it unfolds right here in front of me.

A movement opposite cuts through my thoughts. The medic stands up and I can see that the boy is sitting on his mother's knee. He doesn't look altogether healthy but he does look slightly better than he did ten minutes ago.

He's holding a bag in front of his face and every so often retches into it, his small body quivering with spasms as his body purges itself of whatever bug or toxin is inhabiting his gut. Veronica doesn't seem overly perturbed by this and is talking animatedly to the medic, smiling and nodding at him as he hands her a sheet of paper. Every so often she flicks her hair behind her ears and twists around on the sofa, rearranging her skirt and smoothing out the creases from her clothes. I'm perturbed by this. It seems completely unnecessary under the circumstances. And yet part of me is also drawn to her. Even in difficult situations, she appears glamorous and composed. I'm half tempted to glance in the mirror and take in the image of the pale, wan, lined face that will no doubt stare back at me. I was once like Veronica. I too cared about my appearance and always made an effort to look good. Not wearing lipstick and having my hair styled was an anathema to me. Wearing make-up and stylish clothes was akin to breathing. It was part of my identity. And now look at me.

Perhaps that's why Veronica fascinates me. She's like the

person I used to be. She is pretty and has a husband and family. I like to think that the caring, interesting aspects of her personality outweigh the negative, damaged parts but I don't know that for sure. Maybe she is a complete monster after all. I mean, look at her now, flirting with the medic while her boy heaves his guts up. That's not normal behaviour, is it?

I look away, suddenly exhausted by it all. And besides which, for now, the boy is in good hands. He has a trained professional looking after him. I can step back and have a break from the family at number 19. For the time being, I would like to look at my photographs, see the faces of my children and remind myself of the person I used to be, the person who was once happy and care-free and although it pains me to say it, took their easy life for granted.

I sit at the table and stare down at the smiling faces of Harriet and Dexter, remembering the scent of their skin and sound of their laughter, and before I can stop it, the dam bursts and the tears fall, a river of grief raining out of me until I can no longer see or think or do anything at all except weep endlessly. I hate being like this – weak and useless – but I can't seem to bring an end to it. I'm caught up in a cycle of self-perpetuating misery and hate.

A sound fills the room, a deep, pulsing howling. My head aches, my stomach goes into spasm. I look around for the source of the noise, and that's when I realise it's coming from me.

23

A pair of arms wrap themselves around me. I can't see who it is that's holding me down, pressing their limbs against mine, keeping me from moving. I twist about, my head thrashing from side to side, my feet kicking out until they too are held fast.

I feel myself being transported to a different place and laid out on a bed. People lean in, talking to me, their faces misshaped and warped, their voices a mumble of meaningless sounds. I buck about trying to free myself from whatever or whoever it is that's restraining me but it's no good. I'm trapped. I lift my head and try to bite anybody who is close enough but I end up gnashing at fresh air like a rabid, feral animal. Fatigue threatens my aching muscles. I should lie still, try to conserve what little energy I have left, but then if this is a dream and I shift about enough, I'll wake myself up, which is what I want to do. I don't want to be here, locked inside my own head, pinned down by strangers in an unfamiliar place that exists only in my mind.

I try to speak but a jumble of words pours out of my mouth. Not that it matters. Nobody is listening anyway. I'm not even sure what I'm trying to say. I just want to be free.

One final effort at trying to wriggle away results in more bodies holding me tight, stopping me from moving. I feel my head being tipped forward, a warm hand pressing behind my neck to tilt my head upwards. A cup of water is held to my lips and I'm urged to drink it all. I fear I'm going to choke and I end up spluttering and gagging, water flying out of my mouth as I cough and retch and struggle to breathe. Soft fingers continue to hold my head forwards and more water is placed on my lips until I'm drinking it with no gasping or choking for air. The cold liquid travels down my throat, soothing me, lulling me into a more peaceful state of mind.

I'm allowed to lie flat again and I feel myself drifting off into a deep sleep. A sleep within a sleep. A dream within a dream. I smile at the thought of it. The hands begin to move away from me, the pressure on me lessening as my body grows heavy. Darkness falls, covering me, blanketing me in its warmth, protecting me. Then nothing.

I wake up in bed. Sitting bolt upright, I look around. How did I get here? I was at the table looking at the photographs, that much I do remember, and now I'm here. I think back to the dream. I was being held down, forced to drink something I didn't want to drink. I gaze around the room. No cups of water, no splashes anywhere. So how did I end up here in bed? Have I had another sleepwalking episode? That has to be it. There's no other rational explanation for what I've just experienced. I don't want to admit to it, but that has to be it. There's no other reason that would account for how I ended up here.

My legs are weak and almost buckle under me as I stand up and make my way into the living room. I pass a mirror and daren't even contemplate looking into it. The stale tang of unwashed skin and hair wafts around me. My mouth is dry, my teeth coated in a gritty film. I need to get clean, to get out of these clothes and scrub myself until the memory of the last few days has been washed off my flesh.

The shower is hot as I stand under it. The water runs over my back and down my legs. Soap suds gather at my feet, a small carpet of white bubbles swimming around me, spreading and swirling as I rub at my back and arms with a sponge and then lean back and wash my hair. It feels good to be clean. The sweet aroma of lemons fills the air; water and soap cascade over my body as I lather myself with the foam-covered sponge.

By the time I step out of the shower, the bathroom is filled with steam and the surrounding scent is wonderful. I don't open the window. I want to savour the heat and the smell for as long as I can, to inhale it and let it cleanse and purify me.

I put on fresh clothes and comb my hair, then look in the mirror. I don't look quite as bad as I expected. I've got some colour in my cheeks, which is probably a false indicator as I've just stepped out of a steaming hot shower, but still, I look better than I have in a while. I'm happy to go with that thought. Not brilliant, but better. I'm a forty-five-year-old grieving widow and mother. This is the best I'm ever going to look. I'd best just accept what is staring back at me.

A noise somewhere in the house alerts me, sending an icy chill over my recently warmed skin. I push my feet into my loafers and move out of the bedroom, my senses now acutely attuned to every little noise. After so many inexplicable events lately, I'm not taking any chances. I lean down and pick up the first thing I can find with some weight to it – a hardback book. Not the most effective of weapons but enough to protect me from any intruders should I need to use it. I run through a scenario in my head – lifting my makeshift weapon high above my head and bringing it crashing down on anybody who means to harm me. I'll do what I have to do to protect myself.

Creeping into the hallway, the book held tightly between both my hands, I shriek as I see her standing in front of me. I let go and the book drops to the floor with a clatter, lying there, its cream pages flung open like a gaping mouth parted wide in a scream.

'Charlotte?'

She steps closer to me, her stick tapping on the floor next to her.

'I thought you were in Scotland?' I say.

'We've delayed it for a few days. I had to come and see you, Esther. Can we sit down? I want to talk to you about something.'

My heart starts up an erratic, uncomfortable beat as we sit opposite one another in the living room. She's looking tired. For the first time ever, I can see signs of ageing on Charlotte's perfect, porcelain skin. Her nails aren't long and painted and rather than the immaculate layer of make-up she normally wears, she appears to only have on her face some blusher and a smear of pale lipstick. I'm not sure whether to feel concerned or vaguely smug. It's about time she started feeling the strain. I want to shout at her that this is what it's like in my world. But even then, I don't think she would truly comprehend it. Her life has been absent of rough edges for most of her life. What would she know about suffering and injustice? She may have lost her partner at a young age, but she soon got over her grief, shoved it all aside and did her utmost to replace her lost love with mine.

'So,' I say with a sigh. 'What brings you back here?' I'm trying to sound indifferent and nonchalant when all the while blood is pulsing through my ears, making me dizzy with its speed and intensity. Why is she here? Has she finally come to confess and grovel at my feet? Or does she have more bad news to throw my way?

Charlotte twists her hands together on her lap, her fingers white, the skin on the back of her hands stretched and taut as she sits with a nervous expression on her face. She looks at me, apprehension etched into every line and crease on her skin as she clears her throat and begins speaking.

'I found some photos while I was packing. Photos of us as kids. And pictures of Mum and Dad. I got most of the family photos after they died and they've been stuck in the back bedroom in a cupboard. I dragged them out a few days ago and went through them.' She watches me closely and pauses.

Is she waiting for me to say something? I have no idea what she's getting at. What has some old photographs got to do with anything that's happened recently?

'And it got me thinking about Mum. And the way she was with you when we were younger,' she says.

I swallow and clear my throat. I'm not sure I like the way this conversation is heading. I want to get up and walk away but I seem to be fixed in position, my body unyielding and rigid when I try to move.

'Do you remember that, Esther? How Mum treated you when you were little?' Her face is serious. Too serious. She's talking about things that aren't relevant. I don't want to hear whatever it is she has come here to say. In my mind, I'm screaming at her to stop it, to get up and leave, but in reality, I'm sitting here, frozen to the spot, mute and unable to stop the memories that are now flooding into my mind.

I try to nod but don't seem to have full control of my muscles. My eyes fill with tears and my chest suddenly feels tight.

'Do you remember the time she went into hospital?' she says.

'For the stomach problem?' I whisper, fragments of memories flitting around my head as I think about how well our father coped while she was in there. I do recall the house being much quieter without Mum around. Less shouting, fewer arguments. More laughter.

Charlotte laughs and shakes her head. 'It wasn't a stomach problem, Esther. As far as her body went, our Mum was as fit as a fiddle. Her mind, however, was another matter entirely. She had mental health problems for most of her adult life. She didn't have any sort of stomach problem at all. She was sectioned.'

I feel as if a balloon has been inflated inside my abdomen. Breathing is difficult and I can't seem to think straight. Sectioned? Is this just another of Charlotte's lies? How have I gone through my life not knowing that?

'Anyway, I wanted to apologise for what she put you through as a kid. It wasn't right. You got blamed for everything even when it obviously wasn't your fault. And I was too young and frightened to do anything about it. I should have and I didn't and I'm so sorry for that.'

'What kind of things was I blamed for?' I say, my voice croaky with shock.

'You really don't remember?' A line appears between her eyes, a thin groove of surprise at my question.

I think I do remember. Somewhere, tucked away deep in a dark corner of my brain, are memories that have never resurfaced, memories that have very probably shaped my life, made me the person I am today. I've kept them hidden away for a reason. I don't want to think about that time of my life. And now Charlotte is here, dredging it all up again, making me see those images and hear my mother's voice screaming at me that I was useless and that she never wanted me anyway. Charlotte was all she ever wanted. I was an afterthought, a mistake. The unwanted child.

I recall one time I had done something wrong, something inconsequential, probably dragged mud into the house or fallen over and ruined my new trousers, and she grabbed my arm and told me that if I'd been a puppy, she would have drowned me at birth, held my head in a bucket of water and kept me there until I stopped breathing.

'You do remember, don't you?' Charlotte says, her eyes half closed and soft with what – compassion? Sorrow? Regret?

We sit for a few seconds in silence, the air thick with our shared past and the misery it brings.

'Why was she sectioned?' I ask finally, my breathing taking on a staccato rhythm as I attempt to control it and think straight.

'She was found wandering along the road in the early hours of the morning, naked and unable to remember where she lived.' Charlotte's voice is shaky. I wonder if she's going to lose her composure, if her mask of serenity will finally fall away to reveal the real Charlotte underneath? She suddenly appears fragile, like a china doll, small and pale, and ready to shatter at any second.

'I just thought that with everything that's happened, you should know. I realise that you're starting to remember things now and I thought it might help if I told you about Mum and your childhood,' she says as she stands up abruptly and starts to walk away. 'Because I'm sure all of this now is because of what happened to you when you were little. You never stood a chance. Not with the way she was with you.'

I have no idea what she means. Why did she come here? What on earth has Mum being sectioned got to do with what happened to me? And what does she mean about me starting to remember things? How did I not stand a chance?

'Hang on a minute!' I shout after her but she doesn't stop. She continues walking, her body tipped slightly to one side as she limps to the door. 'Remember what things?' I say feebly. 'What sort of things am I starting to remember? You said all of this happened because of the way Mum treated me. All of what?' My voice threatens to break any second. I take a deep breath to try and compose myself. 'And what about those photos you promised me last time you were here?' I shout, referring to the pictures of Harriet and Dexter that she said I could have, but she doesn't reply.

Charlotte turns and gives me a smile that isn't really a smile at all. This time, her face positively radiates compassion and sorrow. Her eyes brim with unshed tears as she points to something on the table in the hallway.

'What are you talking about, Charlotte? What's going on? What happened and what am I starting to remember?'

But she doesn't answer. Instead, she turns away from me, opens the door and leaves.

24

NUMBER 19

Things are finally going her way. Her husband is so busy fawning over his son, he appears to have forgotten all about his other life and his mistress. He is sitting by the boy's bedside, stroking his forehead and murmuring softly in his ear.

She stares in the mirror and applies a slick of lip gloss, smacking her lips together. They've called an ambulance and now just need to wait. She suggests carrying the boy downstairs and he agrees.

Easier access for the medics, she says softly.

They carry their son down, a blanket draped over his small body as they head into the living room. He begins to retch and convulse, his body rocked by the contractions that take hold in his belly. A puddle of vomit lands on the carpet, the stench taking her breath away. Immediately, the daughter is on her feet, offering to clean up, disappearing and coming back in with a bucket of hot water and a scrubbing brush.

Husband and wife sit side by side on the sofa, the small child laid out on their knees. He's pale and feverish. She leans down and strokes his face. She can feel her husband watching her, admiring how strong she is, how caring and nurturing she is. A buzz runs through her veins at the thought of it. She lifts the boy up off her lap and slips up off the sofa.

Where are you going? her husband asks.

To get him a drink. He'll be dehydrated after being sick.

He nods and she scurries away to the kitchen, checking behind her to make sure he isn't following. She closes the door and leans against it briefly to catch her breath. A small pulse hammers at her neck as she opens the cupboard and grabs a tumbler. She fills it with lemonade and places it down on the kitchen table before reaching up into the top cupboard and rummaging at the back, shuffling tins and jars about in a bid to reach the packet she's after. It's stashed behind the spice jars, nestled amongst the bags of flour – the packet of salt that she hides away. She rests her fingers over it and clutches it tightly, before lifting it up and bringing it out onto the kitchen top. There probably isn't any need to conceal it but she does anyway, just in case anybody monitors how quickly the quantity seems to drop. She can't risk being caught out. This is her secret. That boy and his illness are the only things she can dominate and take command of. She can't lose that element of authority. It's all she's got.

Taking it to the table, she measures out a level teaspoon and sprinkles it into the tumbler of lemonade, stirring it quickly until it's all dissolved. He'll complain again that it tastes odd but that doesn't worry her. She's already got her story sorted in her head. She'll tell him that he needs to replace the salts in his body after throwing up, that it's doing him good, helping him to get better. Nobody will question her. She's in control of this. This is her plan, her child, her home.

She carries the tumbler back in the room and gives it to the boy. As expected, he complains about the taste. She tells him it'll help make him better then she informs her husband about the couple of grains of salt she put in it to replace the essential body salts he's lost.

Doctors recommend it after a sickness bug, she tells him.

He strokes the boy's forehead, watching as the child drinks from the long, pastel-coloured tumbler. Every so often, he stops and pulls a face. She stands over him, urging him on, telling him it's like medicine.

Mummy's helping you to get better, sweetheart, she whispers as she takes the empty cup from him and places it on the floor at her feet.

A knock alerts her. She marches off to let the medic in, straightening her hair and checking in the mirror as she passes. He strides past her as she opens the door, asking her questions about her son's condition before entering the living room and kneeling down next to the boy.

She sits back down next to her husband, doing her best to look unperturbed as her son begins to retch once more before falling into some kind of lifeless daze.

I'm going to recommend he be admitted back into hospital, the medic says as he stands up and shouts through to his partner, a young woman who bustles in and stands next to him, listening to his instructions.

There's no time to voice any concerns or disagree. Their minds are made up. The woman tips her head to one side as they speak to her, telling her what's going to happen, asking her how long he's been ill for and what his symptoms are. She responds accordingly, nodding and talking in a soft, barely audible voice. Pretending to fight back tears.

The boy is as light as air as they wrap him up and transport him into the back of the ambulance. The woman holds his hand and clambers in the back with him before anybody has a chance to object. They won't move her now. She's his mother. And every child needs their mother when they're ill, don't they?

25

ESTHER

My entire body is shaking as I listen to the door close with a dull click. I stand for a few seconds, raking over Charlotte's words in my mind and what they mean, but no matter how hard I try, I simply cannot work out what it was she was getting at. What on earth am I starting to remember? I know I've had a few strange incidents happen lately but I've no recollection of hidden memories springing unbidden into my mind. I would know if such a thing happened, wouldn't I? They would present themselves to me and I would suddenly realise that they were real, that they actually happened, because they would slot into place in my head. Wouldn't they? After the accident, things were a bit hazy, I grant you, but I didn't lose whole chunks of the event. I know the main facts. I know that Julian and my children are gone and that Charlotte was injured. What else is there to know?

I turn and rest my eyes to where she pointed. There's a small box sitting on the table that wasn't there before she arrived. I snatch it up, unable to decide whether I'm confused as hell or just downright bloody furious, and carry it through to the living room.

I sit with it on my knee and hold it for a few seconds. It

contains photographs of Harriet and Dexter, I just know it. Charlotte promised me pictures of them and now here they are, ready for me to open. My children, shut away in a small box. My sweet, adorable children and this is all that's left of them. I wait for a few seconds, my hands hovering over the lid. I want to take my time, to savour the moment but in the end, I'm too impatient and desperation gets the better of me. I end up tearing off the lid and pulling out the contents, spreading them over my lap, the small but immediately identifiable snapshots of the children that I brought into this world.

There are three or four photographs of them spread about on my knee, pictures of Harriet and Dexter smiling and posing for the camera, but like the many other things that have happened lately, they don't make any sense. The anachronistic array of pictures causes me to catch my breath and swallow down a feeling of confusion that refuses to fully reveal itself. These are smiling images of my beautiful children wearing clothes that I've never seen before in a setting I'm certain that I've never been to. How can that be? A dull pain fills my head, beating and throbbing behind my eyes as I blink repeatedly, hoping an answer will jump into my mind. Because there has to be one. These pictures are real. I would know if they were doctored in some way. And besides, why would Charlotte give me something like this if they weren't real? She has her faults for sure, but is my only sister really cruel enough to pass on images that had been photoshopped, knowing they would upset me? I don't believe she would. Not because she cares about my feelings but simply because she wouldn't gain anything from it.

I trace the outline of their faces with my finger. I can almost feel the softness of their skin, smell the heady aroma of their freshly washed hair. The longing for them is so great, I could tear out my own heart and claw at my insides with my bare hands until there is nothing left and even then it wouldn't be enough. It wouldn't be greater than the cavernous ache that currently sits within me.

I continue to stare at the pictures. They're my children all right, Harriet and Dexter, and yet they're not. They're different but I don't know what it is that's awry. Something definitely isn't right. Just like Charlotte's unfathomable statement before she left, these images leave me feeling bewildered and slightly dazed. Why can't I work out what's wrong with them? It's not just the clothes or the setting. There's something else as well. Something that's niggling at me and won't stop until I realise what it is that's wrong.

The cold in the room seems to wrap itself around me, covering me with an icy shroud. I place the photos back in the box and put it to one side. I'll have another look later, see if I can apply any logic to this strange anomaly. It's just another abnormal event in my life that has left me scratching my head and questioning my own sanity.

A memory of Julian suddenly pushes itself into the forefront of my thoughts. He's saying something to me. His eyes are set in an expression of abject horror and he's pleading with me, his hands outstretched towards me, his skin pallid and lined. I can see that his mouth is moving but I can't put any words to what he's saying. I can get the gist of his mood by the look he has on his face, however. I place a clammy hand across my forehead and press down to relieve the pressure that's starting to build there. I want to see it clearly, to relive this image and remember everything, because this isn't how I thought it was. This memory doesn't match the one I have in my head. I'm almost certain our last few weeks together consisted of me pleading with him, begging him to stay with me and not leave me for Charlotte. But for some odd reason, this memory doesn't feel like that. It has a different impression to it, as if I'm the one who has committed some awful deed and Julian is upset and begging me, asking me why I did what I did. My breath is rapid and I feel hot as I try to recall what it was I purportedly did that made him so distressed and angry, but nothing comes. My mind is a complete blank. Even my own body refuses to cooperate and lets me down when I need it the most.

My fingers drum against my thigh as I try to conjure up an image so elusive, it's as if it is non-existent. But it has to have happened, otherwise why would I have suddenly remembered it? I close my eyes and think about Julian and how much I miss him. The loss of the children hit me so hard, I've barely had time to think about my husband and how much I miss him. And I do. He was the other half of me and now he's gone. I think I've subconsciously done my best to block all thoughts of him out of my mind, which is probably why I'm having problems getting them to resurface. I have yet to visit his resting place. It's something I've said I would like to do on a few occasions but never quite gotten around to it. Guilt tugs at me. Soon I'll visit, take some flowers and spend some time by his graveside. It's what I should have done already. Any decent wife would have.

But you were anything but decent...

My eyes fill up and I let out a gasp. Where on earth did that thought spring up from? The small stuttering pulse in my neck suddenly speeds up, turning into a pounding bass drum that batters against my throat, hard and relentless. A spread of heat covers my face, prickling at my scalp. I shiver and tell myself it was a rogue thought that is apropos of nothing. I should ignore it. God knows, I've had plenty of strange things occur to me lately. Some weird, unexplainable thought should barely register on the scale.

I take a deep breath and try to clear my mind. It's the only way. I have to rid myself of all toxic thoughts and memories. There's nothing to be gained from looking back – being positive and moving on with my life is the best way to deal with things. I'm confused enough as it is with all the weird events that have happened lately. I don't need to clutter up my thinking with any extra memories or recollections that I don't even understand, or focus on a negative phrase my own mind has thrown at me without any solid evidence to back it up. What's the point of sitting here going over things again and again? All it does is leave me feeling miserable and perplexed. I'm going to ignore Charlotte's cryptic message and any undesirable lurking thoughts, put the photos to one side and focus on the future. I've got plenty here to keep me occupied. I'm just going to shut my mind off to everything else or I risk being submerged under a sea of guilt and hopelessness.

Craning my neck, I peer out of the window over to number 19. The road is empty. In the distance, the hiss of traffic tells me it's busy in town. A small pulse of excitement crawls up my chest at the thought of keeping a check on Veronica. She's something concrete in my life, something that I know for sure is real. I sit up straight and position myself so I can't be seen. I make a promise to myself that I'll go over there and intervene if I see anything remotely abusive taking place. While everything else seems to be caving in on me, making me doubt my own mind, at least I can rely on her to be consistently inconsistent with her cruel, impulsive behaviour. It may sound just a bit voyeuristic and completely crazy but at this moment in time, the woman at number 19 is the one thing that's stopping me from completely losing my mind.

26

NUMBER 19

The boy begins to heave and convulse as the ambulance roars into life. The sound of the siren is drowned out by his crying and the noise he makes as he vomits into the receptacle that is being held under his mouth. The woman feels herself go cold as the medics step in and take over, tending to the boy's needs and turning their backs on her. She listens as they bark out medical jargon to each other.

Do you need me for anything? she asks one, trying to angle her way past his bulk. *I can hold his hand and talk to him, keep him calm and soothe him.*

The medic doesn't reply and instead continues attending to the boy, taking his temperature and placing an oxygen mask over his face in between the child's bouts of sickness. She stares at the saline drip attached to her son's arm, at his pale skin that appears to be almost translucent and thinks about what she'll say when they get to the hospital. They'll all want to speak with her, all the doctors and nursing staff. This is her son, an extension of her own body. She knows absolutely everything about him. Everything.

The journey seems to go on for an age. She's sore and uncomfortable and the suspension does nothing to protect her from every bump in the road and every sharp corner they take.

She is ignored once again as they pull up outside the doors of the emergency department. The medics bustle her out of the back of the vehicle and propel her inside where a small group of staff are waiting to take some details. At last, people who are prepared to pay her some attention and listen to what she has to say. Not before time.

She talks to a doctor, telling him of her son's bouts of vomiting and listlessness. He seems eager to listen. Nodding and probing her for more details. She notices how young he is and almost laughs out loud. What on earth will he know about her son's symptoms? He's barely out of college. Probably a junior doctor and not even fully qualified. Running her fingers through her hair, she looks him in the eye and reels off the latest illnesses, telling the young doctor that it's probably just a bug and nothing to be too concerned about.

Let us be the judge of that, the doctor replies sharply.

She feels her face burn and itches to slap his smug face. He turns and speaks to his colleagues then marches away from her. She runs beside him to keep up, watching as her child is whisked away, his small body surrounded by a team of nursing staff.

Where are you taking him? she asks. *I need to go with him.*

She walks alongside her son who begins to convulse, his body bucking about violently as the team pick up speed and lean in towards him, the sudden scurry of activity obliterating her view of him. Out of nowhere, a nurse appears and guides her back to a waiting area, telling her they'll speak to her soon and that she shouldn't worry.

They need to carry out some tests, the nurse says, her manner a little too detached for the woman's liking. *As soon as we know what's happening, we'll inform you of his condition.*

This is her son they're talking about. She should be by his side, instructing the medical team on his symptoms, not ignored and left in some scruffy little waiting room while they prod and poke at her boy. He is her son. He belongs to her.

She starts to voice her concerns but the nurse's thoughts are already elsewhere as she stands and makes her way out of the room, leaving the woman alone to muse over what has just taken place. This isn't how it's meant to be. Everything has moved too quickly. She needs to be near her boy, to control the situation and be in charge.

The room is silent, exacerbating her sense of anxiety. A tic takes hold in her jaw as she bites at the inside of her mouth, nibbling on a loose piece of skin. How long is she supposed to stay here? Surely there must be some sort of protocol for the parents of ill children? Don't they deserve some attention too?

Outside the room, a sudden buzz of activity takes place, the metallic rush of trolleys being pushed along corridors, people talking in clipped tones before their voices disappear into the distance, leaving her in silence once more. Is this how she's supposed to spend the day? Being isolated and knowing nothing of her son's progress? What if he comes around, opens his eyes and asks after her? What will they do then?

She stands up, determined to take things further. She could actually take her son and discharge him if she wanted to. He belongs to her, after all. She can do whatever she pleases with him. These people don't seem to know what they're doing and that young doctor didn't appear to know anything at all about what was going on.

She strides towards the door and peers out, disappointed to find the corridor empty and the nearby desk devoid of people. Her feet clatter on the laminated flooring as she paces up and down the long passageway, the sound of her footsteps bouncing around the empty space, heightening her anger.

Walking back into the room, she sits down again and drums her fingers on her thigh. Time passes slowly, every minute feeling like an hour, until she can stand it no more. She stares at her watch in disbelief. It's been over forty-five minutes. Where the hell are all the professionals? All the staff who are purportedly caring for her son? Has nobody asked about his parents or the lady who was by his side when he was admitted?

A distant squeak and shuffle of feet alerts her. She stands up and walks to the door, ready to give them a piece of her mind. They've no right treating her like this. No right at all. She is the boy's mother, after all. She deserves better.

A dark-skinned, older man is standing right outside the door as she steps into the corridor. Beside him is the young doctor who whisked her son away from her.

Well? she says sharply, her gaze firmly fixed on the younger man as she thinks how hard she would love to slap him across his arrogant little face.

We've run some blood tests, the older man says, *and there's something we're concerned about.*

Take a seat, the younger doctor says. *We'd like to speak to you about your son.*

27

ESTHER

I'm gasping for breath. Without realising it, my hand is clutching at the base of my neck, my fingers fluttering against my collarbone in a desperate bid to slow down my racing heartbeat. Something about that living room, those people – *her* – has resonated with me. I can't pin it down but whatever it is, it has unearthed something in me that once brought to the surface, can't ever be put back in place again. I don't know how I know that. I just do. It's such a strong feeling that I can't shake it off or dismiss it. It clings to me like a pernicious disease, digging deep into my body, refusing to leave.

That poor boy must have some sort of serious condition. Twice now he's been admitted to hospital. And yet something inside my brain is nagging at me that that isn't the case at all. I don't know why I think that. I have no evidence or information to the contrary but I do have a deep sense of unease about the whole situation. Whether it's Veronica's strange reactions or some sort of deep-rooted intuition after spending so many years being around children, but my instinct is nagging at me that something is very wrong here. The worst part of this whole dreadful scenario is the fact that I still can't pass on anything significant to anybody in a position of authority. What would I say – that I've seen her admonish her children and her son has been hospitalised on more than one occasion? I may be out of touch with the world outside my window, but even I know that social services are stretched to capacity and it would take a lot more than that to warrant a visit from one of their team. And what is it about this family that has struck a chord with me anyway? Besides wanting to protect those poor kids, I feel a strong and possibly unhealthy attachment to the whole family and know that no matter what, I have to keep watching. Watching and biding my time for the right moment. It's like some sort of sick addiction, me sitting here, spying, taking notes. I can't seem to stop it. Correction: I don't want to stop it.

I stand up, a streak of determination coursing through me. I know exactly what I'm going to do. I may not have enough information to get in touch with the relevant authorities but I'm not going to sit here and do nothing.

Pulling at the door handle, I head over to see Dr McRae. I don't care whether she's busy or not, I'll sit in the waiting room until she agrees to see me. What are they going to do – throw me out? I'll refuse to move and sit there all day if I have to. They'll have to find a slot for me then. They can't just close the surgery and lock me in, can they?

I'm surprised to find the place almost empty of patients. I can't help but let out a light guffaw. This surgery is hardly ever empty. For once, I've struck lucky. A nurse saunters past and stares at me. I give her a brusque nod and she responds by nodding back and giving me a thin smile.

I sit with my hands placed lightly in my lap, waiting for somebody to ask me what I'm doing just sitting here. Right on cue, Dr McRae walks across the room. She stops and raises her eyebrows when she sees me, then comes and sits down, her body angled to one side as she turns to speak to me.

'Esther! I wasn't expecting to see you today. Is everything okay?'

I can't remember when she started addressing me by my first name rather than using my surname. She's acting as if we're extremely familiar with each other when in fact, we're really not. She's only been my doctor for a short while, right at about the time of the accident, actually. She doesn't know how I was before my world was ripped in two. She doesn't really know me at all.

I want to tell her that I wouldn't be here seeking her help if I was okay, but I don't. Of course I don't. That would be churlish and pointless. Instead, I ask if I can speak to her in private. I watch as she glances over to the nurse who is standing close by, pretending to busy herself with the water-dispensing machine.

'Of course,' she replies in a way that irks me. Her manner is artificial, as if she's putting on an act for my benefit. Or maybe it's got something to do with my unexpected presence and I've just caught her unawares. Either way, I don't care for her tone.

We walk into her room and sit opposite one another. The door is left wide open and she appears uncharacteristically relaxed as she leans back in her chair and waits for me to speak. Why are the words we are able to formulate in our heads so damn difficult to say out loud when the perfect opportunity finally presents itself?

A breath rattles in my chest as I exhale and try to stem the feeling of awkwardness and disquiet that is crawling through me. To her credit, Dr McRae doesn't give off an air of impatience or try to hurry me in any way, sitting instead with a look of mild concern on her face while I work out what it is that I actually want to say.

My body eventually allows me to speak, the words coming out in a stuttering stream of unpunctuated syllables. I find myself telling Dr McRae everything, all about the woman at number 19 and the people calling my name outside my house and the photographs Charlotte gave me. I tell her about the visit into town and how we ended up somewhere completely different. I also tell her about finding the holdall full of clothes and the lack of houses at the end of the road. I didn't plan on informing her of all these things when I came here but they seemed to just find a way out and now that they've been released, there's no taking them back. Part of me wishes I hadn't said anything but most of me feels relieved to get it all off my chest.

I let out a long sigh once I've finished speaking, feeling easier about everything. I'm relieved when her expression doesn't change. She simply nods and doesn't appear to be judging me in any way when many would think me completely unhinged.

'I can see that this has caused you some worry and that's not surprising. Unexpected events and things happening that we can't explain can make a person feel deeply uncomfortable.' She looks down at her notes and then back at me. 'The last time we spoke, you said that you didn't want to go back to see the therapist. Do you still feel the same way about that decision?'

I don't nod. I think perhaps seeing a therapist may actually help with my increasing bouts of anxiety and confusion but I'm too proud to admit it. I'm not one for baring my soul and not sure how much it can help me, but I do know that I need to do something about this whole sorry situation before the worry of it eats away at me, leaving me unable to function properly.

'I'm not entirely sure,' I mutter, a sudden wave of fatigue washing over me. 'What about the woman over the road?' I ask, hoping to shift the focus away from my own failings onto somebody else. 'What should I do about that?'

I sit there, hoping Dr McRae will come out with some magical solution to my problem. She knows more about these things than I do. Perhaps she can put in some sort of anonymous complaint against Veronica. Her word would certainly carry more sway than mine ever could.

'Let's just concentrate on you for the minute,' she says brightly, 'and then we can think about the lady over the road once your own issues are sorted.'

I'm not sure how I feel about that answer. I came here hoping Dr McRae would take charge of this situation and relieve me of the burden that Veronica has unknowingly foisted on me, but now she wants to ignore it all and pretend as if it's not happening.

Straightening my posture, I try to exude an air of authority and project my voice towards her. 'I'm sorry, Dr McRae, but I really want to talk about Veronica. I've seen what she does and I want something doing.'

Her eyebrows hitch up at my words. 'You've given her a name?'

'Of course I have,' I reply, feeling slightly braver than I did just a few seconds ago. 'Why shouldn't I give her a name? Easier than calling her the woman over the road or the woman at number 19 all the time, isn't it?'

She nods and juts out her bottom lip which I take as an acquiescent gesture. 'Okay,' she says softly. 'How about you tell me everything you know and then we discuss what our next move is going to be?'

I get the feeling she's humouring me but I'm prepared to put up with it because I know she'll change her mind once I tell her everything I've seen. She's a doctor and has a duty of care to that family. I don't mind if I have to sit here talking all night, I'm going to make sure it's all brought out into the open – all of the sordid goings-on inside that house, every dirty little secret that's happened in there is about to be revealed.

28

'So you think she's cruel to her children?' Dr McRae is leaning forward, her elbows resting on the desk, her hands cupped around her chin. I hadn't noticed until now just how tiny her face is, with its elfin-like features and wide, dark eyes. This is my doctor in a relaxed state. Not the uptight, efficient individual I'm used to seeing. I wonder if she's letting her guard down on purpose, showing me that I can trust her. I like to think that's the case, that we're finally making some sort of connection after months and months of formality and stilted conversations.

'I know it,' I say with a certain amount of poise. I need to radiate an air of sureness about this if I want her to take me seriously and get her on my side.

'Hmmm.' She lifts her elbows off the desk, leans back and looks away from me before picking up a pen and tapping it on the edge of the table. 'I've got an idea that may help,' she says, the tone of her voice giving nothing away.

A breath is suspended in my chest as I wait, wondering what she's about to say, wondering if she has a plan that will help resolve this dilemma.

'Before I tell you what I've got in mind, can I just ask what made you choose that particular name for her? Why Veronica and not Susan or Debbie or Joanne?'

She catches me off guard with her question. I wonder if that's part of her strategy. Who questions leads. She's got the upper hand now while I'm desperately trying to come up with an answer that doesn't sound childish and stupid. I feel like a little girl who has named one of her dolls and is being riled about it by a smirking older sibling.

'I'm not sure,' I say quietly, my recently found confidence rapidly leaking out of me as she watches me with her big, dark eyes. I get the feeling she's probing for something, some elusive scrap of information that will unlock everything in my mind and provide the answer to the unexplainable events that still mystify me, but I have no idea what it is she's after.

'Well, why Susan and why not Veronica?' I say with a tinge of acidity to my voice. 'It's a perfectly acceptable name, isn't it?'

'It is indeed a perfectly acceptable name. I'm just trying to go through your thought processes,' she murmurs. 'That's all it is. I just want to get everything straight in my head before we go any further with our conversation.'

I have no idea what she is up to or what her plan is or why she is going off on a tangent like this, trying to detract attention away from the real issue. 'Right. So what do you suggest I do about all this?' I get the feeling I'm being analysed. Either that or she's stalling because she doesn't actually have any idea of what I should do next but is too proud to admit it.

'Well,' she says with a deep sigh as she briefly looks away and then turns her gaze back to me. 'I think writing everything down will be a real help.'

'Already doing that,' I bark at her, pleased that for once I'm actually ahead of the game. I was hoping for something more than this. I was hoping for a well thought out, educated answer to stop my psychotic neighbour and explain my weird and wonderful hallucinations.

'You're writing it all down?' Her eyebrows are arched and her voice laced with cynicism.

'I'm writing the stuff down that happens in number 19.'

'I meant write everything down,' she says brightly. 'Everything you see that upsets you or things you encounter that you don't quite understand or can't explain.'

'Like expecting to see a row of houses and being faced with a brick wall?'

'Yes, exactly that!' Her voice is shrill. I can't work out if she's annoyed or overexcited. 'And try to include everything. Go back to the very first thing that happened, whether it was seeing your neighbour or something strange happening, and write it all down, as well as how it made you feel.'

I have no idea why she has suggested such a thing but it can't do any harm, can it?

'Writing down your feelings can often help you deal with traumatic experiences.' She's watching me closely now to see what sort of reaction her words will provoke.

'Okay,' I say, as cheerfully as I can, rather impressed at how well she is able read me. 'I'll certainly give it a go.' Perhaps Dr McRae and I are finally making some sort of connection, which is no bad thing I suppose given the current circumstances. I need her on my side if I'm to get to the bottom of what's going on at number 19. At this moment in time, being nice to her is in my best interests so I'm willing to go with her suggestion.

I stand up and then immediately sit back down as Charlotte's words pierce through my brain. Dr McRae doesn't stir, sitting instead in the same position, her large inquisitive eyes boring into me.

'There's something else,' I say quietly. Saliva fills my mouth and I gulp it down, the sound of the mechanism in my throat rattling in my ears and seeming to fill the silence in the room. My respect for Dr McRae grows by the second as I watch her face soften. She doesn't try to hurry me or look at her watch or worse still, roll her eyes and smirk. She just sits there, her face impassive, her features gentle and reassuring as I take my time and try to find the right words.

'My sister, Charlotte, spoke to me about my childhood, more specifically about our mother and her mental health. I'd forgotten all about it. How could I have forgotten something as significant as that?'

'What exactly did she tell you?' Dr McRae replies.

'Well, she mentioned about how Mum was sectioned. Once she said that, it all started to come back to me, but prior to that, I'd got it in my head that she was in hospital for a stomach operation. I have no idea why I thought that. Also, she said that Mum treated me differently when we were growing up and as soon as she said it, I knew she was right. I had a memory come back to me recently you see, and not a pleasant one. It involved me being found with a dead cat.' I stop to catch my breath and to give myself some time to think about that incident.

'And you think you may have done something to it?' Dr McRae is still sitting in the same position, her face still giving off the same look of stoic encouragement.

'I... I honestly don't know.' Tears prick at the back of my eyelids. I close my eyes for a second and swallow. I won't cry. I won't let it happen. Not here, not now. 'I like to think not, but I'm not entirely sure.' I stare down at my hands as if the answer will appear there. Are these the hands of somebody who could kill another living being? Perhaps they are. I feel like I no longer really know myself. Maybe none of us truly knows ourselves completely.

Maybe we all have hidden depths that should never be brought to the surface because they're too dark and troubling to deal with.

'The brain is clever at hiding things that are too distressing for us to cope with.'

'Are we talking about repressed memory here, Dr McRae?'

She stops and takes a breath, then thinks for a few seconds before continuing. 'This isn't really my area so I don't want to speculate too much. Can I suggest you go back to see the therapist, Esther? I really do think it would help you.'

'And what about Veronica?' I say shakily. I won't let her forget about Veronica. That was my initial reason for coming here. Everything else was just a follow-on, things that poured out before I had a chance to stop them.

'Don't worry. You keep writing it all down and then get back to me and we'll take it from there. In the meantime, I'll get onto Daniel Burridge and make an appointment for you.'

My heart does a slight flip in my chest. 'Daniel Burridge?' I say with a certain amount of trepidation.

'Yes,' Dr McRae replies as she taps at her keyboard. 'Is there a problem?'

'No,' I say quietly. 'No problem.'

It's just a coincidence. It has to be. Daniel is a fairly common name. It can't be the same one who followed me down the road a few days back. Not the same person who tried to strike up a conversation with me in the waiting room last week. The same one who told me he was a therapist. It's just a fluke, that's all it is. Just a horrible, ill-timed fluke.

I stand up to leave, my pulse still tapping away, my instinct telling me something is wrong with this whole situation, that I should question her further.

'Have I met him before?' My skin tightens as I wait for her answer.

She looks up, her brow furrowed slightly. 'Hmm?'

'This Daniel chap,' I say, a tone of exasperation creeping into my voice. 'Have I seen him before?'

Her eyes flick to her computer screen and then back to me. 'It isn't the same person you saw last time if that's what you're asking?'

'Right, okay. Thank you.' I don't know why I'm thanking her. I feel no relief at her answer. It doesn't put my mind at rest or fully answer my question. A distinct feeling of foreboding continues to nip at me. Not the same therapist as last time but is it that man who followed me – the therapist from this very same building?

'What does he look like?' I catch her unawares and her face is a dead giveaway that she is now losing patience with me. She tries to rearrange her expression but it's too late. I've seen right into her soul.

'I'll be in touch as soon as your appointment is made, Esther. He's a very nice chap. Very easy to talk to. Really relaxed but still a consummate professional. I'll think you'll get on well with him.' She stands up, the chair scraping sharply on the floor behind her and I know at that point that that is my cue to leave.

I step away, not wanting to break the tenuous link Dr McRae and I have forged in the last fifteen minutes. I need her on my side if she is to help me with the Veronica problem. I'm not stupid enough to ruin a good thing just because I'm worried and confused over the identity of a man who may or may not have spoken to me last week. Put like that, the whole thing does sound utterly ridiculous.

'Thank you,' I say as I leave the room and quietly close the door behind me.

By the time I get home, I've convinced myself that seeing this therapist is something I just have to do and that the chances of it being the same man are almost zero. Yet again, I'm overthinking things. So why do I feel so uncomfortable and perturbed at the mention of his name?

I twist the door handle and step inside, knowing before I even take one step in there that something is wrong. A waft of perfume hits my nostrils, a scent I immediately recognise. I stop dead in my tracks and hold onto the wall for balance as a shadowy figure appears in front of me.

29

NUMBER 19

I'm not sure what you mean?

She's doing her best to keep the annoyance and slight fear out of her tone. She doesn't care for their abrupt manner and body language and bristles at their proximity to her. She feels like some sort of criminal, which she most definitely isn't. She is his mother, the main caregiver of that child and here they are, making her feel as if she's done something wrong.

Hypernatremia it's called, which means your son has abnormally high levels of sodium in his urine. We need to do further tests to rule out diabetes insipidus and find out what may have caused this. Both doctors watch her carefully, their penetrative gazes making her feel uncomfortable.

She smiles at them and nods enthusiastically. *Okay, what do these tests involve?* She sees them glance at one another before turning back to her.

We would need to carry out more blood tests and monitor his condition over the next twenty-four hours.

The older doctor does most of the talking, confirming her

initial belief that the younger man is inexperienced. Just as she thought, really. She was right all along.

Are you here alone or is the boy's father available for us to talk to? The younger doctor catches her eye.

She looks away, unable to hold his gaze. She doesn't like him, doesn't trust him.

She tells him she accompanied the boy because she's his mother and that her husband is at home looking after their daughter.

Both men nod in unison. *Okay, well, diabetes insipidus is rare in one so young. Once we've ruled that out and get more bloods, we should have more of an idea what has caused your son's condition.*

They leave her alone once more, telling her that somebody should be along shortly to take more details and perhaps offer her a cup of tea. This isn't how she planned it. She wants to be at her son's bedside, speaking with the doctors, watching what they're doing to her child. She wishes she had brought her phone with her. She could ring her husband, let him know of the progress, tell him that she's got it all under control.

She gives it another half an hour then decides to take matters into her own hands. She heads out of the room and into the empty corridor, determined to find somebody who can lead her to her son. She's had enough of being left alone and ignored. She'll walk every corridor and go to every ward in this hospital if she has to. Nobody is going to keep her from her child. Nobody. She's his mother and she'll find him even if it takes her all day. She feels a pang of guilt for having abandoned him and quickly dismisses it. Her sitting here wasn't her idea or her doing. The medical staff are responsible for this separation. If anybody deserves blame, it's them.

She screws her face up at the overpowering smell of disinfectant that permeates the whole building. Her feet squeak and clip as she shuffles off down the narrow passage and through the double doors that close behind her with a resounding bang.

30

ESTHER

'How did you get in?' I feel twitchy and nervous even though I've no reason to.

Amy lets out a slight chuckle and shakes her head at me. 'Honestly, Esther. You are funny sometimes. I just thought I'd give you these.' She's holding out something for me to take.

I step closer, my eyes drawn to the brightly coloured item. It's a small, embossed book with a large pink flower on the front. A variety of green leaves protrude out of the many delicate-looking petals, their stems wild and curling as they snake their way over the multicoloured design. The colours are so vibrant and powerful, I feel transfixed by the pattern, unable to tear my eyes away from it.

'It's a photo album,' she says softly. 'You don't see many around these days, what with everything being digital and pictures getting stored on computers and stuff so when I spotted it, I thought of you and your photographs.'

My face feels hot enough to explode. I want to ask her how she got in here but whenever I pose a question to Amy, she always has a way of laughing it off and changing the subject. If I try to pursue the issue, I'll come across as ungrateful and aggressive, especially since she's brought me this gift, which I do really appreciate. It's extremely thoughtful of her. However, I'm still confused and after racking my brain over the new therapist on the way back, I feel completely out of sorts again. Just for once, I'd like to spend a day with no strange occurrences, no unexplained events or happenings that can't be laughed off or put down as coincidences. The things I've seen and experienced are too striking and too bizarre for me to ignore. And the ironic thing is, the person I'm supposed to be meeting with to help me explain them, this new therapist, is actually included in the whole puzzle that is currently my life. How can he possibly help me when he's part of the problem?

I take the album and thank her but still feel perturbed by her unexpected presence here. As kind as it may be for her to bring me a gift, a little bit of notice would have been nice. I do have a life here – it may not be exciting or particularly adventurous but it is mine and I'm starting to feel that certain people take me for some kind of old fool who can be manipulated and mocked whenever they feel like it, Amy included. I never thought I would ever think like this but things seem to be spiralling out of my grasp and it's putting me on edge. Prior to the death of my entire family, I'd always been in control of things but since then, my life has lapsed into some sort of defective existence where time slips away from me and the unexpected and the unexplained are a normal pattern, a normal part of my day.

'Do you want me to put your photos in it?' Amy's voice has dropped. I suppose she's detected my sour mood and is now treading carefully. I should thank her for my present but can't summon up the energy. Even breathing feels like an effort. I just want to be left alone.

She is standing, waiting for me to respond, her eyes bright with the vivacity of youth, her mouth set in a slight pout. She doesn't understand my plight and never will. I've been kidding myself thinking that Amy and I are close, that we rub along together like old friends. It's superficial nonsense. She's just like everybody else – Charlotte, Dr McRae, Anne and Rose – they all think of me as a nuisance, somebody who needs looking after. A person who can be patronised then cast aside when they tire of me. Well, I've had enough of it. I'm fed up of their condescension and their useless, false platitudes to try and cajole me into thinking everything is okay when it most definitely isn't. It might suit them to think that way but it most certainly doesn't suit me.

'No, I don't want you to put my photos in there. What I want you to do is leave.' Placing my hand in the small of Amy's back, I push her towards the door, propelling her forwards, moving faster and faster as I increase the strength in my arm. She cries out for me to stop, a surprised squawk trilling out into the space between us, but I don't halt with my pushing. I continue on, forcing her forwards, not stopping until we reach the door. The album slips out of her hand onto the floor with a clatter. I need her out of here so I can think straight. I need some space to clear my head of the myriad thoughts and memories that are clamouring for attention in my exhausted, overworked brain.

'Esther, please stop this! What are you doing?' Her voice has risen a couple of octaves but it doesn't stop me.

'Out!' My voice is powerful, belying the inner weakness and fear that I actually feel. 'I want to be on my own. I don't need you or anyone else. Get out!'

She turns to face me once I push her outside and for a brief moment I'm tempted to apologise and to reach forward and hug her. Her face is pale and I can see that she's trembling. I close my mind to it. I've got enough of my own problems to be getting on with without taking pity on somebody who isn't actually a friend at all. I only have so much energy to go around and for once, I've decided to use it all on myself, to employ some self-preservation techniques to keep my sanity intact. The first of those is getting rid of those around me and spending some time alone.

I don't look at her again before slamming the door and stalking through to my chair by the window. Enough with doctors and therapists and fake friends. I'm sick of it all. Finding Amy here was the last straw. First, she lied to me about where she lives and now, she's taken to letting herself into my house without me even being here. It's all got to stop.

I'm too angry to even focus on Veronica at the minute. I take a few deep breaths and then think of those poor children and how frightened they looked the last time I saw them with her.

My hands are trembling as I snatch up my notepad and pen and place them on my lap. I stare over the road, my eyes narrowed in suspicion. There's no Veronica and in her place are two figures sitting side by side on the sofa. I lean forward to get a better view and can now see that it's the young girl and the husband. He's got his arm around her shoulder and is cuddling her in. Seeing the pair of them like that softens my mood somewhat. Not quite enough to forgive Amy but enough to stop me shaking and still my shuddering breathing.

The husband suddenly stands up and walks towards the window. My curiosity is piqued. He usually stays in the background and I've never really had the chance to get a good look at his face before now but here he is, making himself visible, just a short distance from where I'm sitting.

I tilt my head to one side and reposition myself, watching as he strides so close to the glass that I rapidly flinch and duck out of sight, hoping he didn't see me. Taking a few deep breaths, I move back closer to the window and squint my eyes to get a better view of his face. He moves even closer to the window and turns my way, affording me a clear view of his face.

And then I see him. I see him so clearly, it knocks the breath out of me. My pulse quickens and I think I'm going to faint as I stare at his features. Everything blurs in front of me, my vision becoming misted with tears. I place my hand at the window then quickly remove it as he moves away and walks back over to the young girl. An outline of my palm remains on the window for a few seconds, the vision of his face burning deep into my brain.

I stand up and the room rolls and tips from side to side, the walls and furniture swimming around me, swirling rapidly like a carousel. I try to speak but my own voice sounds distorted, the words I want to say making no sense. Before I can do anything, a stream of vomit forces itself out of my throat. I lean forward and place my hands over my mouth to stop it but it spurts through my fingers, thick, hot bile that drips onto the carpet and spreads in a yellow, sticky mess at my feet.

Tears stream down my face. I need to clean everything up. I have to get to the bathroom and wash my face and scrub away this pile of vomit, and I need to do all this to stop me thinking about what it is I've just seen. Who it is I've just seen.

Rubbing at my face with the sleeve of my cardigan, I step to one side to get away from the puddle of sick but I can't seem to keep my balance. The room is still moving. My head hurts and my throat is sore. I grip onto the arm of the chair for balance but it feels as if somebody is pulling me down to the ground, like gravity is forcing me downwards with invisible fingers and I'm powerless to stop it.

I let out a small moan of despair as a bout of dizziness overwhelms me. I must be imagining it. I can't have seen what I think I've just seen. It's impossible. Absolutely impossible.

Taking another small step, I feel myself sinking. I can't sit back down. It's too much effort. And I can't continue standing here. My legs are weak and my stomach is about to go into another spasm. I bend over, my hands wrapped around my belly, hoping it'll pass. If anything, it gets worse. Stars burst behind my eyes, like miniature fireworks going off in my head. A loud buzzing fills my ears. I shake my head to stop it but it's pointless.

The last thing I remember is the smell of my own vomit as I hit the floor. My head lands in the oozing puddle of bile that slowly seeps under my face, congealing against my cold skin as the darkness closes in on me.

31

I wake up in bed. I half expect everything to be back to normal, much like last time, as if nothing has taken place. As if I didn't see that man at the window, his face as familiar to me as my own, and then throw my insides up afterwards. But that doesn't happen. As soon as I start to come around, my eyes slowly fluttering into action, I know for sure it all took place.

I try to sit up but a wave of pain forces me back down. A deep pounding beats at my skull like somebody knocking at my brain with a large hammer. I swallow and wince at the intense ache that pulses behind my eyes. My stomach lets out a sudden growl. It twists and roils and I worry I'm going to be sick again. I close my eyes against another possible bout of vomiting and wait for the sensation to pass. When I open them again, a face is looming over me. A film of fog sits over my eyeballs, stopping me from seeing properly. Everywhere seems to hurt – my stomach, my head, even my legs feel bruised and heavy as I try to take stock of what's happening and who it is that's staring down at me while I lie here like some sort of invalid. I shut my eyes again, embracing the darkness, not wanting to see anything at all.

Voices filter around the space above me. Not just one person. More than that. Two people. Maybe even three. Who are they? I try to speak but all that comes out is a deep, unintelligible groan. My throat constricts and I suddenly feel incredibly thirsty.

The thought of the husband from over the road creeps into my mind but I refuse to entertain it. I shut it out, thinking of other things. Anything but that. Anything but him.

I don't move. I just want to stay here until everybody has gone.

Somebody touches my forehead. I try to recoil away from them but pain lashes at me as I flinch, so I lie still instead, my nerves screaming at me that I need to do something. Anything to protect myself. I can't. I'm unable to move. There's no way I can get away from this person who is touching my head, dabbing at it and muttering under their breath as they drag fabric back and forth over my burning skin. It's a woman's voice, soothing and light. I don't feel soothed. I feel edgy and anxious. I feel as if my life is unravelling, spinning away from me like a gyroscope hurtling off into space, and I'm unable to get it back.

I try to put things in order in my mind. A hazy outline of events beginning to form as I adjust my breathing and tell myself I need to stay calm. I remember hitting my head as I fell. Then blackness, a welcome break from the horror and the fresh memory that had started to force its way into my brain after seeing him.

More muttering above me, indecipherable words. Somebody leans down close to my face, so close I can feel the heat from their skin and smell their breath, a mixture of coffee and cigarettes with an undertone of something sweet. Mints perhaps, to disguise the aroma of nicotine. I stiffen at their proximity to me. I don't know them. Why are these people here in my bedroom? I want them all to leave. I just want to be on my own until everything melts away – the memories, the discomfort, the absolute horror of what has just taken place. I want it all to disappear. For the first time in a long time, I find myself wishing I could go to sleep and not wake up. No more pain, no more longing, no more memories slithering into my head and catching me unawares, making me doubt who I really am.

I feel myself shut off to it all. I clench my fists and pray for sleep to take me. It's the only place where I can be free and not make myself ill worrying and fretting and wishing my family was still alive. Sleep is my escape.

* * *

The pain has marginally subsided when I wake up. I open my eyes and can see properly. No blurred vision, no searing headache. The hammer that had been banging against my skull has eased off and I'm left with more of a mild burning sensation whenever I try to move my head.

As gingerly as I can, I drag myself up to a sitting position in bed, pushing the pillow behind me into the base of my spine to keep me upright. The room still sways but thankfully the nausea has disappeared. I rest my head back against the headboard and let out a few deep breaths, then freeze as I hear a voice outside the room. Despite feeling disorientated and slightly dizzy, it doesn't take me long to put a face to the person who's speaking.

Rose is smiling broadly as she pops her head around the door. 'You're awake! Welcome back to the land of the living, Esther.'

I don't ask her why she's here or how she even got in. I'm done with that line of questioning. I've more important pressing matters to deal with.

I try to return her smile but my face is tight and showing anything remotely resembling happiness feels like a step too far. I've got enough to think about without having to bother with social niceties and going out of my way to avoid upsetting people.

'Where's Amy?' The memory of pushing her out of the door bounces into my brain with sickening clarity. Part of me feels horribly guilty and another part of me thinks she deserved it, letting herself into my home without my permission. We may be close but everybody needs boundaries. This is my personal space and she crossed a line.

'She's here. Just making you a cup of tea. Nice to see you're feeling better.'

'I need to speak to her.' I sound rude, I know I do, but I'm beyond caring. I've got some questions I need to ask her. Ideas and thoughts are jockeying for position in my brain that I want to clear away as soon as possible. I need answers and I need them right now.

As if by magic, Amy bustles in carrying a mug of tea, steam curling up from it, misting and blurring her features. 'There you go, Esther. Just what the doctor ordered.'

She places the tray down on the bedside cabinet next to me and perches her bottom on the edge of the mattress. 'And speaking of doctors, Eleanor McRae said you'll be right as rain in no time at all. Just a small bump on your head.'

'How did you find me?' I try to keep the ice out of my voice but it's difficult. Everything feels like one huge conspiracy at the minute, as if everybody knows everything about my life and they've decided to keep me in the dark as to what's going on, colluding amongst themselves whilst omitting to tell me their findings.

'Oh, the usual way,' Amy chirrups as she passes me the tea and busies herself with straightening the bedsheets. 'And it's a good job we did, isn't it, Rose?' she says, glancing over to the young woman opposite her who is nodding in agreement. 'Or you could have been down there for ages on your own. How's the tea? I made it nice and hot, just how you like it.'

I don't reply and sit instead, eyeing her suspiciously. She's right. The tea is piping hot and it is exactly how I like it. I take a couple of sips, formulating the words I want to say to her in my head. I have to get it right. The last thing I want is for the pair of them to think that bang on the head did me more harm than first thought.

The silence in the room becomes deafening. Every breath we take, every rustle of fabric from our clothes becomes accentuated in the stillness that surrounds us. Blood roars in my head as I shift about trying to find the right words to say until eventually, I just open my mouth and come out with it. No more prevaricating, no more sitting here crippled with fury and apprehension. I simply clear my throat and speak.

'Amy, this might sound rather ridiculous, but my husband Julian... he is really dead, isn't he?'

I can see Rose as she widens her eyes and sucks in her breath. Amy is better at hiding her inner feelings and is able to keep a poker face as she nods her head and places her hand over mine. I want to pull it away. I know I should, but her touch is comforting and I so rarely receive any sort of affection from anybody these days that I when I do, I want to lap it up like a desperate, overzealous puppy.

'Esther, you remember what happened, don't you?' Her voice is soft, like delicate, silken petals blowing in the breeze.

'The car accident,' I reply.

'That's right,' she says. 'A car accident.'

'But you only know that because I told you. What if I'm wrong? What if he really isn't dead at all? What if he's out there living another life without me?' My voice is getting louder and more frantic by the second. I'm aware that I'm beginning to shriek. I can't help it or stop it. I'm not even sure I want to.

Out of the corner of my eye, I can see Rose as she stands up, obviously uncomfortable with the way this conversation is going.

Amy's face is slightly flushed, a pink hue colouring her cheeks and covering her throat in a fine web that dips below her collar. I neither know nor care what they think about me and my question. I need an answer and I need it now.

'I want to see his death certificate.' As I say this, I suddenly realise that I don't even know where his resting place is or indeed whether he was buried or cremated. Why don't I know this stuff? What is wrong with me?

I begin to move about the bed in a bid to get up. My head still aches with every movement I make, but I'm determined to do something and not sit here like a bloody useless lump surrounded by people who treat me with condescension and pity.

Amy removes her hand from mine and shakes her head at me, her eyes bulging with worry. 'Esther, I'm not so sure you should be up and about just yet. Dr McRae said—'

'I don't care what Dr McRae said!' I'm almost screaming now, my voice reverberating around the room, savage and fierce. 'I want to find out where my husband is buried! I need to find out right now!'

Rose springs into action as I throw the covers back and stand up. She moves closer to me but I'm too fast for her. It's as if she's moving in slow motion, her limbs heavy and clumsy when she tries to block my way. I push past her, our bodies colliding, our limbs clattering into one another. I feel a sharp pain shoot up my shoulder and stop to catch my breath. I see her stop and turn to face me. I also see Amy catch her eye and put a hand up to halt anything she was about to do. What is this? I'm a grown woman in my own home. Who the hell do they think they are, treating me like this?

An image abruptly flashes into my head: me shouting, my hands grasping at something, some sort of document. My fingers pulling at it, tearing, shredding until it lies in torn pieces at my feet.

And then it's gone. As quickly as it came, the image has disappeared, leaving me feeling utterly bewildered once more. It's fast becoming a regular state of mind and I don't like it, not one little bit.

Suddenly stripped of all energy, I slump to the floor, my muscles aching, my spine locking into position. I don't cry. It's pointless. Shedding tears is a sign of weakness. It's bad enough being treated like a second-class citizen in my own home; I'm not about to lower everybody's opinion of me even further by sitting here weeping like a helpless child.

I drag myself up, slapping Rose's hands away as she tries to help me, and sit on the side of the bed, my head dipped in shame and anger. 'I want you both to leave.' My voice has a brutal quality to it. It's menacing and brimming with pure rage and if I were Amy or Rose listening to me, I would just get up and go.

There's a moment of quiet with neither of them responding to my request. They think I'm stupid. They think I don't know my own mind. They think they know me. They don't.

I turn around to face them, not caring what I look like, not caring if I scare them. 'Get out!' I scream. 'Get out of here and close the door behind you!'

I watch as they troop out, their faces scarlet and stricken, their feet shuffling along the floor. I don't care. All I want to do is find out who that man is over at number 19. I want to find out exactly who he is and why he looks just like my dead husband.

32

NUMBER 19

The nurses are inept and the doctors are as stupid as she initially thought. After trailing through the hospital and asking numerous members of staff, she eventually finds her child in Ward 16. A woman at the nurses' station calls after her as she marches past but it doesn't stop her. By the time she gets to his bedside, her son is awake and a better colour than he was earlier, before he was whisked away from her. Before she was shoved in a room like a spare part and forgotten about.

He gives her a weak smile as she approaches his bed and sits down next to him, taking his hand and running her fingers through his thick, dark hair.

Ah, okay, I see you found us. The young doctor is standing at the foot of the bed as she looks up. Their eyes briefly lock before she turns her attention back to her boy.

When can he go home? She tries to keep the impatience out of her voice, even though she is fighting the urge to rip the cannula out of her son's arm, carry him down through the double doors and jump into the nearest taxi. These people know nothing of what a struggle it is to look after young children and keep a family together when outsiders are doing their utmost to rip it apart.

Well, he seems to have made a remarkable recovery in the last hour or so. We've taken more blood tests and are awaiting the results.

Which means what? She's trying to stay calm, to keep the aggression and bitterness out of her voice. Being rude to these people will solve nothing. She knows they have the power to keep him here if they suspect any wrongdoing on her part so it's in her best interests to be polite even though she'd like nothing more than to slap the pair of them until her hand aches.

A rustling noise behind her and somebody placing their hand on her shoulder causes her to spin around.

You took some finding. Her husband is standing there, his features twisted with worry. His hair is askew and his face has a slightly rosy hue, as if he's been running.

Where is…?

Don't worry. She's fine, he says quickly. *She's being well looked after. How is he?* He nods towards their boy who, after spotting his dad, tries to clamber over to him, the child's face lighting up with glee.

He's a lot better. I'm hoping we can take him home as soon as possible. Her voice is clipped, her words directed towards the young doctor who is still standing close to the bed, listening to every word that passes between them.

Her husband turns to face the man standing behind him, who smiles and holds his hand out to shake. The woman bristles. The same courtesy wasn't afforded to her.

Hello there. You must be his father? I was just saying to your wife that he seems much brighter. We've run some more tests and are just awaiting the results. As soon as we have them, we'll speak with you both.

Before either of them can reply, he strides out of the room, his heels clicking on the floor, a slight odour of sweet-smelling after-shave trailing in his wake.

They sit side by side on the boy's bed. The youngster squirms about, the joy at seeing his father evident in his expression. They make small talk, promising ice cream and milkshakes as soon as he's discharged. She can feel the heat from her husband's body. She inhales his scent. Wants to wrap her arms around his neck and hold him close to her.

Time slips by. They talk about everything and anything, counting the minutes as they turn into hours, waiting for the doctor to reappear. Waiting for him to tell them they can all return home. The husband is sitting closer to her now. He smiles, holds her hand. She wants to tell him she loves him, that everything that's happened, everything she has done, it was all for him. To keep him, to show him how much she cares. But she says nothing. The time isn't right. Not yet. But it will be soon. All she needs to do is continue to show him how well she can cope, how adept she is at handling a crisis. How he couldn't possibly manage without her.

* * *

They're allowed to take the boy home. They've got a follow-up appointment in two weeks' time. She sits in the back of the car with her son while her husband drives them back. Like a family. A close, loving family who will stick together no matter what. Through thick and thin. It's what ordinary families do. And that is all they are – an ordinary family doing their best through trying times.

She rests her head back against the leather headrest, strokes her son's face and smiles.

33

ESTHER

I don't know who she is and yet she's been left alone in the living room with the daughter. Her back is turned to me but there's something immediately recognisable about her, the way she moves, the way she keeps flicking her hair back over her shoulders, that once again generates something in me, a stirring of disquiet that shifts about deep in my abdomen. I will her to turn around, to move closer to the window so I can see her properly, but she is sitting with her back to me, talking to the girl, their heads dipped together conspiratorially as if in prayer.

My jaw is locked tight, my tongue practically glued to the roof of my mouth as I watch them. I feel tense yet have no idea why. I just know that I need to keep watching. Waiting and watching until something happens. Because I know it will. I can feel it in my bones. Something monumental is about to occur in that house. Don't ask me how I know that; I just do.

My back aches as I sit tight, waiting for the rest of the family to reappear. I think about how I behaved earlier and how Amy and Rose will be feeling. I'm surprisingly relaxed about the whole incident. There was a time I would have immediately regretted my actions but in the last few weeks, I've begun to change. It's all about survival in times of crisis. I have to have some sort of self-preservation plan in place because it would appear that just lately, nobody is telling the truth. Even Amy has been deceitful. She dodges and weaves, our conversations like a slalom event as she skilfully avoids my probing. Answering questions with questions. Treating me like a dull-witted child.

I rotate my shoulders, remembering Dr McRae's words about my spine. Stress and tension make it worse, my posture turning rigid with worry and anger, my vertebrae sealing together like a rod of iron. My neck clicks like an old wooden football rattle as I twist my head from left to right and back again. I'm an old woman before my time. Even my bones cause me constant pain and suffering.

A slight movement over the road causes me to stop and take notice. I end my exercises and lean forward to get a better view. I think about *him* and what the sight of him will do to me. My heart speeds up as I watch the rest of the family bustle into the room – the husband and wife and the boy who's walking on spindly, unsteady legs like a new-born calf. The girl gets up to greet them, smothering her brother with kisses, ruffling his hair and stooping down to embrace him. The woman stands up and hugs the other woman before they all sit down together, the newcomer still facing away from me. Curiosity nips at me. This whole situation isn't right. I can't work out exactly what's wrong with it but in time it'll come to me. I'll get to the bottom of it if it's the last thing I do.

My face is practically pressed against the glass as I strain to get a better view of this new visitor to the house, this person whose every movement feels as familiar to me as my own skin. The husband turns suddenly, his face still a shock to me. A bolt of horror darts through my stiffened body. I want him to turn away. I cannot continue looking at him, at the shape of his nose, the cut of his jaw, the sweep of his thick, dark hair. I just can't. It's too painful, too jarring for me to see.

I shift back away from the glass, my stomach taut, a hard ball of tension. Why did I think it would be a good idea to sit here and watch, knowing I would catch a glimpse of him – the man who looks exactly like my dead husband? I should have known it would upset me and make me nervy and jittery but I'm like a moth to a flame with this family. I can't keep away no matter how hard I try. It's a compulsion, a habit I can't seem to break. My plan, ostensibly, was to protect those children but it's now grown into something more than that, my need for it morphing into something different, something that is bordering on unhealthy. Part of me wants to stare into that man's eyes, to look directly into his soul, and yet the other part of me is terrified. This isn't normal. None of this is proper or normal but I can't seem to stop it. I don't think that I want to.

Moving back, I steel myself and look once more into the lives of the people over at number 19. They're all still there, milling about, fussing over the boy. Apart from *her* that is: Veronica. She's standing up now, observing them all with a cool detachment, her face blank, her eyes cold. She's surveying them, detached and set apart from the loving huddle they've all got themselves into. I wonder what's going through her mind and what she's thinking as she watches them. The other woman turns and tries to get her involved but Veronica shakes her head and leaves the room.

I let out an exasperated sigh. I need to stop this voyeurism. It's not right. Besides which, if seeing him upsets me, isn't that a good enough reason to draw my curtains and ignore them? Except I don't. I keep on looking. I watch as the man and the other woman eye each other cautiously when Veronica leaves the room. I watch as she comes back in, carrying drinks and food for everybody. And

I watch some more as they all help themselves, eating and swigging back glasses of wine and milkshakes.

A lump rises in my throat at the sight of them. Even dysfunctional families have their good times. I would give anything to have a family, albeit a warring, dysfunctional one. I don't think Veronica realises how lucky she is. I would be her in a heartbeat but I doubt very much that she would want to be me.

I shuffle closer to the window once more. I'm intrigued by this new person, keen to get a good look at her and attempt to work out the family dynamics. She's obviously known to those children judging by the way they throw themselves at her and sit on her knee, nuzzling their faces into her neck with no inhibitions whatsoever. My guess is she's an aunt or a close family friend. As I watch, an image slots itself into my mind. Me and Julian shortly before the accident. We're arguing. I'm in the kitchen and I turn around to see him standing behind me. His face is full of horror and suddenly he lunges at me. We're grappling, him leaning into me, pulling at me, crying and shouting at me.

And then it's gone. The image, the fleeting memory. It's all gone, disappeared out of my head as quickly as it came.

I close my eyes and take a few seconds to let my brain readjust, then open them again. A noise in the distance filters through to me but I ignore it. I want to keep my attention focused on the goings-on over at number 19. It's important. The new woman is standing up and walking over to the window. She strides towards it confidently, her arms lifted as she ties her hair back away from her face. Stopping for a few seconds, she turns to speak to one of the children. The young girl runs over to her and despite the girl being older and larger than her brother, the woman sweeps her up in her arms and swings her around. Then they stop rotating and stand staring out of the window, stepping closer and peering out until it feels as if they're looking directly at me. I can't breathe. Air is locked in my lungs, unable to escape. It's as if my reflexes have shut down, the most basic functions of my body rigid with shock and disbelief.

I stumble back and slump down onto the floor in an ungainly heap. My stomach growls at me, my bowels swirling and contracting, threatening to open any minute as a spasm takes hold and a deep pain sears across my lower abdomen.

The distant noise from earlier grows in volume as it gets closer. I ignore it. I can't focus on anything else right now. It's all I can do to try to hold everything together. To block their faces from my mind. I'm going mad. I know it now. Everything is an illusion, a horrible, sickening illusion. I live in a tiny, insular world where nothing is as it first appears. I've been living a lie for as long as I can remember. That's the only explanation. As hard as I try, as much as I rack my brains trying to come up with a logical reason for all of this, I know that there isn't one and that my entire life is one big fat lie.

'What are you doing down there, Esther?' Amy is behind me trying hoist me to my feet.

I turn on her as she drags me upwards, my voice a murderous roar, flecks of spittle flying from my mouth and landing on her face. They sit there, tiny crystals that shimmer under the glare of the light. She makes no attempt to wipe them away. It's as if she expects this from me. As if it's normal behaviour, part of our everyday routine.

'You're in on this!' I try to move but her hand is tight on my arm. 'All these lies! You're part of this... this fucking charade! All this time you've been deceiving me, Amy. Day after day, week after week of continued lies. And you call yourself a friend.' I'm panting now. My head is pounding and my stomach continues to howl at me, twisting and knotted with pain.

'I *am* your friend, Esther! Come on, let's sit down and we can chat about what's upsetting you.'

I wrench my arm free as she tries to guide me to the chair. I stand next to her, anger throbbing under my skin, heat pulsing out of me as I gasp for breath. 'Don't touch me! Don't you dare bloody well touch me!'

I take a step back and stumble. She tries to help me but I bat her hand away and right myself, keeping my fingers clasped over the back of the chair to steady myself as my legs begin to buckle under me. I refuse to crumple. I want answers and I want them now.

'You're a fucking liar, Amy!' I see her grimace and watch as her eyes bulge and turn glassy with unshed tears, but don't care. I've had enough. 'Where do you live? Come on, Amy, tell me where you live! Because I've been out looking for your house and it definitely isn't where you said it was. In fact, nothing is where it should be.'

She doesn't reply but I can see that I've got to her. I've broken through her veneer. Her eyes flicker slightly and a flush begins to creep up her neck. I'm not giving up. I'm so close to getting answers. I thought I had my life sussed but I was wrong. I've been horribly wrong about everything. I've been too accepting and didn't question enough. But not any more. This is the turning point. I won't rest until I start getting answers.

'Come on!' I shout. 'Start answering me! I deserve to know what's going on. And before you say anything else, I also want to know how and why you keep letting yourself into my house.' Her hand flutters up to her chest. She turns to look behind her. I wonder if she's considering looking for an escape route. I won't let that happen. She's not leaving here until I find out what's going on. The big question being – what is my sister doing over the road and why is she holding my daughter, Harriet, who is long since dead?

34

NUMBER 19

Everything is back to normal. They're alone once more and the children are tucked up in bed. The woman breathes out heavily and rests her head back on the sofa. It was good of her to come over and to babysit while they were both at the hospital but she never seems to know when to leave, overstaying her welcome and fussing around the kids until they're so hyper, they can't settle and get to sleep.

Her husband is next to her, his breathing low and steady. She almost laughs out loud. That's how he is. Everything about him is slow and steady to the point he's almost in a coma. They still haven't spoken about the obvious. About *her* – his girlfriend. If she's being truthful, she hopes it's all over, that their recent trauma has shown him he's needed here with his family, not wherever she is, the pair of them together, ensconced in each other's arms. The woman shudders at the thought of it.

Above them, the sound of footsteps starts up again. She bites at the inside of her mouth, tugging at a loose piece of skin angrily until it comes away, a burst of pain causing her to suck in a breath.

I'll go and settle them, he says chirpily.

She watches him go and shuffles along to where he was sitting, savouring the warmth left behind after his departure, and inhaling the woody scent of his aftershave. Her hands drift to the edge of the cushion and land on something solid. An object is lodged down the side. She pushes her fingers deep into the rim of the sofa where the back meets the seat, knowing immediately what it is she has found.

Plucking it out, she holds it tight in her palm. His phone. Buried treasure right here in her living room. She cocks her head and listens to the shenanigans upstairs. He's got them playing games, running around the bedroom like lunatics, then he'll read them a story. His idea of settling them in bed takes ten times longer than it should, which most evenings drives her to distraction, but not tonight. Tonight, his over-the-top, protracted bedtime routine with the kids is perfect. It gives her time to scroll through his phone and find any incriminating evidence. She'll know whether or not he's still up to his devious tricks or if it's all over between them. She prays it's the latter but it's so hard to tell. He is a closed book to her and so damn difficult to read nowadays. She hopes she's done enough to make him see that she's all he'll ever need and likes to think he has noticed how strong she is in a crisis and that their son's illness has brought them closer together. She was the gutsy one in the hospital, the one with the backbone who stood up to those doctors. Not him. It was her, his wife, the one who's willing to stick by him through thick and thin. For better, for worse.

A creak above her drags her out of her thoughts. She has to use this time wisely, find out as much as she can. Be sure that her life is back to how it should be without another woman tagging along like an extra limb, trying to pull her husband away from her.

His phone is locked. Damn! It's asking for a PIN. That's a recent addition. The last time she checked, she got straight in. Her stomach flips. He's obviously got something to hide.

She controls her breathing and quickly enters the date of their wedding anniversary. Wrong number. Panic begins to grip her. She has to get this right or it may lock her out, then he'll know she's tried to access his phone. She types in the number of their house twice. Nothing. Her heart begins to thrum steadily in her chest. She takes a deep breath and as a last resort, types in the year of his birth. Bingo. She suppresses a snort. It's so typical of him to use something pertaining to him as a password rather than something connected to her or their family.

Her fingers are trembling as she scrolls through his messages. Most of them are work related. Annoyance ripples through her as she continues searching. So many unnecessary texts, so much rubbish and nonsense that means nothing to her. Texts to friends about football results, messages about deliveries at work. Even one to his brother in South Africa about the economy and some article he's been reading in *The Times* about how the UK is due another recession.

She grits her teeth as she drags her finger over and over them all until at last, she finds it. Her brow furrows into a deep groove as she sees the name of the contact and reads the message, her heart battering wildly against her ribcage so hard and fast, she starts to feel physically sick.

Things not great here. Could do with seeing you if you have the time? I really need you here.

Her blood boils, pumping through her body like lava, burning her veins as it travels around her system. She is consumed with rage, completely eaten up by it. She wants to kill them both. How did she not see it before? It's obvious now. So bloody obvious. All this time, she's been blind. But not any more. She's seeing everything clearly now, so fucking clearly, it's terrifying.

She puts the phone on her lap and rests her head in her hands to stem the nausea that's rising. She has to do something. She is losing control and doesn't care for the feeling. Not just losing control of her own body at this moment in time, but of her life and her family. It's all coming undone right in front of her eyes. She needs to do something to rein it all back in, to make sure her husband stays with her and doesn't leave her to be with the one person she trusted implicitly. Not in a million years did she think it would be her. And yet it is.

Her stomach clenches. How did she not see it before? It's obvious now, but hindsight's a wonderful thing, isn't it? Answers are always obvious once they're in plain sight.

She gives herself a couple of seconds to collect her thoughts, to work out what her next step is going to be. Because she's not going to let this one go. And she's definitely not going to let him leave her. He's her husband. She belongs to him. They made a commitment and she intends to stick to it even though he's betrayed her in the most despicable way possible.

Standing up, she heads into the kitchen, her legs heavy with disgust and shock. Shock at finally discovering the identity of the other woman and complete and utter dismay at being deceived in the worst way possible.

Reaching up into the kitchen cupboard for her secret stash, she rummages about and pulls it out, then places it next to her. She then reaches over for a tumbler and fills it with milk. Holding a spoon steady, she pours the salt onto it, her eyes focused on the small mountain of white powder that rapidly fills the spoon. A smattering of grains spill onto the counter. She tips the spoon into the tumbler, then scoops up the stray grains in her palm and pours them in as well. She hums to herself. It feels so good to regain control of things. She is no different to anybody else. Nobody likes the thought of losing their family. Nobody wants to be alone.

She holds the packet of salt aloft and opts for a second teaspoon, mesmerised as the grains gather into another small mountain, pearly white against the silver surface of the cutlery. Bending forwards, she moves her arm, ready to tip the contents into the tumbler of milk and jumps when a hand grabs her elbow and a voice bellows in her ear.

What the hell do you think you're doing? Jesus Christ. Oh my God! No!

35

ESTHER

Before Amy can do anything else, I run at her, grabbing her arm and yanking it up behind her back. Pulling at a fistful of her hair, I hear her howl as I drag her head back with as much force as I can. I spin around. I need something – something heavy. Anything will do but there's nothing close by. No paperweights, no sharp objects, absolutely nothing of any substance to use as a weapon should I need to. I have my hands and I have my fingernails which are strong and sharp. I let go of her arm and jab one of my nails into Amy's hand to check. I push hard and trail it downwards. She lets out another grunt and I watch, satisfied, as a trickle of blood oozes out of her flesh and snakes down her porcelain skin. Sharp enough to do some damage. That's good enough for me.

'Right,' I say, my voice low and controlled as I take hold of her arm again and hitch it high up her back. 'I want to know what's going on.'

I hear the patter of feet, the shuffle of bodies and know that others are coming. Of course others will come. I'm starting to put it all together now. Some pieces are slotting neatly alongside each other in my head while some of the other incidents don't quite fit.

There are bits of the puzzle that continue to bewilder and frighten me. Like why the people over the road look just like my dead family. And why Amy keeps coming here and lying to me. It seems like everywhere I turn, she's there. Like a bad smell. A disgusting odour that continually wafts about the place. A noxious stench I can't seem to get rid of. I almost laugh out loud.

Amy doesn't answer me but then the angle I've got her head tipped at is probably making it difficult for her to even breathe, let alone speak. I should care, yet I don't. I feel oddly detached from it all. It's just as well, otherwise I would possibly end up capitulating and letting her go without getting any of the answers that I need.

I grip her even tighter and feel the small bones in her body creak under the strain. She wriggles about, trying to free herself of my grip, but I'm stronger. She's only slight and obviously inexperienced. I'm bigger and tougher and have more stamina than people realise. I can do this. Whatever it is I'm experiencing, I can see it through to the bitter end. I know it now. Maybe I've always known it. I've been in some sort of fugue state for God knows how long but I'm slowly coming out of it. It's as if I'm emerging from a thick, wintry mist back into the sunshine. It's not completely clear to me yet exactly what's going on and I know that I don't have the full story but I soon will. I just need a bit of time to receive some answers and get my head around it all and then I'll know for sure.

'Okay, Esther. Let go. You're hurting Amy and you don't want to do that, do you?' Dr McRae is standing in the doorway. Rose is next to her, her cheeks red with fear, her eyes bulging with panic.

'Don't come near me. If you try to do anything, anything at all, I'll ram her head into that.' I nod to the nearest wall, just a foot or so away from me. I'll do it. They know I will. I can tell from their expressions and the way they murmur to each other. It's clear that they don't trust me. I'm powerful, that much I do know. I'm also a loose cannon. I can see that from their eyes as well. They're frightened of me. I like that. It makes me feel ten feet tall. It's been such a long time since I've felt anything except anger and misery that I want to stop time, to freeze this moment and bottle this sensation, to remind myself that I'm so much more than a grieving widow and a childless mother.

They continue to whisper, their voices too low for me to hear what they're saying.

'Stop talking!' A throaty screech bellows out of me, causing Amy to jump under my grasp. That's good. I'm the dominant one here, the one calling all the shots. As long as they all know who the boss is in this scenario then nothing will go wrong.

Amy makes a strange gurgling sound from her throat, like water bubbling down a drain. I tug a little tighter. I like the feeling of her hair wrapped around my fist. For so long, I've been the twee, middle-aged lady who potters about aimlessly with no real purpose. A doddery woman with no friends or family who's lived the life of somebody twice her age. A woman who, just lately, doesn't know what the hell is going on in her life. Well, that's all about to change. Why did everybody think they could deceive me, tell me lie after lie, and then not get hurt when the truth finally comes out? If I thought it was possible to just sit down and discuss what's happened lately, then I'd do it. But I know they won't go down that route. I tried it with Dr McRae and all she did was humour me and talk in riddles. And then Charlotte with her cryptic words and esoteric phrases, telling me about my shit childhood and how I'm starting to remember. Nobody, absolutely nobody, has sat with me and told me what it is I'm supposed to be remembering. But they will. By God, I'll make sure they will. I'll use Amy, I'll use whatever it takes for these people to start telling me the truth, for them to explain what's been going on in my life.

Dr McRae and Rose do as I command and stand silently, their eyes watching my every move. I twist Amy's head around so she can't see them. I'm not stupid. I'm not having her mouth instructions to the pair of them, imploring with her eyes and giving them ways in which they can intervene and rescue her, and then turn on me and restrain me, pinning me to the floor like a wild animal. Absolutely not.

She lets out a little moan as I turn her around. I do wish she would stop being so overdramatic. I really loathe histrionics. They're vulgar and unnecessary, used by attention-seekers who'll do anything to thrust themselves into the limelight. I didn't have Amy down as the type to do such a thing but then I didn't expect her to lie to me over and over and she's done exactly that, hasn't she? I pull her hair even tighter and push her arm higher up her back to send her a message – *don't mess with me.* I'll go to any lengths to get what I want. No more chats and hot cups of tea to solve our problems. I won't back down until they start telling me exactly what I want to hear. Until they tell me what's going on with my family and why they're all alive and well and not buried deep in the ground.

I ignore her gasps and the tears that have started to roll down her face. This is no more than a show of amateur dramatics and is, quite frankly, rather embarrassing. She had better stop it before my temper really gets the better of me because what she's enduring now is nothing. I'm capable of so much more.

'Hello, Esther. I was wondering if you'd like to talk with me.'

The voice is familiar but not instantly recognisable. I spin around to see Daniel standing there. Dan the therapist or the counsellor or whatever title he wants to give himself. Here in my room.

He nods to Dr McRae and Rose who both take a step back, their bodies disappearing into the shadows behind him. They don't leave. I can still see their grey forms bobbing about as they mill around in the background, their silhouettes shifting from side to side on the wall next to where he's standing.

I should have known that he was in on it. It was no coincidence him being there in the waiting room and then me bumping into him outside my house last week. He's part of the conspiracy, the plot they've all been planning behind my back. I shake my head and look away. He's as bad as the rest of them – scheming, devious manipulators, each and every one of them.

'I will definitely help you, Esther. I can see you're upset and I can help you sort that out. If you let Amy go, we'll just sit down and talk. Nothing else will happen. You have my word.'

My heart patters out a steady, comforting beat. He sounds genuine but then so did Amy and Dr McRae and look how they tricked me and deceived me and made me look foolish. For all I know, he could be worse than them, saying one thing and meaning another. It's hard to find somebody to trust lately. Do any of them have any idea how upsetting and bloody downright confusing it is when you can't work out who your friends are and who your enemies are?

I want to trust this man, I really do. It's lonely not knowing who the baddies are, who to have faith in and who not to have faith in. It's a dark place to inhabit when even in your own home, there are a stream of nasty surprises waiting for you when you get out of bed in the morning. But if I let Amy go and he's lying, just like they've all lied to me...

No. I grip Amy tighter, her glossy hair a thick bundle in my fist. Her hand is bony and hot as I pull it even further up her back. I feel her flinch and I smile. I'd forgotten how much I relish being in charge, taking control of uncontrollable situations. Such a satisfying feeling.

'Please, Esther. Amy's in pain. I know you don't want to hurt her. You're a good, kind person.' Daniel's voice echoes around the room.

I ignore him. He's just like the rest of them with his well-crafted phrases designed to calm me down and defuse the situation. If only they'd talk to me like a normal person instead of continually spouting those pathetic words that have been lifted straight out of a textbook. Don't they know that real life is very different from theoretical circumstances? Maybe they don't. They all walk about like little robots with no idea of how to treat people. They've never suffered true heartache, been subjected to utter devastation and had their hearts ripped out, have they? All they know and understand is chapter and verse of what they learned at university. They don't know anything about real life.

I shake my head and glare at him as he tries to move closer. He stops and holds his hands up to indicate he means no harm. I don't believe him. If I let go of Amy, a team of people will swoop and I'll probably get arrested and be hauled off to prison for assault. I'm not letting her go.

'Okay,' he says softly. 'Here's the deal. You tell me what you want and I'll do my best to comply.'

I do something instinctively that I didn't even know I was capable of doing, and spit on the floor in front of him, watching gleefully as he recoils slightly. More empty words from him just to placate me. I almost laugh out loud. I honestly didn't know I had it in me. I don't think I've ever spat on the floor in my life. Just goes to show what we're all capable of when our lives begin to unravel. We each and every one of us have hidden depths that unfurl and spring into life when we're cornered and being forced to protect ourselves.

'Esther, at some point you have to let Amy go. She's in so much pain. Look at her face. Lean forward, Esther, and take a look at what you're doing to her.'

For a second, I'm tempted to do as he asks, my resolve almost weakening after listening to him. But I don't. More deceit and trickery, that's all it is. More disgusting lies.

I can hear his breathing. He's either angry or nervous. Or maybe exasperated. Not that I care. All I'm bothered about is being ahead of the game, being able to pre-empt his every move. I need to read his body language if I'm to win this particular battle.

'Who are you?' I say, my words like splinters of ice raining down on him.

'You know who I am, Esther. You've known for quite some time but perhaps you've forgotten. We met last week in—'

'I know where we met, for heaven's sake! Stop patronising me.' I'm panting heavily. I try to act calmly, to regulate my breathing. I can't afford to lose it now. Everything is too far down the line to go back.

'I didn't mean to do that. I apologise, Esther. I'm a therapist and I'm here to help you.'

He tries to move closer. I make a point of tugging Amy's head some more. He stops and sucks in his breath. I raise my eyebrows and smile.

'I want to talk about Charlotte,' I say. 'And my husband and children. They're the ones who are important to me. Not Amy or you or Dr McRae. You don't mean anything to me. I want to talk about my family. And I want the truth.'

Daniel doesn't answer. His expression grows darker. I can practically hear the cogs whirring in his brain. He takes another step closer to me. I let out an annoyed grunt.

'You said to tell you what I want! So I'm telling you that I want to talk about my family. And now look at you – hesitating and lying! You're all as bad as each other. Fucking liars and charlatans, that's all you are, every single one of you. Fucking liars!'

I drag Amy up, our bodies knocking together, my grip tighter than ever just to show them that I really do mean business.

Dr McRae steps out of the shadows. A tall, austere-looking man is standing behind her. I have no idea who he is but I do know that I don't like the look of him, not one little bit. He has an air of authority about him, somebody who can bring a stop to this situation.

'Esther, let Amy go and we'll talk. I promise.' It's Dr McRae talking now. I've decided I don't like or trust her any more. 'There are lots of people here now, Esther. More of us than of you. Please let Amy go.'

I shake my head and let out a moan of desperation. Images of Charlotte and Harriet and Julian over the road at number 19 rise and twist in my mind, their faces leering at me. Charlotte and Julian locked together in a loving embrace while my children sit by and watch. And I'm on the outside seeing it all unfold, watching it all happen, unable to do anything about it. I let out a roar of anguish. Tears escape and slide down my face. I swallow and shake my head. I promised myself there would be no more tears.

Amy's hair feels good in my hand, like a snake coiling its way between my fingers, slithering across my skin, its venom seeping out until I have to do something to release it. With a high-pitched scream, I pull my arm backwards and slam her head into the wall as hard as I can, as many times as I can, before I run out of energy and we both slump onto the floor in a sweaty, mangled heap. Bodies swoop, their large hands pressing down on me, forcing me to stay still, pulling at my arms, grabbing at my ankles until blackness descends. Then nothing.

36

NUMBER 19

You! It's been you all along! What the fuck are you doing to him? What the fuck have you done?

His voice booms in her ears. He rarely shouts or gets angry and now here he is, practically screaming at her, his voice alien and unrecognisable, his face twisted in revulsion and hostility. Her throat closes at the sight of his slack mouth and eyes full of fire and hatred.

She speaks, trying to inject as much authority into her tone as she can. *You've got it wrong. It's not what you think. I'm just helping him to get better...*

Her voice trails off. She's unaccustomed to justifying her actions and suddenly feels all out of energy, her body and mind spent with the tension of pretence. Months and months and months of it. And not just hers. What about him and his continual acts of deceit and lies? That's why she did this – to keep him impressed, to keep him by her side. To stop him running off with somebody else. He left her with no option. This is all his fault.

He rips the spoon out of her hand, tiny grains of salt spreading far and wide over the kitchen worktop and onto the floor. She focuses on them, staring at the tiny, glittery grains rather than at him. She can't bear to look into his eyes, to see how much he hates her for what she's done. It's all gone wrong. So horribly wrong. This isn't how she planned it. It's not how it was meant to be.

You're killing him! Christ almighty. He's our son and you're killing him! His breathing becomes laboured. Tears course down his reddened cheeks. He gulps and steadies himself then lifts her face and stares deep into her eyes. *You're not well. You need help.* His voice has lost its edge, become gentler, softer. He's almost pleading with her. *We can't go on like this. All our married life I've tried to help you, to keep you well, but this... this is more than I can deal with.*

Her chest locks, white-hot anger augmenting inside her. She steps away from him, her teeth gritted, her hands balled into fists. *Help me? Help me? You're having an affair with my sister! How the fuck is that helping me? And don't try to deny it. I've seen the messages!* She holds his phone up triumphantly, her hand waving about in the air as she grips it tightly.

He shakes his head despondently, confusion wrinkling his brow. *I've already told you. I'm not having an affair. Why would you think such a thing?*

She can barely speak, she is so consumed by fury. It builds inside her, growing and growing until she feels sure she is about to explode. *Why would I think such a thing? How dare you insult my intelligence. I've seen and heard you on this phone! Making calls, huddling in corners, whispering down the handset! I know exactly what you're up to, so don't start pointing the finger at me! I'm not the only guilty party here...*

Her flesh burns. Scrolling through the phone, she finds the incriminating message and holds it out on her palm for him to see. She brandishes it in front of him, pointing to the name, grasping it so tight, her fingers are as white as bone.

He sighs and closes his eyes in denial. She wants to punch him, to slap him, to hurt him as badly as he has hurt her. She pictures herself taking his head and slamming it into the kitchen counter until his eyes bleed. How could he?

He grapples with her, catching her unawares. She feels the phone slipping out of her grasp as he snatches it and holds it up in the air out of reach.

Give it back to me! What the hell do you think you're doing? She is shrieking now, her body trembling with rage.

I'm calling her, that's what I'm doing. He taps at the phone and holds it against his ear, slapping her hands away as she tries to take it back from him. *I'm calling her and getting her over here to show you just how wrong you actually are.*

Her blood runs cold at the thought of it, at the thought of having her in the house, being so close to the woman who has ruined her life. *Oh, this is hilarious! You actually think I'm going to sit here and listen to you two spout more lies and shit at me. You really expect me to believe this nonsense?*

But he doesn't reply. He's already speaking on the phone, his voice hushed as she screams at him. She listens to the one-sided conversation, to his stilted words and concerned, fretting voice and is tempted to rip the phone from his hand and smash it on the floor. Instead, she begins to shout at the top of her voice that she hates them both, wishes they were both dead, yelling that she will kill the pair of them. The patter of small feet behind her halts her tirade. She whirls around, her eyes wild, her face scrunched with malice and spite. She hears the cries of her daughter and stops to catch her breath.

Behind the young girl is the face of their son, his mouth wide open in undisguised terror. Fearing that her husband will try and take them away from her, the woman lunges at both children, scooping up the small lad in her arms. The daughter lets out a piercing shriek and the boy begins to sob uncontrollably, his body heaving against his mother's breast.

Grabbing the girl by her hand, she pulls her close and takes both children into the living room. Her husband shouts something incomprehensible into the phone before slamming it down and following her, his footsteps loud and vaguely threatening.

Put him down. His voice is quiet, coaxing. Gentle and calm. Talking to her as if she's a naughty child.

She shakes her head and moves away from him. *You're going to try and take them away from me. I just know it.*

He moves towards their daughter, who is sobbing loudly. The girl tries to go to him but her arm is yanked back. A shrill howl fills the room as she cries out in pain.

I'm not taking them anywhere. We're all going to sit down and have a chat, that's all. We'll just talk, I promise. Please let the kids go. They're frightened. Can't you see how scared they are?

Again, she shakes her head, tears running down her cheeks, hot and unchecked. She has to keep her children close to her otherwise she'll lose them. She's done bad things. Terrible things. She knows that but they're still her children. She loves them no matter what. They belong with her. To her.

The family at number 19 stay like that, the children pulled close to their mother while he sits by pleading and cajoling for what feels like an eternity. The sound of the youngsters' cries continues to fill the room, rattling in her head, reminding her of what she's done. How her life is slowly falling apart. Then another noise jolts her.

The door.

Somebody is opening the front door. She knows who it is. She instinctively pulls the children even closer to her, taking no notice of their resistance, ignoring their twisting limbs that long to be free of her grasp. She presses them to her body, denying them their freedom. They're hers. Nobody else's. She'll keep them close to her, hanging onto them no matter what.

And then she sees her standing there, her sister, his girlfriend, and for a brief second, she slackens her grip. A second of shock and the children are free, running to the figure, throwing themselves at her, screaming her name over and over and over...

37

ESTHER

I wake up in a room I don't recognise. Everything is blurry. I blink to clear my vision. My throat is dry and I ache everywhere. A fog sits behind my eyes, slowing me down and stopping me from thinking properly. I just need a couple of minutes to get everything straight in my head. Rubbing at my eyes, I try to sit up but it's too painful. I can't work out how I got here or why I'm in pain. I swallow and take a few deep breaths.

And then it hits me. I remember.

Charlotte, my sister, was there, over the road at number 19. And Harriet. My dead daughter. She was with her. Amy came. And that's when everything started to go wrong. I remember grabbing her, being so completely consumed with anger that I didn't care what I did to her, whether she got hurt or not. Whether *I* got hurt or not. I was reckless and thoughtless, driven on by fear and frustration. I probably would still feel that way if I wasn't so exhausted and weak. I have an inner fury inside me, a burning desire for revenge.

So much dishonesty. So much deception. My life is a web of

lies, crushed beyond recognition. If I thought things were bad before, they're a million times worse now.

I rest my head back and look above me. A strip light runs the length of the ceiling. I blink and let out a shuddering breath. I don't have a strip light in my house. My heart begins to thump: a rapid, thick pulse beneath my breastbone, a reminder that all is not right with this situation. I don't know or care where I am but I do know that I want to go home.

Using my hands, I force my body upwards in the bed, shuffling my bottom into position. I ignore the pain that whistles through my skull, circling and clawing at my nerve endings, and look around me.

I'm in hospital. I must be. The room is almost bare – clinical and sterile. Definitely a hospital. Maybe I have concussion. I strongly suspect that Amy does too. I think about her and the damage I may have done to her. Part of me feels guilty and yet part of me thinks she deserved it – stringing me along, telling me so many lies. Pretending to be my friend. If I'm being honest, that's the part that hurts the most – thinking we had some sort of bond when in fact she was nothing of the sort and the bond I thought we had was no more than a façade on her part. A smokescreen to get me to comply with her wishes. And I'm also certain she knows about what's going on over at number 19. I'm sure of it and I won't rest until she starts telling me what it is. Amy knows about lots of things, I can just tell. I may be confused but I'm not a complete fool.

My head continues to pound as I swing my legs out of the bed and place my bare feet onto the cold, tiled floor. There's nothing here to give me any clue as to where I am. They must have drugged me and taken me from my house to this place, this soulless environment. Well, they can't keep me here indefinitely. I want to go home now. Unless they're going to charge me for assaulting Amy, then they can't keep me here against my will. I have every right to leave.

Out of the corner of my eye, I see a shadow. My eyes travel to the door, to the glass in the centre of it. To the face watching me on the other side. My stomach leaps as I see a pair of eyes follow my movements when I stand up and walk around the bed, looking for my shoes or slippers.

I walk over and try the handle. As expected, it's locked. I know to remain calm, to not show any anger or fear. If I do, Dr McRae and Daniel the therapist will see it as a reason to keep me here. Wherever *here* is. So instead, I do the right thing, the placid, docile thing, and knock gently then step back and wait for somebody to let me out.

The face on the other side of the glass disappears out of view, probably looking for somebody in a position of authority to let me out. All I have to do is wait. Keep my temper in check and wait.

I'm at an immediate disadvantage. We're sitting in a room I don't recognise. There's two of them and one of me. I guess that's for their own protection after what I did to Amy. If they started telling the truth then maybe I wouldn't have had to hurt her. All I want to do is see my family. I want to leave this place and see my husband and children. Surely they can understand how distressing and frustrating it is for me, knowing my loved ones are so near and yet so far? They're out there and I'm stuck in here and it's eating away at me. Resentment and frustration are such corrosive emotions. Even worse than misery, although nowhere near as bad as grief. I thought they were all dead, my family, but I saw them. And if they're not dead, then why were they there, in that house with that woman? Who is Veronica and why has she got my husband and children with her?

I feel like a small child as I stare up at them from my low armchair. Dr McRae and Daniel the therapist are both seated on higher chairs opposite me. I was told to take this particular one for comfort but again I'm almost certain it's to allow them an air of authority and a chance for them to wield their power over me, for them to let me know that they're superior, in charge and pulling all the strings.

'I want to go home.' I need to be submissive, I know I do, but I also have rights. I'd feel more at ease if I were in my own living room, seated in my own armchair by the window. They can't deny me that. I've done nothing wrong. The sensation of Amy's head crashing into the wall pierces my thoughts. I swat it away. I was only defending myself. She had entered my home without permission, caught me off guard. I was frightened and didn't know what else to do.

'Let's talk about what happened, Esther.'

'Let's not,' I say defensively. I cross my arms and stare at them. 'Let's talk about my family instead. My dead family who I now know aren't actually dead at all.'

They quickly glance at one another then back at me. I can do this. I can play this little game of theirs and even win if I manage to think logically and not lose my temper. Staying focused and keeping calm is the key. I can do this. I'm so close to ending this terrible, sickening charade of theirs and they don't seem to even realise it.

'Okay. What is it you want to say?' Daniel takes the lead, shuffling his seat forward in front of Dr McRae and staring directly into my eyes. His elbows are resting on his knees and his legs are splayed open. He has such a pitiful look on his face I almost laugh. Do these people not realise that this level of sincerity is painful to watch and quite obviously disingenuous? It's also deeply insulting. I grit my teeth and focus on my breathing. So hard to remain on an even keel and not lose my temper when I'm surrounded by faux concern and low levels of intelligence, but I do my best.

'Dr McRae,' I say a little too loudly as I look over Daniel's shoulder to the small, dark-haired woman sitting slightly behind him. 'You've known me since the accident that involved my husband. I want you to tell me truthfully what happened.'

She clears her throat and shifts forward into view. 'What do you want to know?'

I wiggle my jaw about to release the tension that's building. More prevarication every time I ask a perfectly reasonable question. More time for her to carefully plan her answers and dodge the truth.

'Is Julian Nesbitt, my husband, still alive?

'Why do you ask?' Her voice is crisp, full of authority.

'Just answer the damn question!' I can hardly contain my anger but I know that I have to try. 'Stop answering my questions with more questions and tell me if he's actually dead or not.' My pulse throbs and pounds in my ears as I wait for her reply. 'Please,' I add meekly, my desperation for the truth leaving me drained of all energy. 'Please, just tell me the truth and then let me go home.'

38

NUMBER 19

You fucking bitch! I've seen your messages! How could you? she says.

Her husband speaks first, his voice urgent and desperate. She listens, wondering if he's going to cry.

There's nothing going on. We've been communicating for some time now. About you. We're really worried. He looks at the children as they continue to sob and cling to their aunt. *She's going to take the kids for a while so we can talk*, he says, nodding to his sister-in-law as she slowly begins to back out of the room.

The woman leaps to her feet, her ear-piercing shriek causing everyone to flinch. She launches herself at her sister, her fingers hooked into claws as she tries to pull the two terrified children away, pulling and pawing at them, hollering for them to come to her. They stay rooted to the spot, their arms locked tightly around their aunt, their faces buried deep into her midriff.

It all happens so quickly, she doesn't have enough time to do anything to stop her children being ripped away from her. Taken without her consent. Taken by her. Her own sister.

The sister carries the boy and coaxes the girl away, then turns and runs out of the room. The woman tries to follow her but the husband grabs her, his big, strong arms wrapped around her entire body as she thrashes about, yelling to be set free.

How could you? How could you? She's my sister and you've been fucking her behind my back. I hate you! I hate you both!

She feels weightless, as light as air, as he sweeps her up and carries her to the kitchen, kicking the door shut behind him. The slam echoes throughout the house, accentuating the emptiness, reminding her that her children are gone. They've been taken, kept from her, kidnapped by her own sister. The one person she trusted, the one person she thought she could rely on.

His voice is neither angry nor contemptuous as he speaks. She wonders how he does it – managing to stay in control even in the midst of a crisis. But then as he speaks to her, something changes. As she listens, she hears a slight crack in his voice and begins to realise that the emotions that are slowly creeping into the timbre of his words are caused by her. She knows this and despite not wanting to admit it, she also knows that it's all her doing. His tone is flat, laced with exasperation and defeat. He sounds like a man beaten down by all that's happened. She's pushed it too far. Pushed *him* too far. But then, didn't he start all this with his unforgivable philandering with her sister? Maybe he's pushed *her* too far, left her with no option but to lash out and screech and do the terrible deed that she has done with their son. She's been put under undue stress and can't be held accountable. This is all his fault. Correction: it's all *their* fault. Her husband and her lying slut of a sister.

I'm not going to say this again. I have not slept with your sister. I've been ringing her to talk about you, about your declining mental health. She's been helping me – helping us. Because you do need help. I can't do this any more. You have to listen to me, to cooperate if we're going to get through this. I knew you had problems and always tried to help, to do the right thing, but I can't do it any more. I just can't...

He lets go of her and holds his hands out to her. She slaps them away and spits in his face. A thin trail of bubbling, frothy saliva trickles down his cheek. He doesn't flinch and makes no attempt to wipe it away.

Where has she taken them? Her voice is savage. Demon-like. She's beyond hysterical now, driven on by some primal urge that she can't control.

But before he can answer, the sound of an engine starting up outside fills the kitchen. Free of his grasp, she darts to the door and is outside and heading around the side of the house to the driveway at the front with him in close pursuit behind. She hears his footsteps closing in on her and steps up a gear. She's lighter than him, nimble and able to dodge between the many obstacles that litter their path: wheelie bins, recycling boxes, children's toys. She jumps over them and listens to him stumble and fall, swearing and cursing as he scrambles back to his feet.

By the time he catches up with her, she's at the car, her hands frantically yanking at the handle to open it. It's locked. Of course it's locked. What did she expect – for her sister to stop the engine and hand her children back over to her? That was never going to happen.

She steps back and then tries again, watching as her children flinch away from her, their small faces filled with fear and horror. This is what it's come to. Her own children don't want her any more. They've done this – her philandering husband and conniving shit of a sister. They have turned her own children against her. She's on her own now. No husband, no children, no sister. Nothing left to live for.

Without warning, the car splutters into life, the sound of rubber squealing against tarmac hitting her ears as it reverses off the driveway and onto the road. She follows it, her screams still able to be heard above the sound of the roaring engine. She shouts for her children. She shouts for her sister to come back. She shouts that she wishes she were dead. She's lost everything. Her life isn't worth living. She's nothing without her husband and family. Nothing.

She breaks into a gallop, watching as the vehicle does a three-point turn, sees her sister slam it into first gear and set off at a lick with her children inside, the engine howling under the strain. Without giving herself time to think, to consider the ramifications of her next decision, she watches and waits. Waits until the car is almost upon her, then she closes her eyes and steps out into the road...

39

ESTHER

I rest my head in my hands. I feel utterly defeated. I'm an empty shell. A husk of a person. Nothing left inside. I just want the truth. I thought all humans had a right to know the truth but it would appear not. I've been to hell and back in the last few months, experienced a whole gamut of emotions, and it seems that even after going through all of that, no amount of begging is going to help me get to the bottom of what's wrong with my life. Nobody can help me. Nobody wants to help me. Being friendless and alone is a cold and desperate place to be.

Despite myself, tears spill out through my fingers. I hate crying. It solves nothing but sometimes my emotions get the better of me and I can't stop the tears no matter how hard I try. Furious with myself for being so weak and pathetic, I wipe them away and rub at my face angrily. I'm better than this, or at least I thought I was. I guess everybody has their breaking point. Even me. Especially me.

'You asked about your husband. You seem to think he might still be alive?' Dr McRae's voice seems to come from miles away even though I know she's close by. Everything feels awkward and strange, as if my entire life has been tipped out of balance. Everything feels perilously close to breaking point, the earth tilting on its axis, sending us whirling off into space.

I look up and nod. My throat feels constricted, too tight to speak. My core body temperature oscillates from freezing cold to hot and back again as I wait for her answer.

She lets out a sigh, looks down at the pad on her lap then back at me. 'Now before you say anything, Esther, can I just say that I'm not avoiding your question and I will answer it, but before I do that, I'd like to know why you even asked. It is, after all, a rather odd question, wouldn't you agree? Asking whether or not your husband is really dead?'

I'm shivering now. There's something big coming, something life changing. I can feel it, see it in her expression and the way she's suddenly tensed up. And as for Daniel – he seems to have suddenly shrunk back out of view. Maybe this is how they do it – a good cop, bad cop routine designed to unnerve me. I think Dr McRae knows me better than that, though. She's well aware I'll be able to see straight through their thin façade and shoddy little games. I may be vulnerable at the minute but I still have a brain.

I nibble at the side of my mouth as I struggle to find the right words. My heart hammers out a thick beat in my chest, making me feel slightly nauseous. I give her a curt nod. She's right. It is an odd question but I know what I saw and I refuse to be swayed or convinced otherwise.

'I saw him – Julian, my husband. It was definitely him. He can't be dead because I saw him.' I feel as if I can't breathe properly. Ice-cold fingers clasp my windpipe. I swallow and fight back more tears. Saying his name out loud has caught me unawares. My hands grab at the edge of the chair to fight the wave of dizziness that's taken hold of me. 'And Charlotte, my sister. I saw her too. She was with him. And there's something else as well.'

I am really having to force air in and out of my lungs now. It's a huge effort, breathing normally and sitting upright when the floor and walls are swaying violently around me and my throat feels like it's shrunk to the size of a pinhead. I shut my eyes tight, afraid to open them again. Afraid of what I just said and afraid of what I might see. I don't want their looks of incredulity and disbelief. I want their help and support but I also know how ridiculous all of this sounds.

'Harriet was there with her. My daughter, she was there in the house with my sister and dead husband.' The words practically fall out of my mouth, a garbled stream of sentences with little or no pause in between them. 'And if they're there, then I'm certain my little boy is with them.'

I look over to Dr McRae and Daniel, my eyes brimming with more tears as I gasp for breath and speak again. 'My family, Dr McRae. They're all alive. They're not dead at all. My entire family is alive and I know exactly where they are.'

Time stands still as I wait for their response. I can't even bring myself to look at either of them or to catch their eyes for fear of what I might see there. They think I'm some sort of basket case, I can just sense it. And to be fair, if I were in their position, I would probably think the same.

A rustling noise causes me to reluctantly glance their way. Dr McRae is opening a small piece of paper and straightening it out on her knee. A tic starts up in my jaw. I swallow and rub at my face to stop it while I wait for her to tell me what it is she's holding. It's something to do with me. I just know it. Something to do with my family and what happened on the day of the accident. If there ever was one. Everything is so confusing. I can no longer trust my own feelings and memories. Even my own thoughts are betraying me.

'Right,' she says breezily, as if we're talking about the weather and not my family who may or may not be dead. 'I have here a report stating your husband died when he was struck by a car.'

My head feels as if a swarm of angry wasps are buzzing about in there. It takes a couple of seconds for me to find my voice. 'No,' I stammer. 'That's not right.'

'I realise how upsetting this is for you, Esther, after thinking you've seen your husband but I can assure you that I've seen his death certificate and—'

'No!' I shout, frustration and a sense of overwhelming disappointment washing over me. 'What I mean is, he wasn't struck by a car. He was inside the car when it crashed.'

Once again, Dr McRae and Daniel glance at each other; the look that passes between them one of suspicion and doubt. They're suspicious of me and it's patently obvious that they doubt what I'm telling them.

'Esther, I don't mean to criticise you or detract from what you've been told, but I can assure you, your husband definitely wasn't in the car. He was a pedestrian and died as a result of a tragic accident involving a vehicle driven by a woman who suffered serious injuries.' Dr McRae's voice is nasally and waspish as she tries to assert her authority and convince me of her version of events.

I shake my head, my thoughts now clouded with confusion and uncertainty. This is not how I remember it. Not how I remember it at all. What the hell is going on? I no longer know what to think. I had a scenario in my head, a solid story as to how my husband died. Then I saw him over at number 19, alive and well, and now I'm being told that he's definitely dead but it didn't happen how I thought it happened.

My world begins to fold in on itself. I can't comprehend what's going on. Julian is dead. He's really dead. A boulder-sized lump is stuck in my throat; it feels like I've swallowed a huge stone. My eyes are dry and my skin is burning like a furnace. I want to cry, to shriek out loud and weep a river to help alleviate the build-up of misery and tension that's accumulating in my body but I don't think I've got any tears left. I haven't enough energy to think, let alone scream and sob. I have nothing left.

'Can I go home now?' All I want to do is curl up in bed and sleep for a hundred years. I long to wake up in a fresh world where everything is shiny and new and there's no hurt or grief or the deep, bottomless misery that is so vast, it's terrifying.

Another surreptitious glance from Daniel to Dr McRae and then back to me. There's another problem. I can sense it. I'm not sure I can take another nasty surprise. I'm all out of resilience and courage.

'Okay,' Daniel says softly, his tone less abrasive than his colleague's. 'But before we take you back, I'd like to know where it was you saw the people who look like your family.'

Goosebumps prickle my flesh. He mentioned taking me home. I'm being allowed back. I allow myself a small smile. Thinking of going back home to Warum bolsters me, gives me a shot of confidence. 'It was over the road from my house. They live at number 19. I've been keeping watch over their lives, especially the behaviour of the woman who lives there. I mentioned it to Dr McRae before. She knows all about it.'

Dr McRae doesn't react as I speak. I expect some sort of movement or recognition but she says and does absolutely nothing except sit, her back ramrod straight in the leather computer chair she is sitting in.

'I didn't tell her about the likeness because I didn't know about it then. But she knows about the woman and the abuse of her children. I told her all about it.'

Dr McRae finally breaks out of her trance-like state and nods, albeit stiffly as if she's embarrassed to be a part of this conversation.

'So, can I go home now? I'm very tired and I'd like to go to bed. It's been an extremely stressful time and I'd like to be alone.'

Daniel looks at Dr McRae who takes it as her cue to speak. 'I asked you to think about why you gave the woman at number 19 the name that you did. Do you remember?'

It's my turn to stiffen now. I sit there, rigid, my posture stick straight as I think about the relevance of her question. I nod. 'Of course I remember. I'm not that stupid. I remember it very well.' If I'm being truthful, after leaving Dr McRae's office, I hadn't given it much thought. It's just a name I thought up. It has no real bearing on any of the events that have taken place lately. Her name is just that – a name. It means nothing to me.

'Okay, so is there any reason why you came up with that name for her?' Dr McRae says, her eyes probing me for answers that I cannot give.

I shake my head and stare at her. Why this? And why now? All I want to do is get out of here and back into my own place. My sanctuary.

Daniel and the doctor steal another glance at one another before passing me a piece of paper with something written on it. I can barely see as I look down at it. It's an enlarged copy of my driving licence. My face stares back at me from the paper. An unlined face – younger, happier, prettier. Next to it is my name. My full name. I swallow loudly and stifle a gasp as I read the words written there.

ESTHER VERONICA NESBITT

My eyes roam over it again and again.

I want to cry out, to gnash my teeth and scream to the heavens that this is all wrong, that there has to be a terrible mistake. And yet I know that it isn't. Because Charlotte was right. I am starting to remember.

Memories are beginning to trickle back into my brain. Everything is starting to make sense. At long last, I'm beginning to see everything so very clearly. Everything is pointing to one cold hard fact, inescapable and terrifying – and that fact is that the woman over at number 19 is me.

40

NUMBER 19

The car doesn't have time to stop. The woman doesn't have time to move. Not that she actually wants to. In that brief, painful moment, all she wants is to do is die, the realisation of everything that has happened, simply too much for her to deal with. Images bounce around her brain, some good, some bad. Some pleasant, some too dreadful to even think about. Death. That's what she craves. An end to it all.

She waits for the hit, the soothing, crushing, searing pain that will release her from this torment. But there's nothing. Nothing at all.

Until she feels the blow. But not from a piece of metal. Not the deathly hit she is expecting from a speeding car, but a soft push from somebody close to her. She feels herself being shoved aside. She feels herself being lifted into the air, her body sailing, being propelled forward until she lands on a grass verge, face down in the mud.

And that's when she hears it. The sickening screech, the slam of metal, the unforgettable thud that tells her the vehicle has finally come to a halt, hitting something solid.

Scrambling up, she has to stop herself from vomiting as the smell of burning hits her nostrils and the groan of twisted metal assaults her ears.

No! NO!

It was supposed to be her. Not them. Not him. Dear God, please don't let it be him...

Her heart thuds wildly as she runs full pelt towards the carnage. The wreckage is close by, the car pressed into the wall under the railway bridge, crushed and bent, its occupants silent inside. She throws herself at the door, pulling at the handle, grasping, clawing, her fingers tearing and scraping at the windows. She screams, her voice a loud piercing shriek that could shatter glass.

She can see everybody in the vehicle. They're sitting there, slumped forwards with their eyes closed, heads lolling, unmoving. Looking like dead bodies. She hollers, she howls, she screams until her throat is tender and raw. Her palms are flat against the glass as she slams her hands onto it over and over. Her voice suddenly cracks and a tight ribbon of pain wraps itself around her skull.

And then she sees him. She looks down, notices the river of blood as it gathers at her feet, dark and viscous, pooling around her. His legs are just visible beneath the bumper bar. Hardly daring to breathe, she creeps closer to the front of the vehicle, the pounding in her head so strong, she thinks she may be about to pass out.

Her eyes are almost closed, terror forcing them shut as she gets closer to the battered body of her husband trapped beneath the broken car, its twisted metal cutting into his skin, severing his limbs and crushing his skull. She screams his name. She screams for help. She screams again and again and again until she has no breath left in her lungs.

The rush of a train echoes around her, the noise a pulsating, deafening roar as it passes overhead. It booms in her ears, cutting through her animalistic howling. Staggering backwards, she yells for assistance. Where is everybody? Why isn't anybody coming out to help her?

The sound of a siren cuts through her thoughts. She twists around, slipping in the puddle of sticky, oily blood, falling onto her hands and knees, dizziness and nausea overwhelming her as she comes face to face with the unseeing eyes of her dead husband. His face is almost cracked in half, clots of crimson pumping out from his torn and shredded skin.

She throws up, her body convulsing and shaking with the effort, then tries to crawl away from the body. Her hands and feet are sticky and wet. She slips and slides, distress and dread blinding her, until she collapses onto the concrete, her head slamming against the ground with a sickening bang.

A pair of strong arms hoists her upwards. She feels herself being laid on the grass, hears the shriek of the siren as it grows closer, somebody shouting something about the police, sees the faces of passers-by looking down on her. Then blackness.

41

ESTHER

My legs are liquid and my stomach is a swirling mass of gurgling acid as I stand up and follow Daniel and Dr McRae out of the room.

'Where are we going?' I can barely find the strength to speak. The words sound warped and misshapen as if I'm speaking a foreign language. My voice isn't my own. I no longer know myself. I'm just a shadow, an entity. No longer the me I thought I was. Seeing those words has changed all that.

'You said you wanted to go home.' Daniel's voice has changed in pitch. It's distant, sharper. Or maybe I'm hearing it differently. Everything is skewed. Out of kilter. I can't think straight or put what he is saying into any sort of context.

We step out of the room into a long corridor, our feet squeaking on the linoleum flooring like nails being dragged down a blackboard. I let out a trembling sigh and traipse behind them like a small child, desperate to go home, desperate to be back in my own enclave of anonymity where I can be alone and not be subjected to any of this.

We walk for what feels like an age even though we don't go far.

Not nearly far enough for my liking. We're still in the same cold, airless building and we don't approach an exit. I get the feeling that once again I'm being played by these people, being lied to and tricked. But for what purpose? Why would they do such a thing and what do they stand to gain from it?

We eventually stop next to a door. I think that I recognise it but perhaps I don't. I reach out and touch the surface. It feels familiar. There's something about it that I can't quite comprehend or put into words. I'm in an alien environment. This place is new to me. I've never been here before. So why does this inanimate object stir some remote memory deep in my mind? It's like somebody is dragging their fingers through murky waters, trying to unearth something that is best left alone. But they won't stop. The sediment of my mind is being brought up to the surface to be observed and analysed.

Daniel and Dr McRae turn and for the first time, they both fix their gaze on me, a probing, razor-like look of contemplation that makes me feel deeply uncomfortable. I get the feeling they're waiting for me to say something, yet they both know that they have the upper hand here. I'm here at their behest and am stumbling about in the dark, unsure of where we are or what it is they expect me to do and say. I'm tempted to turn and run but I'm aware that I'm being closely monitored and scrutinised like a lab rat. If I were to do anything unexpected, a team of people will swoop out of nowhere and pin me down.

'Well?' I say with more confidence than I actually feel. I'm trying to be bold and appear unruffled when all the while, my heart is battering about like a small bird trapped beneath my ribcage.

Dr McRae lifts one eyebrow which I find both annoying and insulting. What is it with this woman? She is either ice cold and impassive or has such a look of incredulity on her face that it drives me into a rage. Where is the help and guidance from these people? I thought medical professionals were supposed to be caring and nurturing. What exactly is it that they want from me?

A torrent of memories push into my mind as I move my hand away from the door. I place it back there and then pull away again as if burnt.

I'm wheezing now. Gasping and panting for breath because I can see it all. Julian's body crushed under the car. Charlotte and Harriet and Dexter trapped inside. Their drooping heads, their tiny, unsuspecting faces...

I lean against the wall, almost sliding down it as desperation takes hold of me. The sirens. I can hear the sirens. And I can see the railway bridge, hear the howl of a train as it passes overhead, the groan of crushed, twisted metal close to me. And the blood. So much blood. I'm swimming in it, choking on it, hardly able to breathe.

I thought there was a police chase. It was simply my confused brain trying to make sense of the nearby sounds. And Julian. Not in the car but crushed by it.

Cold realisation washes over me. I cling onto the wall to stop myself from collapsing. I can see it all now. The minutiae of my life, every bit of detail, every dirty little secret is about to come tumbling out.

It isn't other people who've been deceiving me all this time. It's me. I'm the liar, the great pretender. I'm the one who's been lying to myself.

42

It's Dr McRae who opens the door. She stands back to let me enter but I hang back. I don't think I can go in there. Daniel leans over to me and places a reassuring hand on my arm. A frisson of self-confidence briefly flows through me but it's not enough for me to take that first step in there unaccompanied. As if sensing my fear and reluctance, Daniel places his arm over mine and guides me inside, our feet shuffling along together along the cold plastic floor.

I look around. Everything is as I remember it. And yet it isn't. The walls are a pale-grey colour but everything is smaller. My heart bounces in my chest as I spot my chair next to the window. My pulse gallops as I stride over to it, stroking the fabric fondly with trembling fingers. This part is real. This is the bit that comforts me. My chair by the window.

'Where's the kitchen?' My words are bitter, loaded with resentment. I don't mean them to be, but this confusion is proving too much for me. I know I lied. I know I did terrible things but surely my home is the one thing I can be certain of?

Dr McRae turns and points through the door to some sort of communal area. A handful of people are gathered there. A young woman in a white outfit fills a kettle and I can see immediately that it's Anne, her small young features instantly recognisable even from this distance.

I bring a hand up to wipe my upper lip that is suddenly coated in perspiration.

'They moved my things,' I whisper, remembering the bag full of clothes I found in the holdall. 'And tore my photographs up.'

Dr McRae bites at her lip and speaks so quietly that I have to move closer to hear what she's saying. 'The holdall will probably have been your laundry getting returned, and as for the photographs – well, I'm afraid that was down to you, Esther.'

I blink and fight back tears. 'Down to me?' I want to sit but don't want to appear weak or lacking in any sort of resilience. 'What do you mean, that was down to me?'

She looks as if she wishes she hadn't spoken. But then I've badgered her for the truth for so long now that I need to hear it. No matter how damaging or hurtful or difficult it is to hear, I want to get to the bottom of her words.

'Esther, you have to understand the situation. We've worked really hard to get to this point – all of us – Amy, Daniel and you. Especially you. We brought you here because you've made such good progress lately. But sometimes, well, sometimes you have bad days and things happen.'

It's becoming clearer to me now. I wish it wasn't. I stay silent. I want to hear it all. I want to hear everything.

'And on those bad days, you can get into terrible rages. It was you who tore those photographs up, Esther. We carried out an assessment and decided afterwards that you were still well enough to go out for a visit.'

'To Leyburn,' I interject sadly.

'That's right,' she says with a smile. 'You went there with Amy.'

'I thought I was in Warum,' I mutter, misery and anger at my own stupidity and lack of insight welling up inside me. 'I thought we walked there together from my house. I could have sworn.'

'The human mind is a complex thing, Esther. When we've suffered some sort of trauma, the brain plays tricks on us to protect us from the truth. We live our lives seeing only what we want to see.' Her voice is laced with sympathy now. Now that I know the truth. Now that I can see the horrific reality that is my life.

Snapshots of times gone by flash into my head; Amy constantly letting herself into my home, her talk of working at the hospital. It's all slotting into place.

I slump down onto the chair, hardly able to turn my head, to look out of the window and see what I know isn't really there.

After a couple of seconds, I shift my whole body around and stare out to the house over the road. To the woman at number 19.

She isn't there. I already know that. I'm faced with a small courtyard full of flowers and a high wall that seems to go on forever. It's painted with brightly coloured animals and exotic-looking plants. At the far side is a small, sad-looking sunflower, its wilting head tipped towards the tiny streak of dappled, autumnal sunshine.

I try to speak but nothing comes. I just need a few minutes to gather my thoughts. I rest my eyes for a brief time and when I open them, Dr McRae and Daniel are standing, watching me. I don't want their pity. Daniel clears his throat and looks away. Dr McRae steps back and pretends to be checking her watch.

'I'd like to see outside,' I say, my voice croaky with humiliation and shame.

I expect a refusal, to be told that people like me aren't allowed to go outside and that I'm locked away for a reason. But that doesn't happen. They both nod and wait until I stand up, before stepping back out into the corridor and closing the door to my room behind us.

43

There's no railway bridge, no neighbouring houses. I knew there wouldn't be. Beyond the long corridor is a door leading to a larger outside area. Again, a high wall borders the whole area. This is the same place I went to when I thought I was going searching for Amy's house. The same place I bumped into Daniel. This is the place. I can see it now. I was here all the time.

I stand in the centre of a garden surrounded by rusting leaves and wilting flowers. Even in the weak, autumn sunshine, it's beautiful. Somebody has obviously put a lot of work and effort into making it look this gorgeous. But it's not the road where I live. It's not Warum and it's definitely not my home.

'How long?' I ask at last after waiting there for the longest time, enjoying the feel of the sun on my skin. 'How long have I been here?'

Daniel looks at Dr McRae as if he's asking permission to answer me. She nods and he gets down on his haunches, sniffs one of the flowers and rubs the petal between his fingers before standing up again to face me.

'A year. You've been here for just over a year.'

I suddenly feel faint. A year? How can I have lost a full year of my life, wandering about in a state of fugue, living in an imaginary world and not been aware of it?

It's as if they can read my mind. Dr McRae is the one to let out a protracted breath of resignation this time. She looks exhausted. How did I not see that before? I wonder if I've done to that to her, given her the permanent frown and the dark circles beneath her eyes, or if I'm just one of many who push her to her limits each and every day.

'We've slowly been altering your medication. Some drugs have worked better than others. You've made some tremendous strides in the past few weeks, Esther. We're all extremely pleased with your progress. It's been a long journey but you've done really well and come a long way.'

The garden still swims in front of my eyes. Such a lot of information to process. I'm struggling to comprehend it all and slot the pieces neatly together alongside each other in my mind. I try to walk but the ground continues to move under my feet. Dropping to my knees, I fall forward and sit in the middle of a damp lawn. I feel Dr McRae and Daniel move closer to me and, for once, their presence comforts me. It feels good to have them close by, somebody watching over me.

I stare up at the sky, wondering if I'll ever get home, back to Warum, to the place I love more than anywhere in the world.

I brush my fingers over the grass, wondering who is taking care of my garden and tending to my plants. Everything will need cutting back, ready for the winter. Charlotte's words catapult into my mind. She wanted me to sell my house. My house at 19 Warum Lane. I understand it now. I think about it standing empty and my heart aches for the old place.

The need to get back there claws at me but it's also tinged with fear. I think I've probably become institutionalised and I'm not sure I could cope on my own out there in the big, wide world with nobody around to help me. How would I manage looking after that place on my own?

Julian's face looms in my mind. He's dead. How could I have ever doubted that? The memory is now too vivid, too painful for me to forget. His face, those unseeing eyes the last time I saw him. He was crushed, ripped apart. And he did it trying to save me. I wanted to die and he wouldn't let me so he gave his life to save mine. I obliterated that memory from my mind for a full year. I thought he was leaving me to go and live with my only sister and all he was trying to do was help his unbalanced wife get her life back on track. He loved me enough to save me and get himself killed in the process.

The tears that I hate to shed begin to roll once more. The truth is a painful thing to bear, a heavy burden to carry. I'm not sure I want it. Life felt easier when I remembered nothing of my previous life, my real life. The one that I messed up. It was all so much easier when it belonged to a stranger, a person I conjured up in my head to protect myself from my own evil deeds.

I sit there for a long time. Daniel and Dr McRae don't attempt to speak. I'm grateful for that small mercy. Whilst needing their support, I also need some solitude, even if it is only in my own mind.

Only when the rain starts do we go back inside. The light shower soon develops into a heavy downpour, bouncing off the windows and saturating the lawn. I watch from a chair near the window, mesmerised as the rain floods the small garden. I like the way the water trickles down each and every browning leaf, giving them a healthy shine, making them come alive again if only for a brief time. I watch it for as long as I can. It's easier than turning around and having to look at what's behind me. Easier than having to see what I don't want to see.

I can hear the voices in the distance but I don't want to look at them, at these strangers I'm now being forced to live with. I think about Amy, wondering how she is. I hurt her. And what's worse is, I meant to. It wasn't an accident; it wasn't a spur-of-the-moment thing. I was furious and I deliberately attacked her. Is this how I am now? Or is it how I've always been? I think about the incident with the cat and stare down at my hands, wondering how much I'm really capable of doing, how much damage I've done in my lifetime.

Time goes by and still I sit, not moving, not wanting to look at the environment I'm now living in because of how I am. Because of what I did. Dexter's small face stares at me from the blank wall opposite. I blink and he's gone. Gone forever. All because of me.

Dr McRae has left the unit. I listened to her footsteps as she made her way along the corridor but Daniel has stayed. I can hear his breathing. I suppose he's been asked to stay close by, to make sure I don't do anything irrational or dangerous. Like I have in the past. It's his job to make sure I stay safe and keep others from harm. I used to teach – many of the children I worked with were vulnerable. I know all the jargon. I know exactly what he's doing.

'How long?' I say suddenly, catching him off guard.

He clears his throat as I wait for his reply. 'We spoke about this earlier, Esther. Just over a year. You've been here for just over a year.'

'Not that,' I snap. 'I'm not asking how long I've been here for.'

'So what is it you want to know, then?' His voice is weakening. I don't have to turn around to see that he's looking around for some sort of support. He needs a backup for somebody like me. A contingency plan for my erupting madness. People who will come rushing to his aid should things turn sour.

'How long am I going to be in here for?' I say, a slight growl to my voice. Even when I try to control it, to keep it under wraps, my simmering anger always seems to find a way out.

I can hear his breathing as it grows in rapidity. He's not sure what to say, how to answer me and keep me calm. He knows that he needs to give a measured response to my question but has no idea what to do in this situation. It could go either way. We both know that. Things like this have a nasty habit of escalating in the blink of an eye. He's readying himself, possibly even pressing an alarm button hidden somewhere on his body. I'm sure they have something. They need it with people like me around, don't they?

I allow him this one reprieve and tell him it doesn't really matter. Daniel has been kind to me and he is after all, somebody's son. He is somebody's Dexter.

My face grows hot at the thought of them – Harriet and Dexter. I won't allow myself to think about any of it – the arguments, the hospital visits. The day of the accident when I saw their pale, lifeless little faces in the car. They haunt my dreams, those faces. My children. I think about them every day. Every minute of every single day.

'It doesn't matter now. I'm here as long as you want to keep me here. Isn't that right?'

But he's gone. I'm fine now. He can sense my little nuances and has decided I'm not going to do anything silly or erratic. After all, he knows me pretty well now, doesn't he? Daniel and Dr McRae and very possibly a host of other doctors, therapists and psychiatrists who have seen me at my worst. They know the triggers, can spot every single possible situation or stray word that will tip me over the edge. They know me better than I know myself.

'Everything okay there, Esther?' Rose is standing next to me, sent in no doubt to keep an eye on me. You know, just in case...

'Yes, thank you,' I whisper, my ghost of a voice floating around the space between us.

I stand up but fatigue threatens to take my legs from under me. I need to lie down. I have no idea what time it is, let alone what day it is. I suppose I no longer need to know. Not in this place. Time has no meaning. A minute, a week, a year. It's all the same in here, isn't it?

I want to ask her something but am afraid to hear the answer. I know that I'll sleep a little easier if I can find out though.

'How's Amy?' I brace myself, sucking in my breath as I wait to find out.

Rose lets out a little laugh. 'Ah, she's fine. She's had worse than that in the past. Got a whacking great bruise on her head but she'll live.'

I let out the breath I've been holding even though I don't feel particularly relieved at her answer. I don't actually feel anything at all if I'm being honest. The last few days have seen so many ups and downs that I fear I've become desensitised to most things.

'Tell her I'm sorry next time you see her.'

Rose nods, her eyes hooded with sadness. 'She's got a few days off but I'll be sure to pass it on when I next see her.'

I don't ask whether her time off is due to what I did or whether it's time owed for hours worked. I don't think I want to know. I have enough to contend with at the moment. I'm not about to make my life more cluttered and complicated than it already is. My own problems are enough.

'Anyway, Esther, now that I'm here, shall I take you back to your room? You look a bit tired.'

I think of my room here and the rooms in my house in Warum and feel a lump rise in my throat. A room is a room, after all. I walk beside Rose in companionable silence, neither of us feeling the need to say anything. What is there to say?

We reach my room just in time. She opens the door just as my tears begin to flow. I don't want her to see me. She would have to pass on her concerns and people would come to see me when all I want is to be left alone.

Keeping my back to her, I sit in my chair, the same chair that helped me see myself for what I was, the same chair that allowed me see into the cracks of my damaged life.

I close my eyes, listen to her feet move away and let out a guttural howl.

My sleep is littered with images of crying children and dead people. And blood. So much blood everywhere. When I wake, it's as if a thick cloak of depression has been draped around me. Everything feels different. Dark and heavy. Cold and pointless. A huge void of emptiness stretches out in front of me at the thought of being here with no end point in sight. I was happier before I knew who and what I was. Happier living in blissful ignorance. I look around the room, despair washing over me. This isn't my home. And yet it is. I don't want it to be. But it is. I'm not sure if I'll ever leave here or feel content again.

44

SIX MONTHS LATER

I'm sitting in the garden, my face tilted towards the sky as I stare at the cloudless swathe of blue above. A flock of swallows swoop and dive in perfect formation, graceful and elegant, like tiny ballerinas dancing on the thermals. I watch mesmerised as they twist and turn effortlessly, their small bodies perfectly adapted to their environment. It's one of the most beautiful things I've ever seen. It makes me feel calm and at peace with myself. Not full of rage and angst, not full of murderous intent, just relaxed and at one with the gentle forces of nature.

The distant song of the blackbird floats closer, a soothing, light chirrup carried on the breeze. It's like having somebody close by, their warm breath next to my skin as they whisper poetry into my ear. It's the small things that count, isn't it? Being amongst the flora and fauna soothes me, giving me a brief respite from my thoughts – the torturous ones, the dark, intense ones. The same thoughts that constantly remind me of who I am and what I did.

I blank it all out. I don't want to think about it. Those terrible days. Those awful, unforgivable deeds...

Letting out a deep sigh, I continue gazing upwards, breathing in the gentle warmth of the sun that gently kisses my face. A series of smoke trails criss-cross the cobalt sky thousands of feet above. I think of how wonderful it would be to be one of those passengers, to be transported somewhere exotic, somewhere beautiful. Somewhere far away from here.

I close my eyes, picturing the exquisiteness of it all, the decadence of having people wait on me hand and foot, catering to my every demand, speaking tenderly to me, smiling and asking me if everything is to my liking. Making me feel as if I were the most important person in the world. My eyes abruptly snap open and I let out a small gasp.

No.

I cannot permit myself to feel that way. If I do that, then I'll be playing into their hands, allowing myself to feel trapped and desperate by dreaming of another world where I am free. It's all about making the best of what I have in here. That's the only way I'll make it through, the only way I can carry on living my life as a prisoner. Because for all the fancy terms applied to the reasons for me being held here, that is exactly what I am. I'm not a patient – I am a detainee, a captive interred here against my will. And if I allow myself to dream about how much better my life would be if I were elsewhere, I know for sure that I will undoubtedly go mad, my mind too fragile to face the truth, to live up to the realisation that I am well and truly trapped, stuck at this place indefinitely until they decide what to do with me. Until they decide whether or not I will ever be able to leave.

So I shut out dreams of happiness and contentment – the thoughts I have where I can fly like a bird, soaring through the skies like the swallows that feed on the wing, dancing as only creatures that are free can, and I force myself to be happy, to make do with what I have in this place that I have been forced to call home.

I close my eyes and open them again, blinking repeatedly. And what is that? What exactly do I have?

That is a very good question.

What I have is a roof over my head, a bed to sleep in at night, food to eat, and my thoughts. At least they are my own. Nobody has control over them. As much as the people here in this place would like to climb inside my head and work out what I'm thinking, I can rest easy on that score, knowing that I'm the only one who has the key to that particular area of my life. And as long as there is breath in my body, it will stay that way.

My thoughts are all I have. They are mine and mine alone.

I lean down and carefully bends the stalk of a nearby daffodil towards my face, the silken, golden petals yielding to my touch, its pale, light scent billowing up in an invisible haze and enveloping me in its delicate, perfumed beauty.

Inhaling deeply, I let go of the thin stem and sit back up. The welcoming arms of spring reach out, temporarily lifting my mood. Soon it will be summer. I smile, my face tight, unaccustomed to feelings of happiness. Summer reminds me of good times, better times. A time when I was loved and content. A time when my family was still together.

And then it's gone. My brief moment of happiness in that moment vanishes like the last gasp of breath uttered from a dying man, and in an instant, a thick veil of misery descends, shrouding me, suffocating me, slowly killing me as it hooks its talons deep into my soul. One small memory, one tiny rogue thought, is all that it takes to burst my bubble of brief contentment – the sound of birdsong, the smell of a garden, the memory of my fragmented family and shattered life. My life before I came here. The life I lost and will never get back.

Suddenly, I'm consumed with sorrow, swamped with raw anguish as it rushes up my abdomen, travelling up my throat and forcing its way out of my mouth. I see them out of the corner of my eye, the people who are up and out of their seats, racing across to where I sit, alerted by the noise escaping from my burning lungs.

My scream gains in pitch, a hollow, distorted wailing sound, growing and growing until it reaches a crescendo. Their faces are full of fury and frustration when they reach me. They don't like it when I do this, when I allow my demons to escape. They want me to stop, to keep it all under control, and I'm all too aware that they'll do anything to make that happen.

But then, they don't truly understand my plight or how I think. They don't understand that I don't want to stop the noise, or for the dark thoughts to subside and simply vanish into the ether. I want them all to hear, to listen to my raw anger and terror and be subjected to the desperate shrieks that emerge from the pit of my stomach.

Because this is how I am now and how I will always be from this point on. The spells of happiness and calm I experience are short-lived. The memories of those painful, murky days have dug deep into my brain and refuse to leave, pushing any fresher memories and feelings aside, stomping on them and grinding them underfoot.

So these people need to listen to me, to be sympathetic to my cries and howls, because they're the ones who made me this way. They are the people who forced me to see what took place, to make me realise what actually happened. This is all their fault. They are the ones who made me see what a monster I had become.

And I hate them for it.

I can hear them as they talk to me, their voices distant, detached from reality, their pleas and whispers for me to calm down washing over me. Their pedestrian, persuasive techniques are a waste of time. I won't respond. I know it and they know it and yet still they persist. It's just another hoop to jump through, a ticked box that says they tried with me, that they did their utmost to talk me around and it didn't work so they were forced to restrain me.

So I continue to scream, roaring into thin air at the injustice of it all. I bring my hands up and use my long, ragged nails to scratch at my bare skin, tearing them down my arms, tugging and digging until I feel a rush of adrenaline and I am completely smeared with blood.

And still the people plead with me. Still they try. And still I scream and tear at my own flesh, ignoring their pleas for me to be silent and to listen to them.

Only when their begging and talking doesn't work do they eventually move towards me. I thrash about, bucking and bending my body as they pin me down and restrain me. I scream some more, swearing and cursing. They don't stop. The small gang of people wrap their big, strong arms around my thin, frail body, pulling at my shoulders to stop me from moving. An arrow of agony rips through my spine as my upper body is held fast.

It doesn't bother me. I embrace the burning pain that shoots through my body. I deserve this. I deserve all of this and so much more.

In the end, they're too strong for me. I can't keep it up, that level of resistance. No energy left. No fight left in me. Exhaustion swamps me, wraps its tight arms around me and refuses to let me go. I feel myself go limp and being hoisted into the air, then carried inside. Soon I'll be given sedatives and fall into a deep, synthetically induced sleep. I will drift off into a world of darkness, into a place where the full reality of my life repeats itself over and over again. And then I will wake into a hell of my own making. A hell from which there is no escape.

45

EIGHT WEEKS LATER

Amy is brushing my hair, her touch so gentle I can barely feel the bristles as she pulls it through, her fingers freeing up the slightly knotted strands. It's grown such a lot in the past few months. I haven't had long hair for years and years. It's a new look and a new feel for me. I'm still getting used to it, forever flicking it back out of my eyes and over my shoulders like a pouting, vain teenager.

She insisted I wear some make-up as well. She said it helps a person to feel better about themselves if they take care of their appearance, so I've relented and she has helped me to apply some blusher and lipstick. It doesn't look too garish as I've got a bit of a light tan from working in the small garden with a few of the other women in the ward. I've become quite the green-fingered expert. We've planted some magnolia trees, a handful of rose bushes and an acer, which is growing faster than we can cut it back. I don't mind, really. It gives me a reason to get out of bed every morning. Because I'm not going to pretend that everything is hunky-dory in here. It isn't. It's been an uphill struggle to get to this point but I think I'm getting there. Some days are better than others but isn't that just life?

I've been attending the therapy sessions and learning a lot about myself. I'm still not sure I like Esther Veronica Nesbitt very much but we're slowly becoming acquainted with each other, and perhaps sometime soon we'll become close friends.

'There, that's a lot better. Here you go – have a look at the back. I've put a comb in at the side to pin it out of the way and to stop it falling into your eyes so much. It's given it a lot more body at the back. You look really glam, actually!' Amy hands me the mirror and I surreptitiously glance at my new self. The self I never thought I would see emerge after finally coming to terms with who I am and what I did.

I let out a gasp. Is this person really me? I actually look healthy and – dare I say it – happy?

'We must be sitting in a good light,' I say with a slight laugh as I tip the mirror to get a better view of my reflection. It's good to see a chink of light, a possible new me in the near future. I picture myself as some sort of reptilian creature, a snake shedding its skin and a new, fresh person stepping out of it with the promise of some sort of life ahead of them. Otherwise, what is the point of it all?

'Well, you're obviously right. A bit of make-up and a new hairdo and I feel and look like a different person.' I can't stop staring at myself. I'm a real person. Not a monster. Not some sort of pathetic creature who doesn't deserve to live alongside decent people.

Forgiveness is everything, isn't it? Forgiving others is one thing but forgiving yourself is a different thing entirely. That is so much more difficult. I have to live with myself knowing what I did and for months and months, I've avoided looking in the mirror, afraid of what I might see there. But now I can see that I'm a real person, not a two-headed monster. I haven't completely healed – I'm not sure I ever will – but I'm trying.

'Right, let's get you to the café. She's coming soon and I want a cappuccino with chocolate sprinkles so let's get there early and get a good table and get settled, shall we?' Amy sounds more excited than me. Her voice is light and delicate, like the sound of china being gently chimed with a silver spoon.

We stand up and make our way out of the unit and into the corridor that leads to the café where the smell of coffee beans is so rich and powerful, it makes my mouth water. That's another thing. I've started eating regularly and put on some weight. I had no idea how painfully thin I had become. My clothes were falling off me and my hip bones protruded through the fabric. How had I let things get so bad? But that's all behind me now. I am, as Amy keeps telling me, on the up and up.

I get a frothy latte and Amy gets her cappuccino with a healthy helping of sprinkles as promised. We sit in the corner at a circular table. Amy disappears for a few seconds and comes back with a plate of cookies. I shake my head at her and laugh.

'Not long until the wedding,' she says quietly. 'It's my last treat before I give it all up so I can get into that bloody slim-fitting wedding dress!'

'I want to see some pictures,' I murmur, secretly jealous of Amy, of the fresh, new life that lies ahead of her. I had that once and I messed it up. But then, after what I've discovered about my childhood and formative years, I guess it was always going to happen. Some things are out of our control.

I stop myself from going down that route. As Daniel has told me on more than one occasion, we're all responsible for ourselves and our actions. It's just that some of us manage it better than others. It's my job to manage what goes on inside my head and deal with it in an appropriate way.

'Oh, I can promise you, I'm going to bore everybody to death with them.' Amy laughs and drinks her coffee like she doesn't have a care in the world. That's why I envy her. I know I shouldn't, but I do.

She looks at me, turns her attention to something over my shoulder and then turns her gaze back to me. 'She's here, Esther. I'm going to sit over there by the window and read my book. I'm close by if you need anything, okay?'

I nod and grip onto the edge of the table with my fingers. All of a sudden, I feel nervous. I have no idea why that is. I knew she was coming. This visit has been planned for weeks and weeks, if not months. Time still has a nasty habit of slipping through my fingers and before I know it, another season has passed me by.

I clear my throat and watch Amy as she saunters off to the corner and places a book open on her lap. I feel like a small child, vulnerable and exposed, sitting alone without her parents. Nobody close by. Nobody to protect me.

My breath comes out in small irregular grunts as I slowly turn around to see her standing there.

'Hello, Esther. You're looking great.'

I smile and pull a chair out for Charlotte to sit down next to me. 'Amy did my hair and I've got some make-up on.' I give an embarrassed eye roll and pull at the fabric on my sweater.

'You've put weight on too.' She leans forward to hug me. My instinct is to flinch. I'm unaccustomed to being touched but as she moves closer, I find myself melting into her arms and once again the tears come thick and fast.

46

It takes some time for the sobs to subside. I've missed her. I didn't know how much I'd missed my only sister until she strolled in and I saw her standing there. I've spent so long hating her, so many wasted years with resentment and anger and malevolence eating away at me, that I'd forgotten how much I actually love her. Hatred and fury are such powerful and damaging emotions that they leave little or no room for anything else.

'You look amazing too,' I sniff.

And she does. She hasn't got her walking stick with her and her gait is less wobbly, straighter and steadier than the last time I saw her.

'I've been having physio and it really seems to be working. The exercises I have to do are hilarious. I've gone from being one of the laziest people on the planet to being a contortionist.' She makes an attempt at wiggling her leg in the air and we both collapse in a fit of giggles.

It takes a little while for us to stop and catch our breath. I'm so pleased Charlotte came. Seeing her has given me a glimpse of how life could be for me, a snapshot of a possible future.

She shuffles her chair closer to me, so close I can smell her perfume – a deep, musky scent. Chanel perhaps. It always was her favourite. I used to tease her that she had expensive tastes and was a high maintenance kind of lady.

'It would be lovely if you could come up to Scotland and visit our place, Esther. It's been hard work doing it up but we're getting there.' She moves her hand and gently strokes my hair, her fingers resting on the back of my neck. 'There's room there for you. When you're ready.'

Her words say everything we both need to know. My future is still uncertain but I'm working on it. I'm trying to secure it. One day at a time.

'We still need to talk about your house,' she says, as she watches me for a reaction. She needn't worry. I'm not going to throw some sort of tantrum and shout and scream like last time. I've had a long time to think about what to do with my house and I've spoken to Dr McRae about it at length. We both agree that going back to Warum wouldn't be good for me. It could have a detrimental effect on my well-being, so I've already made up my mind to put it on the market. I'll need Charlotte's help to do that. Being sectioned means I got to keep my house and don't have to sell it to pay for my care. Silver linings and all that.

I tell her that letting it go is the best option and we can get the ball rolling as soon as possible.

She nods and takes my hand. 'I also wanted to talk to you about things that happened. You know, stuff from when you were small.' She bites at her lip and watches me carefully. It must be tiresome for her, having to pre-empt my every move, to think carefully about what she should and shouldn't say in my presence. How long has it been like that? Since I was a child or did my behaviour only begin to deteriorate once I reached adulthood?

'It's okay,' I say softly, wanting to reassure her. 'I don't mind talking about this stuff. I've been going to talking therapy and it's really helped me.'

A small stray tear slips from her eye and rolls down her cheek. She briefly looks away then back to me. 'You know now that Mum had mental health problems?' I nod again and she continues. 'Before she was, you know—'

'Sectioned,' I say quickly. 'It's okay, Charlotte. You can say that word. I've come to terms with it now.'

'Right,' she whispers, 'before she was sectioned. Well, I've thought long and hard about this and I need to tell you. I'm almost certain it had an effect on you. You may remember it.'

I shrug my shoulders, unsure of what it is she's about to come out with. No more dead animals. I don't want to hear any stories about how I possibly tortured helpless creatures as a child and grew into a deeply damaged woman who tried to kill her own son.

'Mum never believed you were her child. She had a breakdown after you were born and rejected you. I didn't know this as a child. We were just kids but I've done a lot of research and found out a lot of things from relatives and from reading old documents that I found in Dad's stuff after he died.' She stops to take a breath. I think back to when we were small, to Mum's cold demeanour and aloof ways and how she would do strange things, such as sitting in the garden shed for hours and hours when we came in from school, refusing to come out until our father came back from work.

'Anyway, there was one time when Dad came home and the house was empty of kids. I had gone to a friend's for tea but you should have been there. Except you weren't. When you got in from school, Mum had put you in the car, driven you up to the moors and left you there, then she drove back home and cooked a meal.'

I shut my eyes, the memory of it slowly coming back to me.

Being alone, frightened. And the cold. The wicked, biting cold clawing at my bare legs as I sat in an exposed area with no idea of where I was or how to get home.

'He drove straight back to where she had left you and fortunately you were still there, sitting on the side of the road on a large rock, crying and terrified.' Charlotte stops and takes a deep breath. 'Stuff like this went on for most of your childhood. You started sleepwalking and suffering night terrors and would often wake up in weird and sometimes scary places.'

'Like in the garden or in the kitchen after emptying the knife block,' I add sadly.

'Yes, exactly like that,' she replies, her eyes suddenly unable to meet mine. 'I wish I'd done more to help you.'

Her voice sounds so horribly sad and I don't think I can bear to see her so upset. Clutching at her hand, I make sure she's looking at me as I say my next words. 'Charlotte, you have been my rock. You were always there for me as a kid. You were the one I turned to, not Mum. It was always you. Every single time. And you're still here for me now we're adults even though I...' It's my turn to stumble over my words now. I don't think I can finish what I was going to say. Not that I need to. We both know what I believed. What I accused her of and what happened next. Some things are best left unsaid.

We hug again. I think we're making up for lost time. It certainly feels that way. I can't remember the last time anybody embraced me. How could I have forgotten how good it feels?

'Anyway,' Charlotte says after a while, 'there's another reason I came here.'

A shadow suddenly appears over our table. I look up to see Amy standing there. Charlotte pulls out a chair for her to sit on. My stomach plummets. This means Charlotte's time is up. Our allotted slot has come to an end. My skin shrivels at the thought of her leaving. I feel as if she's just arrived. I have so much I want to tell her. I'd like to let her know that I'm doing well in here. I want to tell her about my little team of fellow green-fingered helpers and how the little garden we've established is doing really well. I want to show her the recently planted saplings and tell her how the roses are flourishing now we've placed them next to the wall. But it appears we've run out of time.

'And now for the next part,' Charlotte whispers as she looks at Amy and then at me.

I shake my head, unsure how to interpret her cryptic message.

'I don't know what you mean.' A pulse is hammering at my throat. I widen my eyes until they feel as if they're about to burst out of my head. I need to know what's going on. I don't like uncertainty. It makes me nervous. I like my routine.

Amy and Charlotte stand up. I instinctively do the same, my legs weak as we walk into a small room next to the café. Dr McRae is in there, sitting in a low chair by the window. She greets us with a warm smile. I don't return it. I'm feeling frightened now.

'What's happening?' The question fires out of my mouth in a garbled stream. I can't help it. Things were going so well too. And now... well, now I don't know what to think.

'Take a seat, Esther.' Dr McRae gestures for me sit down. I obey her, like a small child. Charlotte sits next to me and takes my hand. Her fingers are warm next to mine. I suddenly feel like ice, my skin cold as it clings to my bones. What if they're going to discharge me? Let me leave this place and venture out into the big, wide world? Despite complaining about being detained here, I don't think I'm ready for that. The thought of it fills me with terror. I'm safe here. Safe and protected within these walls.

Charlotte rubs my hand softly. We're back to being children

again. She's the big sister taking care of me, looking after me, doing her best to make sure I come to no harm.

'Okay, Derek,' Charlotte says loudly, her voice projecting behind us to the doorway. 'You can come in now.'

I swivel around in my chair and feel the blood drain out of my face as I see them standing there.

47

I'm hallucinating. I must be. This is some sort of drug-fuelled dream. I've been administered a sedative and this is the net result. There's no other explanation. So why does it seem so real? There's a starkness to this image, to the whole scenario, that doesn't ever accompany drug-related incidents.

I stare at them, at the vision of beauty standing right in front of me. I want to reach out and touch them but the fear of them vanishing if I make contact is too great, so I sit and watch as Harriet and Dexter – my children – come and sit by Charlotte with Derek wedged in between them on the other side.

Breathing feels arduous. Every pocket of air, every exhalation of oxygen, sticks in my throat like sandpaper. My reflexes have forgotten how to work properly. I've forgotten how to control my own body.

'Here, drink this.' Dr McRae hands me a glass of water and I glug it back greedily, the cool liquid alleviating the dryness in my dry throat and burning lungs as it travels down to my stomach.

I want to ask how they got here, where they came from, who's looking after them. I want to ask a million different things but nothing will come. In my head, I'm screaming that they're dead. And yet they're not. They're here, sitting near me in this room. My precious, darling children. Still alive. Here. Right in front of me.

I try to stand up but the floor is an undulating mass under my feet. 'I think I'm going to faint.' My words sound distant. Stars burst behind my eyelids. Nausea rises.

A hand guides my head down between my knees. I'm told to take deep breaths. In through my mouth and out through my nose. In. Out. In. Out.

'That's it,' Dr McRae says, her voice a whisper in the distance. 'You're going to be fine. You've had a bit of a shock, that's all.'

My head thumps. I can hardly breathe. *A bit of a shock...*

I thought my children had been killed in a car accident, the same accident that took my husband, and she's telling me I've had a bit of a shock when I see them standing next to me. I've had over a year of thinking they were dead. Almost eighteen months thinking they were in their graves.

'Why didn't you tell me?' I finally croak as I turn to face Charlotte, who's looking at me with such concern that I am blinded with torment and grief.

'We tried,' she replies quietly. 'We really tried, but it was so difficult...' Charlotte looks to Dr McRae for backup, her eyes pleading for assistance.

'I don't want to go into too much detail here for obvious reasons but please believe us when we say that we tried to tell you but your mind was closed off to the idea and nothing we did or said could persuade you otherwise.'

I nod and wipe a lone tear away. 'The photos,' I say, my voice now no more than a squeak.

Charlotte squeezes my hand. 'I hoped that would help you understand and see how much they'd grown.'

It did. Or at least it helped me take small steps to understand.

At the time, I couldn't work out why the children looked so different. Now I know.

Shifting forward, I lean over to get a better view of them. *My children*. The more I say that, the better it sounds. I try to act reserved even though my heart is hammering and fit to burst. I know that I'm being watched. I can also see that both Harriet and Dexter are wary, if not a bit scared of me. Who can blame them? The last time they saw me, I was hysterical. Violent and completely out of control.

Their eyes dart from Derek to me and Charlotte, and then back to Derek again. Harriet is dressed in navy-blue leggings and a checked overshirt. Her hair is pulled back in a silver bobble and she is wearing a pair of fingerless gloves. Dexter is wearing a pair of black joggers and a denim jacket. He looks so much like Julian, it takes my breath away. They've changed and grown so much, Harriet especially looking no longer like a child, but more like the young adult she will soon become.

I want to move close to them, to cuddle them in and tell them how sorry I am but I know it's not allowed. Instead, I give them a weak smile and a surreptitious wave. Harriet tries to return it but her eyes fill up and she turns her head away. My heart almost breaks in two. Dexter smiles back and then looks to Derek to make sure he did the right thing. Everything is so fragile, like the petals of a flower – beautiful to look at but so terribly easy to ruin and damage irrevocably should an infinitesimal shift occur; a stray word, a slight change in mood and it could all disappear. I could lose everything. And then where would that leave me? I don't want to go back to that dark place when I thought my children were dead. I want them alive. I want to think of them running and playing and doing all the things that children should do. I want them to be happy. I was far from a perfect parent but I desperately want them to be happy. Believe it or not, it's all I've ever wanted.

'Right, you two. Let's get you that hot chocolate that we talked about.' Derek claps his hands together and Harriet and Dexter jump up and let out small, excited squeals. I should feel grateful to him for his avuncular manner and for looking after my children but I don't mind admitting that I'm actually consumed with envy. A dreadful way to feel given the circumstances, but I can't help how I feel.

I watch as they skip away, Derek giving me a curt nod and a curl of his lip when he passes. I suppose I've earned that after what I did. He has every right to hate me. I hope in time, we can grow to be friends but at the moment, I'll have to make do with being tolerated.

A silence descends as they leave, Charlotte sitting nervously, her hands twisting in her lap. Amy gives her a reassuring smile. Dr McRae gets up and closes the door then sits back down, dragging her chair closer to mine.

'They look so mature,' I say quietly. 'So grown up and content.'

Charlotte nods and lowers her eyes.

'Thank you for letting me see them. And say thank you to Derek from me, for taking care of them.' I do actually mean it. Despite feeling jealous, I'm delighted they look so healthy and happy. That's all any parent wants for their children, isn't it? Even me, the worst parent ever.

'Right. We can talk a little more freely now Harriet and Dexter are enjoying their chocolate drink.' Dr McRae is leaning forward, her hands clasped together over her knees, something she does when the conversation takes a serious and more official turn. Dr McRae is no fool. Her body language is telling me that she means business.

I swallow nervously and clear my throat, waiting to hear what she has to say.

'We need to tell you this, Esther, just so you know. Charlotte and Derek are now the legal guardians of Harriet and Dexter. You can have supervised contact but you're not allowed to be left alone with them,' she says in her official voice.

'Does that mean I'm leaving here?' My voice is shaky. I'm trembling.

'Not just yet, but with your recent progress, it's something we're considering. We need to monitor you for a little while longer.'

I'm relieved to hear this. I'm not brave enough to leave here. This unit has become my security blanket and I'm not quite ready for the world. Not just yet. Truth be told, I'm not so sure it's ready for me. It's a fast-moving society out there and I've led a slow-paced existence in here over the past year or so. It's suited me, helped me remember. Helped me heal. I want that to continue, not stumble back out into an unfamiliar environment and slip straight back into that dark place. I want to be completely well.

'They live in Scotland now?'

Charlotte nods and smiles. 'They're at the local village school and have settled in really well. Harriet has made some lovely friends and went bowling last week, and Dexter has started playing in the school football team. He scored the winning goal at the last game. Derek's got some photos. We'll bring them in next time we visit.'

I squeeze her hand and we sit for a couple of minutes while Dr McRae tells us more medical jargon about my condition and legal stuff pertaining to the children and Charlotte and Derek's guardianship of them. Apparently, I suffered trauma, both as a child and an adult. I have been diagnosed with various mental health conditions including having a personality disorder. Talking therapy is helping me with this, getting me to manage my own emotions and control my impulsive behaviour. I also have clinical depression. I'm on medication for it and according to Dr McRae and Daniel, my condition is improving all the time.

I think about this and wonder, did my mother drive me to this point or is it in the genes, given her history? Was my path in life preordained and no matter what I did, nothing would have stopped it from happening? I guess we'll never know.

I do know that I have one request. If I'm considered well enough to have contact with my children, then I'm hoping I'm considered well enough to be granted this one wish.

'I need to see him,' I say quietly, making sure I catch Dr McRae's eye. 'I need to go and see Julian.'

48

There's a clear sky and slight a chill in the air despite it being summer. The cold breeze seems fitting for the occasion. Amy and Anne are watching me from a safe distance, making sure I don't scream to the heavens above and collapse in a heap. I pull my scarf tighter around my neck and tug at my collar to stop the cold air from creeping in and spreading down my back. Dr McRae says I need to put on some more weight. Perhaps she's right. Even in the midst of summer, I feel chilly.

I look at the vast space around me. This isn't where I expected him to be. In our younger years, we used to laugh and say we wanted to be buried side by side in All Hallows Church graveyard where there is an ancient oak tree that spreads its gnarled branches over the dead, keeping them safe and protecting them from the elements. But instead, he's here in the local crematorium with a small headstone to mark the place where his ashes are buried. There's no oak tree and the headstones are jammed so close together, there's barely room to manoeuvre my way around each grave.

The stone isn't the one I would have chosen, but then I was in no fit state to be involved in the decision-making process. I didn't even go to his funeral. My own husband's final memorial service and I was absent, busy having a massive breakdown in the local mental health unit. Charlotte was in hospital having surgery on her leg injuries, thinning out the numbers even more, leaving Derek and a handful of Julian's friends and work colleagues present in the church.

I place the bunch of flowers I brought along in the centre of the small mound of earth and take a couple of minutes rearranging them and tidying up the graveside. I scrub at the stone with the small nailbrush I was allowed to carry with me, and throw a vase of dry, dead petals and wilting stalks onto the nearby compost heap. I presume the caretaker distributes flowers evenly on each of the graves. Either that or Charlotte and Derek visited here recently and placed them on Julian's grave. Another thing to thank them for. If I live to be a thousand years old, I know I'll never be able to repay them for what they've done and how they've helped me. It was Charlotte who told the doctors and the police about Julian finding me in the kitchen and the ensuing argument afterwards. She told them about my fractured and difficult childhood, Mum's hatred and mistreatment of me and how she believed it impacted on me deeply enough to radically change my behaviour. It was possibly Charlotte who saved me from prison, helping doctors to fill in the gaps when they assessed me, telling them what a terrible time I'd had and how Mum had done her utmost to damage me both physically and emotionally.

We speak often, Charlotte and I, and there may even be a chance of me visiting them in Scotland sometime in the near future. I'm not getting my hopes up but when things get on top of me, it's one of those thoughts that gets me through the day, helps me to get out of bed when I feel like curling up in a ball and weeping. Because although I'm making enormous strides, some days are still difficult. Some days feel weeks long – hour after hour of torturous thoughts about my family and my home and where I'm now housed, and how it all came to this. Some days are endless. But not today. Today, I've been allowed out to see my husband. The man who gave his life to save mine.

A rustle in the nearby bushes causes me to jump. A cat slides out from between the branches and edges its way along the perimeter of the cemetery. Its fur is matted with wet leaves and mud and its ears are pricked up in readiness for predators. I close my eyes and turn away, then stand up and rub my clothes clean with my gloved hands.

I make my way over to where the two young women are standing.

'All done,' I say, trying to inject an air of cheeriness into my voice when I actually feel extremely glum and subdued. I knew this visit wouldn't be easy but neither did I expect it to feel so downright depressing. I guess it's to be expected. This is my first visit and I don't know how I'm supposed to feel. There are no handbooks and offers of guidance on how to conduct oneself in these situations. Nobody to turn to when the grief becomes overwhelming.

'Look at that,' Amy says incredulously, pointing at the build-up of traffic next to the cemetery. 'They need to widen this stretch of road. It's too congested and everybody drives far too quickly.'

We shout over the roar of the passing vehicles as we head out of the high, wrought-iron gates, a scribble of ornate black metal that points skyward, and make our way back to the car.

'We need to get through this lot to the other side.' Amy points to where she parked up on the other side of the road.

'Ah, it'll be fine,' I say dismissively. 'Somebody is bound to slow down for us.' A convoy of HGVs power past, the strength of the slipstream almost knocking us sideways. I take in a lungful of dust and carbon monoxide and let out a splutter.

'Tell you what,' Amy says brightly, her eyes narrowed against the rush of air caused by the speeding traffic. 'Why don't I cross on my own? I'll get the car, turn it around and if you two make your way to that layby farther up, I'll nip in there and pick you up. Easier to get one person over the road than three, isn't it?'

Anne nods eagerly. I suspect this is also to do with looking after me and making sure I come to no harm while I'm in their care.

We watch as Amy waits until there's a clearing and then dashes over the road, her face pinched with concentration as she practically throws herself onto the pavement. A car speeds past a second or two later and honks his horn at her as if the near miss is her fault even though it's patently obvious that he is well over the speed limit.

Anne and I set off towards the layby. She chats excitedly as we make our way along, her voice a shriek above the howl of the traffic. 'What about the plans to extend the unit then, Esther? Sounds rather exciting, doesn't it?'

I shrug my shoulders and shake my head dismissively. 'Not to me it doesn't. I like the place just as it is.' I don't tell Anne that it's taken me quite some time to adjust to living there and that I'm starting to feel a level of familiarity for the place that I never in a million years thought I would ever feel. I don't want any changes, regardless of whether they will improve the facilities or make it bigger and brighter. I want things to stay exactly as they are. Change doesn't work for me. Never has.

'I'm sure you'll get used to it once it's all finished,' she says as a bus rushes past us, its wheels throwing up a cloud of grit from the gutter.

'I'll just ignore it all and spend as much time as I can out in the garden,' I reply tersely. 'I don't care how hot it is or how cold or rainy it might be; at least I'll be away from all the disruption and noise.'

'Oh, there won't be any disruption or noise. They're building it on the side of the unit and knocking through when it's all done. And I know you'll love it because you're going to get a new garden area.'

I stop walking, a slight buzzing beginning to build in my head as I stare at Anne. Hurt and anger pulses through my veins. 'I don't want a new garden. I like the one we've got.'

'It's nothing to worry about, Esther. Honestly, as I said, you'll love it. From what I've heard, the new garden will be bigger so there'll be more room for your plants and stuff.'

Her words ring around my head. So cold and unfeeling. *Plants and stuff.* That's how she thinks of it. None of my hard work means anything to her. Nothing at all. It's all just fluff and nonsense in her infantile, uneducated head.

'I don't want a bigger garden. I just want it to stay exactly how it is.' I sound like a petulant child but I don't care. I've worked damn hard for everything in that garden. It's a place of solace, not something that can just be ripped up and replaced on a whim.

'Well, I'm sure you'll love it once it's all done. And after all, it's just a garden, isn't it?' She turns and smiles at me then carries on walking, unaware of what she has just said, oblivious of the damage her words have caused.

I'd like to say I have no idea how it took place, how such a horrible, tragic accident happened, but we all know that's utter nonsense, don't we? I'd also like to say it was painless but I very much doubt that as well. But at least it was fast. That's one thing I can say with a degree of certainty. It was definitely fast.

It happens so quickly. A split-second decision. A flick of the wrist. A swift move disguised as a stumble. I hear the growl of a large engine coming up behind us, stagger to one side, make a grab for Anne to save myself from falling and then stumble some more before giving her a sharp push as the huge tanker approaches.

I watch as she falls into the road and under its wheels. I hear the screech of rubber on the tarmac and the grate of metal as the driver locks the brakes up and grinds to a juddering halt. The whole episode is over in seconds. I stagger back onto the pavement and let out a long, drawn-out scream before crumpling into a heap on the kerbside and rocking backwards and forwards like a terrified child. It sounds and looks authentic. That's because there's years of practice behind my behaviour. Years of perfecting my art. And I'm really good at it too, all this lying and deception. I'm one of the best. It's what I do. It's part of who I am. I lie to everyone, even myself. Especially myself.

ACKNOWLEDGMENTS

Authors, like parents, shouldn't really have favourites, but I imagine that there are hundreds of writers that have that one book that they really love and enjoyed writing. *The Woman at Number 19* is mine. Set in the North East of England in a fictitious town that was based on a place only a few miles from where I live, its characters and setting were so easy to create. So, with that in mind, I would like to show some gratitude to the wonderful town of Yarm for inspiring me to write this book.

Once again, I would like to thank my editor Emily Ruston and the team at Boldwood Books for giving my book another chance, for republishing it and refining it and making it the absolute best it could be. All stories deserve a second chance and I'm so grateful that my book is one of those that has been chosen.

I feel honoured to be a writer. There are many (and I mean many) highs and lows in this game. Interacting with other writers has helped me through those times, as has coffee and chocolate, so thanks to my other writer pals, Nescafe and those lovely people at Cadburys. You all rock.

I write full time and love chatting with readers so please feel free to get in touch with me on social media at:

www.facebook.com/thewriterjude

www.twitter.com/thewriterjude

www.instagram.com/jabakerauthor

Bring coffee and cake...

MORE FROM J. A. BAKER

We hope you enjoyed reading ***The Woman at Number 19***. If you did, please leave a review.

If you'd like to gift a copy, this book is also available as an ebook, hardback, large print, digital audio download and audiobook CD.

Sign up to J. A. Baker's mailing list for news, competitions and updates on future books.

https://bit.ly/JABakerNews

Explore more twisty psychological thrillers from J. A. Baker...

J.A. BAKER
LOCAL
GIRL
MISSING
Who will
be next?

J.A. BAKER
THE
LAST
WIFE
A fresh start
could cost them
everything....

J.A. BAKER
THE
WOMAN
AT
NUMBER 19
What secrets lie
behind closed doors...?

J.A. BAKER
THE
OTHER
MOTHER
Three troubled women.
One deadly secret.

ABOUT THE AUTHOR

J. A. Baker is a successful writer of numerous psychological thrillers. Born and brought up in Middlesbrough, she still lives in the North East, which inspires the settings for her books.

Follow J. A. Baker on social media:

facebook.com/thewriterjude
twitter.com/thewriterjude
instagram.com/jabakerauthor
tiktok.com/@jabaker41

Printed in Great Britain
by Amazon